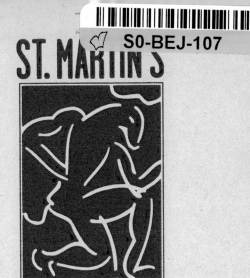

PRAISE FOR **KAREN HARPER** AND HER ELIZABETH I MYSTERY NOVELS

THE FATAL FASHIONE

"Entertaining. . . . Harper skillfully interweaves fact and fiction, presenting a heroine who is as intelligent and gutsy a crime solver as she was a real-life monarch." —*Publishers Weekly*

"Harper brings the period vividly to life, develops characters from the earlier tales, and makes the Virgin Queen a sympathetic, ambitious, and patriotic woman. . . . [O]ne soon is swept up in the rush of events in a turbulent time skillfully described. Recommended for all collections." —*Library Journal*

THE FYRE MIRROR

"An appealingly courageous detective." —*Kirkus Reviews*

"A truly vibrant protagonist, thoroughly satisfying characterization, attention to detail, and credible plotting mark this as an outstanding historical." —*Library Journal*

"Fabulous . . . a thrilling reading experience . . . Fans of the Ursula Blanches series by Fiona Buckley will definitely love this glimpse into a bygone era." —*Midwest Book Review*

THE QUEENE'S CHRISTMAS

"Wonderful historical detail mixed with intrigue . . . a real treat for those who enjoy historical mysteries." —*Booklist*

"Nicely blends intrigue, humor, and period detail."
—*Wall Street Journal*

MORE . . .

THE THORNE MAZE

"Brilliantly plotted and authentically detailed." —*Booklist*

"The novel's true pleasure is the re-creation of Elizabeth I's court, the manners of the day, the fêtes, the sumptuous clothes, all of which Harper brings wonderfully alive." —*Miami Herald*

"Harper is to be commended for keeping to what we know about Tudor history. . . . and for making the factions of Elizabeth's court clearer than many history books have done."

—*Chicago Tribune*

"A wonderful web of drama and deceit that would make Shakespeare envious . . . this is great stuff."

—*Toronto Globe and Mail*

THE QUEENE'S CURE

"A neatly plotted mystery with genuinely terrifying scenes."

—*Publishers Weekly*

"Fully rounded, sometimes baroque, but always engaging . . . the plot quickens to the very end." —*Booklist*

"Superb . . . a winner." —Amazon.com

"[A]n Elizabethan fan's delight . . . [with] several red herrings that will delight the heart of mystery lovers."

—RomanticTimes.com

THE TWYLIGHT TOWER

"Harper's exquisite mastery of the period, lively dialogue, energetic plot, devious characters, and excellent rendition of the willful queen make this a pleasure for fans of historical mysteries." —*Library Journal*

"The sleuthing is fun but what makes *The Twylight Tower* comparable to the fine works of Allison Weir is the strong writing of the author." —*Midwest Book Review*

"Exciting . . . and as cleverly crafted as only Karen Harper can be . . . a hugely appealing and fast-paced tale that keeps the reader satisfied and yearning for more."

—Romancereviewstoday.com

THE TIDAL POOLE

"A nice mix of historical and fictional characters, deft twists and a plucky, engaging young heroine enhance this welcome sequel." —*Publishers Weekly*

"Harper delivers high drama and deadly intrigue . . . she masterfully captures the Elizabethan tone in both language and setting . . . Elizabethan history has never been this appealing."

—*Newsday*

THE POYSON GARDEN

"Impressively researched . . . the author has her poisons and her historical details down pat." —*Los Angeles Times*

"Intoxicating . . . whether you love history, romance, adventure, or mystery, you will be intrigued by this view of Elizabeth as queen and as a brilliant detective." —*Romantic Times*

"A walk side-by-side with one of history's most dynamic characters." —Anne Perry, author of *Half Moon Street*

Elizabeth I Mysteries by

KAREN HARPER

THE POYSON GARDEN
THE TIDAL POOLE
THE TWYLIGHT TOWER
THE QUEENE'S CURE
THE THORNE MAZE
THE QUEENE'S CHRISTMAS
THE FYRE MIRROR
THE FATAL FASHIONE

AN ELIZABETH I MYSTERY

THE FATAL FASHIONE

KAREN HARPER

St. Martin's Paperbacks

THE FATAL FASHIONE

Cover design by Royce M. Becker Design. Illustration of building © Guildhall Art Gallery, Corporation of London/Bridgeman Art Library, London. Queen's cameo © Hatfield House. Gown with eyes © Rainbow Portrait, Hatfield House.

Library of Congress Catalog Card Number: 2005049770

ISBN: 0-312-94193-5
EAN: 9780312-94193-2

Printed in the United States of America

St. Martin's Press hardcover edition / January 2006
St. Martin's Paperbacks edition / December 2006

St. Martin's Paperbacks are published by St. Martin's Press, 175 Fifth Avenue, New York, NY 10010.

10 9 8 7 6 5 4 3 2 1

To Don
for help in visiting London
and the English countryside again

And to Linda Fildew,
the only person I know who lives in Mortlake,
for the tour of the ruins of Richmond Palace

Earlier Events in Elizabeth's Life

1533 Henry VIII marries Anne Boleyn, January 25. Elizabeth born Greenwich Palace, September 7.

1536 Anne Boleyn executed in Tower of London, Elizabeth disinherited from crown. Henry marries Jane Seymour.

1537 Prince Edward born. Queen Jane dies of childbed fever.

1544 Act of Succession and Henry VIII's will establish Mary and Elizabeth in line to throne.

1547 Henry VIII dies. Edward VI crowned.

1553 Queen Mary (Tudor) I crowned. Tries to force England back to Catholicism; gives Margaret Stewart, Tudor cousin, precedence over Elizabeth. Queen Mary weds Prince Philip of Spain by proxy.

1554 Protestant Wyatt Rebellion fails, but Elizabeth sent to Tower for two months, accompanied by Kat Ashley.

1558 Mary dies; Elizabeth succeeds to throne, November 17. Elizabeth appoints William Cecil secretary of state; Robert Dudley made master of the queen's horse.

1558 Elizabeth crowned in Westminster Abbey, January 15. Parliament urges queen to marry, but she resists. Mary, Queen of Scots, becomes queen of France at accession of her young husband, Francis II. Elizabeth knights Thomas Gresham, who writes economic plan for her reign.

1560 Death of Francis II of France makes his young Catholic widow, Mary, Queen of Scots, a danger as Elizabeth's unwanted heir. Thomas Gresham becomes queen's unofficial financial advisor.

1561 The widowed Mary, Queen of Scots, returns to Scotland.

1565 Mary of Scots weds Lord Darnley.

1566 Mary, Queen of Scots, bears son James. Elizabeth defies parliament about marriage.

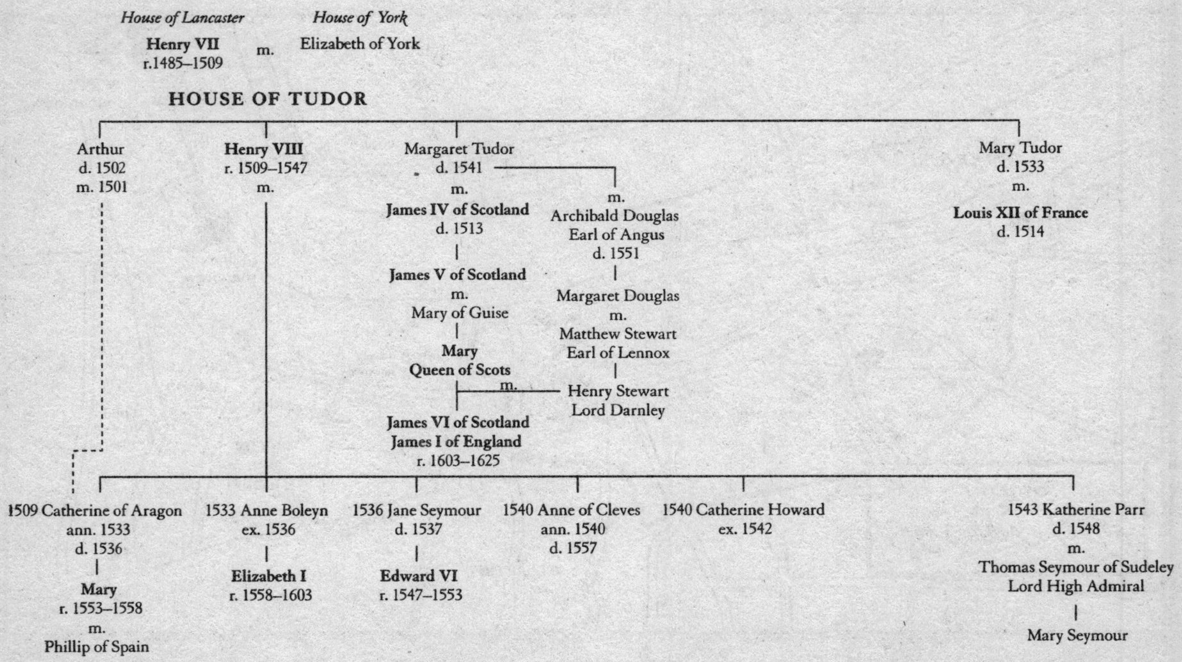
House of Lancaster
House of York
Henry VII
r.1485–1509
m.
Elizabeth of York
HOUSE OF TUDOR
Arthur
d. 1502
m. 1501
Henry VIII
r. 1509–1547
m.
Margaret Tudor
d. 1541
m.
James IV of Scotland
d. 1513
James V of Scotland
m.
Mary of Guise
Mary
Queen of Scots
m.
James VI of Scotland
James I of England
r. 1603–1625
m.
Archibald Douglas
Earl of Angus
d. 1551
Margaret Douglas
m.
Matthew Stewart
Earl of Lennox
Henry Stewart
Lord Darnley
Mary Tudor
d. 1533
m.
Louis XII of France
d. 1514
1509 Catherine of Aragon
ann. 1533
d. 1536
Mary
r. 1553–1558
m.
Phillip of Spain
1533 Anne Boleyn
ex. 1536
Elizabeth I
r. 1558–1603
1536 Jane Seymour
d. 1537
Edward VI
r. 1547–1553
1540 Anne of Cleves
ann. 1540
d. 1557
1540 Catherine Howard
ex. 1542
1543 Katherine Parr
d. 1548
m.
Thomas Seymour of Sudeley
Lord High Admiral
Mary Seymour

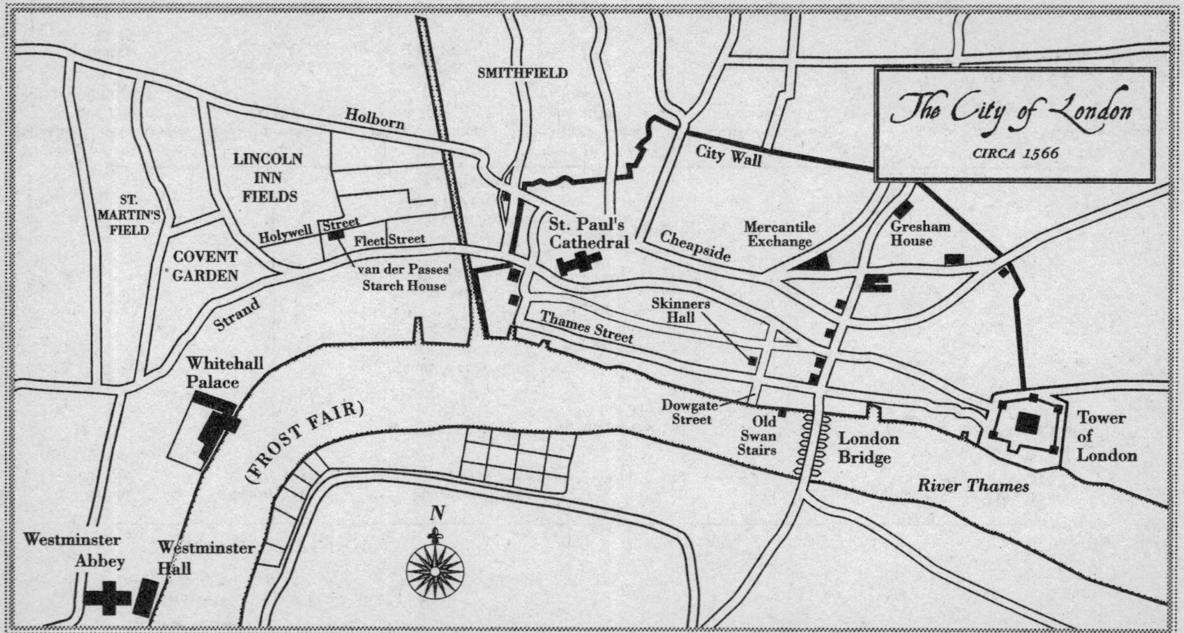
The City of London
CIRCA 1566
SMITHFIELD
Holborn
City Wall
LINCOLN INN FIELDS
ST. MARTIN'S FIELD
COVENT GARDEN
Holywell Street
Fleet Street
van der Passes' Starch House
St. Paul's Cathedral
Cheapside
Mercantile Exchange
Gresham House
Strand
Thames Street
Skinners Hall
Whitehall Palace
Dowgate Street
Old Swan Stairs
London Bridge
Tower of London
River Thames
(FROST FAIR)
N
Westminster Abbey
Westminster Hall

And hereby it appeareth that no people in the world are so curiouse in new fangles as they of England be.

—PHILIP STUBBES
The Anatomie of Abuses

Oh, how much cost is bestowed nowadays upon our bodies, and how little upon our souls!

—WILLIAM HARRISON
Description of England

The Fatal Fashione

Prologue

WHITEHALL PALACE, LONDON

OCTOBER 21, 1566

"IF THE MEMBERS OF PARLIAMENT ARE HERE, THEY may cool their heels for a while!" Elizabeth Tudor announced the moment William Cecil, her trusted secretary of state, was admitted to her withdrawing room. "They have come to urge me to marriage and motherhood, but I know what they are thinking even beyond that impertinence."

"That if—when—you refuse," Cecil said, "they will urge you to name your cousin Queen Mary of Scots as your heir, even if she is a Catholic?"

"Exactly. And I'll not play into their hands."

"They do await your presence, Your Grace. But you sent for me?"

Though she had been attired in her bedchamber, her ladies were still arranging her large neck ruff and long strands of pearls. She'd wanted to see Cecil before she faced down the men who forever tried to tell her how to govern. At least Cecil merely advised.

"I cannot abide their audacity," Elizabeth went on, flinging gestures despite her women's attempted ministrations. "They think, because my cousin Queen Mary of Scots has wed again and produced a son, that I must wed posthaste and go to breeding, too. They believe they have me trapped. For if I choose not to wed and do name Mary my successor, I risk my safety, because my death would place her on the throne. 'S blood, my Catholic shires to the north could rise in open rebellion. And my Parliament is one step from that, I swear they are!"

"Yes, Your Grace, but I believe their concerns about the succession have some validity and merit, and their words to you—"

"Were rude and rash so far." She took the last loop of pearls from Lady Rosie's hands—Rosie always panicked when her queen raised her voice—and finished the job herself. Leaving her ladies behind, she strode toward Cecil with her huge black satin skirts swishing.

"You saw what they dared write to me!" she told him. "'It sets a fatal fashion if a young queen does not wed, and endangers the realm.' *I* set the fashions here, my lord, not only for garments and ornament, such as what they are calling these 'pearls of the virgin' set off against my favorite black, but for manners, behavior—even morals."

"I understand, Your Grace."

"Do they think I am some green girl or schoolroom dunce to be lectured and set aright? I'll not be preached to about suitors, foreign or domestic, nor about who should get my throne if I departed this earth. For I do not plan to do that for years, God willing!"

He seemed to have no retort to that, or else he realized she needed to vent her ire and would calm down if he but listened. Yes, she and Cecil knew each other well after all these years working together, first to attain the throne and then to preserve and use it well for her people. Elizabeth knew she had been the cause of most of the lines on his long face and the gray hairs in his shovel-shaped beard, which made him look older than his forty-six years.

She heaved a sigh and turned to glance into her new Venetian looking glass. Good—her appearance was startling, even stark, with the black bodice and skirt and the huge white satin and gold-embroidered sleeves. Her starched neck ruff was so stiff and large it almost looked as if her red, bejeweled head were on a platter—which her enemies, and there were many, would love to see.

With a decisive nod to Cecil, the queen preceded him out. The two yeomen guards at the door fell in behind. She might be a woman, Elizabeth thought, a *mere* female as her father had said more than once, but she still—thanks to a good and gracious God—looked young and strong at age thirty-three after eight years on England's throne. Graceful, tall for a woman, and slim, with sharp dark eyes and gold-red hair, she was still what her court favorite, Robin Dudley, called "fetching".

Yet, though she never told even her closest friends and advisors such, not even Robin or Cecil, she intended to live and die unwed, but for her marriage to her country, of course. From her toddling days, she'd seen at too close range what dreadful things men could do to women, even their wives—even queens.

Flanked by her crimson-clad guards, Elizabeth Tudor stood beneath the scarlet canopy of state on the dais before her throne, facing sixty parliamentarians, thirty from the House of Lords and thirty from the House of Commons. The nobility had donned their best attire for the occasion; even the others wore their best. The few Puritan members, led by Hosea Cantwell, were in their somber black and white, as if following her fashion, when in truth all they did was carp about it.

She had expressly forbidden the speakers of the two houses of Parliament to attend, for she meant to do the speaking on this day. If they thought her so-called weaker sex would make her entreat or retreat, they were much mistaken. Did they not know she had learned—though sometimes from afar and under fire—from her sire, Henry VIII, that talented builder and terrible destroyer?

"Lords and men of England," she began, in turn staring directly at each man in the front row. "You write to me of my 'fatal fashion' of not wedding and pronounce it dangerous to crown and kingdom. And so you try to coerce and force your queen to obey your will."

She leveled a straight arm and finger at them in a slow arc. The northern earls Northumberland and Derby, both covert Catholics who could raise a rebellion, stood next to her dear Robin, Earl of Leicester. All visibly braced themselves and flared their nostrils as if they were stags scenting a wolf on the wind. A frown furrowing his brow, Hosea Cantwell from the Commons glared back at her.

"How have I governed?" she plunged on, clasping a fist of dangling pearls in her free hand. "I need not say much, for my deeds speak for me. And do not use the words 'fatal fashion' to me. Fatal fashions are treasons, greed and lust, adultery and murder—and rebellions—in my kingdom. England must take a stand for justice. You must see to the proper punishment of lawbreakers and even to your own sins. Best tend to the safety of your country and your queen—and not by trying to force her to wed and bed, but by helping her, not hindering."

More than one man shifted his weight or shuffled his

feet. Several turned their caps about in their hands. This utter refusal was obviously not what they had expected. 'S blood, did they not know her yet?

"Some of you have whispered that I fear death in childbirth. Oh, yes, I know your thoughts, that and others," she added, looking directly at the northern earls whose shires bordered Scotland. "I do not fear death, for all men are mortal, and though I be a woman, yet I have as good a courage as ever my father had. I am your anointed queen. I will never be by violence constrained to do anything. I thank God I am endowed with such qualities that if I were turned out of the realm in my petticoat, I would be able to live in any place in Christendom."

Robin looked amused by the petticoat point, yet her stare wiped the smile from that handsome face. Cecil seemed almost smug, while the others stood stunned by her defiance. No doubt those who'd had to settle for the back of the crowd now blessed their good fortune.

Elizabeth of England said no more but stood for several moments, as if daring them to gainsay her. She only prayed no one guessed that her pulse pounded and the velvet neckband of her cartwheel ruff was soaked with sweat.

She glanced at the massive portrait of her father, hanging behind her audience. They probably thought she nodded to them before she turned and strode from the chamber. She thanked God they could not see that, beneath her skirts, her silk-stockinged legs shook like a child's.

Chapter the First

"JUST EVERYONE IN THE CITY IS TALKING ABOUT what you said to the deputation from Parliament, Your Grace," Meg Milligrew told the queen the next morning. As Her Majesty's strewing herb mistress of the privy chamber, Meg scented the draperies and bedclothes with fresh, fragrant herbs each day.

They were more than queen and servant, for Meg had been with Elizabeth in the difficult days before the throne was hers. Now, with select others, she sometimes helped Her Majesty in dangerous situations that had to be kept private. The young woman resembled her monarch, and that had served the queen's purpose more than once.

Meg had recently returned from a week at Hampstead Heath, a rural area just north of London. She had gone to gather autumn herbs, but also to see her ten-year-old daughter, Sally. Years before, though Meg had been told by her now deceased husband that their only child had died of the small pox, he had actually given the baby away to a country couple. Later Meg learned that her child lived, though her little face was horribly scarred. Meg visited Sally at her family's small farm several times a year, laden with gifts from the queen so that the child would know, as Elizabeth had said in a note to her, "that you are special to us."

"Then what are they saying about me today?" the queen asked, looking up from the letter she was writing.

"That you are as strong as your sire, old King Henry, even if you are one-tenth of his size, that's what I heard the bargeman say."

Elizabeth shouted a laugh. "I like that. What else?"

"That no matter if the Scots queen has a son, they prefer their virgin queen since she is pure English."

Elizabeth threw down her quill and stood. "Their virgin queen is pure English," she echoed as Meg began to rub the bed curtains with sweet cicely and woodruff. "I'd wager my people are pleased I am pure English because of all the foreigners coming to our shores these days. Our island is becoming quite a stew of strangers and their ways."

"But that means new fripperies and fancies," Meg said, as she sneezed at her own scented dust. She jammed a finger under her nose and spoke nasally. "I've smelled that new nicotine smoke the sailors inhale from their pipes, 'drinking tobacco' as they call it. Others are trying it, too, though I don't s'pose it will ever catch on with proper people."

"You never know about the passion for fashion, my Meg."

"Like the Dutch ladies started with their starch. Oh, by the way, Your Grace, I brought back baskets of cuckoo-pint roots for Hannah von Hoven's starch. I'm grateful you let me sell to her, as it gives me extra money to send to Sally's family. I'm hoping to harvest enough of the roots next year to visit your other starcher and see if she'll buy some, too. Hannah's been arguing with me about the prices lately, saying the cost is too dear, when I work hard to find and dig up those roots. Still, what would she do without starch, and what would we all do without the Dutch ladies bringing in their secrets of it?"

"What indeed? Keep to our limp little ruffs or start a new trend, I warrant. But as for fancy foreign imports, I draw the line at French cooking. They actually eat frog legs," Elizabeth said with a shudder, "and who knows what else they try to hide under all those strange sauces. The Earl of Leicester's looking for a Frenchie cook, and I told him I don't trust one of them worth a fig in a kitchen I'm eating from."

"But won't there be French stuffs to buy at the shops in Sir Thomas Gresham's new mercantile exchange when it's finished? That's what else is on everyone's lips in London, how your money man, as they call him, looks like he's building a place bigger even than his house on Bishopsgate. After he's lived abroad in Antwerp all these years, they say he's building a barn house just like the Flemish built there."

"Not a barn house, my Meg—a *bourse.*"

"That's right—a bourse, just like the foreign one."

Frowning, Elizabeth leaned on an elbow into a recessed window overlooking the Thames. She pushed the mullioned pane farther ajar to catch the crisp breeze off the river. The autumn sun felt fine, but with it in her eyes, even leaning out a bit, she couldn't see far in the direction where Gresham's great endeavor was under way.

"Sir Thomas Gresham's new financial and shopping establishment," the queen said, "may be inspired by the mercantile exchange in Antwerp, but it is to be an *English* exchange house, with shops to sell *our* goods as well as some of the finer imported ones. But predominantly English, not foreign, for that belief has always undergirded his philosophy even when he's lived abroad."

Sir Thomas Gresham was her chief financial advisor and

one of the new breed she was relying on in her reign: men of exceptional talent, not necessarily of noble birth; men like William Cecil himself, who had been Thomas Gresham's mentor. Brilliant and adept in international finance, Gresham had risen fast and far under her brother, King Edward. Elizabeth's sister, Queen Mary, had dismissed him because he was not Catholic, but Hugh Dauntsey, the man Mary had put in charge, made such a botch of England's foreign financial affairs that she had eaten royal crow and brought Gresham swiftly back.

In Elizabeth's reign, Thomas had helped her pay off foreign debts at good rates and strengthened English coinage, which her father had debased with all his wild spending. Gresham had been her eyes and ears abroad, living in Antwerp in Flanders but traveling widely. She admired and relied on him so heavily she had knighted him. Even though her lord treasurer, William Paulet, who had served the Tudors even longer than Gresham had, often spoke against the younger man as rash and too freethinking, she would bet her kingdom on Gresham. More than once, when it came to the fashions of finance, she already had.

"Meg, when you go out, have the guards send a secretary and a rider to me. I believe I will inform Sir Thomas that I will come myself to see this new wonder of our age."

The queen set out that afternoon garbed like a prosperous merchant's wife in a sturdy, dark worsted gown, the hood of a cloak pulled over her red head. With three others, she went by unmarked barge to the river steps at Dowgate Street. Lady Rosie Radcliffe, likewise attired, attended Elizabeth with two plainly dressed, armed guards. These were her most trusted yeoman, Clifford, and her longtime protector, Stephen Jenks.

Sir Thomas Gresham, with two of his men waiting with horses, met the *incognito* party at the landing. He was dressed in somber black, not in mourning for his son or to match the current style but because he always wore that practical, businesslike hue.

Gresham at forty-seven was beginning to show his age. Furrows lined his brow, and crow's-feet perched at the corners of his gray-blue eyes. His taut lips were framed by a trimmed silvered beard. Thinner than usual, almost gaunt, he leaned on a walking stick and limped markedly from being thrown and nearly crushed to death by his horse six years ago.

The queen realized her money man had also been aged by grief. Two years ago he had lost his only son and heir at age twenty from malignant fever. Thomas and his wife, Anne, had a young daughter they had adopted in Antwerp, but she could hardly inherit the massive Gresham fortune. So Sir Thomas had decided to spend part of his wealth on his huge building project to help his homeland and perpetuate his name.

"Thomas, I am pleased you recognize me without the fabulous pearls you brought me," she jested as they huddled together at the windy watergate. "I thought it best you give me a tour without a lot of to-do and hangers-on."

"I am honored, Your Majesty. I believe this exchange will be a star in the crown of your capital city, and I am proud to show it to its crowned queen, even in fledgling form as it is. And, I must say, this project has begun a building boom in other parts of the city."

The mutual admiration between the financial genius and his queen ran deeper than many knew; theirs was a meeting not only of minds but of memories. Thomas had been one of the first to pledge allegiance to Elizabeth when she became queen, and he had served on her first council. He, too, had lost his mother when he was but three and knew what it was to have a stepmother. Like the queen, he'd had a powerful father, albeit a commoner, in whose footsteps he walked: His sire had been high sheriff and lord mayor of London as well as founder of the Gresham family fortune through trade with the Merchant Adventurers.

Jenks cupped his hands to give Elizabeth a boost up to her mount, and she lifted her knee over the horn of the sidesaddle to settle herself. With a guard before and behind her, the party strung out along Dowgate, heading north toward Cornhill in the most mercantile part of town, crowded with shops and livery company halls. This late in the day, the hawkers' cries were few, as many were already home. By now goodwives or servants had purchased whatever would grace the tables of London this evening before darkness fell.

"To clear the area for your visit, I gave the crew an early good day," Thomas explained as he rode beside but slightly behind her. "There are but a few necessary watchmen about the place now."

People made way for the mounted party, though some stared up at them. Elizabeth kept her hood pulled close to her face. She startled as a pan of slop from one of the overhanging stories above just missed her skirt. She urged her horse toward the middle of the street, despite the fact it then walked in the shallow sewer ditch. Just ahead, she saw the large cleared site, looking clean and spare with great marble stones rising from its base.

"This will be very grand, Thomas, bigger than I imagined it when you explained your plans," she said as they reined in.

Both he and Jenks helped her down. Three men were on the site, guarding stacks of materials and supplies, but only one seemed to pay them heed.

"It was shameful the way merchant traders had to meet in the open on Lombard Street for years, Your Grace. There we were much subject to the weather and to the possibility that someone lurking nearby would overhear us. Yet I am keeping the tradition of a bell rung twice a day to summon traders. Only this bell will hang from a high tower—there," he said, pointing skyward. "And it, like the dormers of the fourth-floor slate window, will be graced with the sign of the Gresham name."

"Your grasshopper insignia?" she asked, for she recalled the name Gresham came from two old English words for "grass" and "farm," a farm no doubt full of the high-jumping insects. Now, as never before, that sign seemed a perfect symbol for this ambitious, loyal man who leaped fast and high in her service and esteem. Thomas's notes to her always had his grasshopper crest pressed into the wax from his signet ring; he wore a gold one now on his left index finger.

He took her on a tour, pointing out sites whereon would stand outer colonnaded arches supporting second-story rows of shops for mercers, smiths, and tradesmen. Within the future colonnades would lie the open space for a vast inner courtyard where merchants and traders from England and all of Europe could meet and bargain for personal and national fortunes.

"No more, I pray," he told her solemnly, "will the focus of financial power be on the Continent, among our foes as well as friends, but here, in the heart of our England. By the way, Your Majesty, second-floor niches will each be graced by the bronze and painted statue of an English ruler, with yourself in the very center. And, of course, your royal arms will hang over the Gresham arms at the front double-arched entry."

"All that pleases me mightily, for this grand edifice must be not be a mere copy of a foreign bourse but English to its foundation. As you say, it will bring the control of capital and trade monopolies to our very door."

"But the future of our mercantile power lies in competition, Your Grace, not in monopolies," he corrected, then looked as if he'd like to snatch his words back. "Though I realize," he added hastily, "that the monarchy keeps powerful noble factions loyal by bestowing monopolies."

"I've always encouraged competition and then granted monopolies to the best man. In the case of the fledgling starch industry, however, my approval shall go to the best woman."

"Forgive me, Your Majesty, but monopolies in the financial future I—we—envision *must* rely on open competition."

"As I do now," she insisted, her voice rising. Though she was hardly dealing with stiff-necked parliamentarians, she faced him squarely. "Here is my credo on all of that, Thomas. Competition—and perhaps monopolies, if they are best—is for deserving men and women. Why, if I didn't believe in competition for all, I'd still have Lord Paulet handing out consignments and gratuities as my father did. I keep Paulet as treasurer of state in name only, a figurehead. It's you I consult, not him, though I know he fumes at both of us for that."

"More than fumes, Your Majesty, now that you bring him up. I warrant he tries to do me damage in the eyes of others—including my queen—at each turn."

"But I am onto him, and he still serves his purpose to

keep my conservative-minded men in line. They've been seething since we stripped to the bone that bloated bureaucracy of Paulet's friends my father left behind."

"I have often been grateful you are so bold and clear-sighted in assessing people, Your Grace."

"Though there have been a few who have hoodwinked me," she muttered, as they began to stroll again. "But, Thomas, as for my fostering competition, even foreign if need be, take the burgeoning new starch industry. Mrs. Dingen van der Passe and her hovering hulk of a husband have more than once tried to suggest I bestow upon them the right to control all London starch houses, and I've told them no. I cannot see shutting the door on such young talent as her competitors, someone like Mistress Hannah von Hoven, who also—"

Though Thomas had seemed sure-footed, he stumbled, grunted, and almost pitched into her. She caught his arm as his walking stick clattered to the cobbles. One of his watchmen, a short, sinewy man with eyebrows that seemed knit together as one dark slash across his face, darted to pick it up, then backed away again. Elizabeth was surprised that anyone had stood so close, for she had not seen or heard him. But she noted now that the man emanated a strange acrid scent she had smelled earlier, no doubt the residue of mortar or resin on his person.

"Forgive me, Your Majesty," Thomas said. He turned away a moment and called to the man—perhaps a personal guard, she thought—"My thanks, Badger."

"Thomas, I will forgive you on the condition that you visit both of the starch houses I've mentioned, Mrs. van der Passe's large one and Hannah von Hoven's small establishment, to see what I mean. I've been sending ruffs to both, encouraging both. Indeed, Hannah's small shop is holding its own in the burgeoning business."

Suddenly, he seemed more distressed than his near fall had made him. "Your Most Gracious Majesty, I keep so busy here—"

"I will only be a *gracious* majesty if you humor me on this. I'll not have you believe your queen is not forward-thinking. I will inform both women that the illustrious Sir Thomas Gresham, financier and builder of the English exchange, will honor them with a visit. My herb mistress sells Hannah the roots of the cuckoo-pint herb to make starch, so everyone profits, you'll see."

Thomas nodded, but she could see she'd upset him. Perhaps, despite the numerous industries he had personally encouraged, one run strictly by women to promote style was beneath him. If so, her heartfelt admiration of the man would suffer. Too, she had heard that he and his wife were not getting on of late, and she never approved of marital discord among her closest subjects.

"I shall look forward to the visits and encourage both ladies," Thomas assured her, but he still looked annoyed. Men would ever be men, she thought. She told herself again: Though she could hardly rule without them, she'd never take one on as mate or king.

Carting four hemp sacks of walnut-sized cuckoo-pint roots, two sacks knotted over each shoulder, Meg Milligrew left the palace through the kitchen block and headed for Kings Street at midmorning the next day. Under the Court Gate, she nearly bumped into Ned Topside. Ned, whose real name was

Edward Thompson, was the queen's principal player for court entertainments.

With roguish green eyes, chiseled nose, curly hair, and well-turned legs, Ned was beguiling and knew it. Talented, too, for the clever thespian could become a prince or a pauper in the blink of an eye. When Elizabeth Tudor was still a princess and struggling simply to remain safe, Ned had taught Meg not only to read and write but to mimic the queen in stance and speech, so that she could serve as Her Majesty's counterpart upon occasions of the queen's choosing.

Ned was witty, besides, with his glib tongue and teasing ways, a man women adored on stage and off. Though she'd lied to herself about it for years, Meg knew she not only hated but loved Ned, and had since she'd laid eyes on him eight years ago. She considered herself a reasonable person, but, curse the man, he always managed to make her sound like a ninnyhammer.

"Mistress Milligrew," he declaimed, and swept off his cap in a bow, "as they used to say in days of yore, whither goest thou?"

"Where you'd like to go, you blackguard, but Her Majesty has sent me this time instead. To Hannah von Hoven's with roots to make starch."

"Her Grace only sent me once to her with your cuckoo roots when you were puking, as I recall. After all, I deem you the real stiff and prickly Mistress Starch, not her."

"That isn't funny. And one official visit doesn't mean you didn't go back to see her on your own and more than once, smelling of pomade, I heard you did."

"Did Jenks tell you that?" he inquired, taking two of the

sacks from her shoulders so fast that, suddenly unbalanced, she almost tipped into him.

"What if he did?" she challenged, her voice rising.

"Jenks is still sweet on you and wants you to be angry with me, that's all. I don't love Hannah."

"Love?" she screeched, snatching back her sacks. "When did that ever enter into the talk between you and one of your—"

"I missed you, too, the week you were away," he interrupted, and darted a quick kiss on her forehead. He wedged her in with one arm on the arched wall of the gate, heedless of how people stared. To her amazement, he tenderly brushed her flyaway hair from her face and tucked the loose tresses behind each ear.

In a silky voice, he said, "You always did have the most lovely skin, and your ears are like little sea shells. Meg, Hannah may be fair of face and form, but you are—"

"—onto your seductive flatteries, Ned Topside, actor *extraordinaire.* Save your lip for Her Majesty—or both lips for Hannah. Now leave off and let me pass!"

Instead, he stepped closer and put both big, warm hands on hers where she gripped the tied necks of her sacks. Her voice came out breathy this time. "Don't trifle with me, Ned."

"You are not a trifle to me, lovey." His voice, too, was husky, which only made the butterflies in her stomach beat their wings harder in her wretched need for him. "Let me go with you," he whispered, "and after we can—"

"I have business with Hannah and don't need you underfoot!" She wrenched herself from his touch. Devil take it, she should have wed Jenks when she had the chance two years ago, but she feared then her heart would be untrue not only to herself but to dear Jenks. And after he had saved Ned's life, they both owed him dearly.

"Her Majesty," Meg said in a calmer tone, noticing that several palace servants upon their own errands had stopped to stare, "has sent me to tell Hannah that Sir Thomas Gresham will visit her soon with some questions and she's not to think aught is amiss. Now, if you please, let me pass."

She was certain Ned, too, realized they had an audience, because he dramatically lifted his hands, palms out, to his shoulders, as though he would never touch her again.

"If I pleased, you would not pass," he said. Those green eyes seemed to devour her. "I had hoped for a softer tone and sweeter touch after your week away. I only hope things went much better between you and your little Sally than between us. Good day then, Mistress Milligrew, alias Mistress Starch."

With a half-bow and a flourish of his hand, he disappeared into the small crowd that had gathered. Her cheeks aflame, Meg turned and hied herself up Whitehall toward Charing Cross just west of the royal mews, berating herself with each step.

Ned had seemed so sincere when he'd mentioned her daughter and bid a hurt farewell. Why did she always have to act the shrew with him when he made advances? If he didn't care for her one whit, wouldn't he have given up long ago? Or did he just like the challenge? For the love of heaven, why couldn't she feel this swept away by solid, sturdy Jenks?

She saw a little girl about Sally's age sitting in a doorway, cutting scraps of cloth with a small knife. Tears filled Meg's eyes. Sally. She must keep her thoughts on Sally, not Ned.

Though she made her way through the crowded crosstraffic of Charing Cross, Meg saw again the day—last

Wednesday, it was—when she and Sally had gone off alone to cut the cuckoo-pint roots she now bore on her shoulders.

Look in the shaded spots for the telltale bright red berries, but don't eat any, Meg heard her own warning voice say to her daughter. *All parts of the plant are poison. Why, even touching the starch made from the roots turns the hands of laundresses and starchers chapped and red.*

But it won't hurt us to just pick them, Mother Meg, before the starch is all boiled up?

Meg smiled even now at the way the girl called her "Mother Meg" and her adoptive mother "Mother Susan." They both tried hard to keep anything from harming or even frightening the child. Her poor face was so scarred from the small pox that had nearly killed her as a baby, but her adopted family owned no mirrors, and the child knew she was cherished.

Meg prayed that would be enough to sustain Sally when her parents told her—soon but reluctantly, they would, they said—about her disfigured face. Meanwhile, Meg feared the girl would see her image in a polished kettle or horse-trough water. At least Sally was living on a small, isolated farm on the fringe of the heath, not here in London where a woman's face could be her fate. Gracious, if Hannah's starch business didn't make her name and fortune, surely the blessing of her beauty would.

Even though the cuckoo-pint plant is cursed to be poison, Meg had told Sally, *the Lord God gave it a special blessing.*

Sally had looked up into Meg's face, breathless to hear. *What blessing, Mother Meg?*

The pollen—the seed dust—of the plant glows in the dark, like fairy lamps. Can you see it on the leaves in the deep shade there?

Oh, yes—pretty fairy lamps! she'd cried, clapping her hands.

The fen folk call them shiners, my dearest girl, and can even find them at night by their glow. I think the stuff is so pretty, I've collected it over the years, and keep it in a little box. In daylight it is mere dust, but at night—bright magic!

Isn't it silly, then? Sally had said with a giggle. *Poison that glows and draws one to it . . .*

"Eh, watch where *ja* going, *ja* clay-brained baggage!" A man's voice jolted Meg from her reverie.

She'd bumped into him, a tall man with hulking shoulders. Though he was all in black, he sported a flat taffeta cap of striped red and blue. He sounded foreign, but then, so did too many in London these days. As he, fortunately, turned away and hurried off, Meg noted she'd somehow walked a few doors past Hannah's. From here she could see laundresses and bleachers, called whitsters, guarding their linens spread to dry in St. Martin's fields just beyond, so many sheets it seemed to have snowed. She turned around and went through a narrow alley to the entrance of the young Flemish woman's starch house.

Compared to the large establishment Mrs. Dingen van der Passe owned over on Holywell Street, Hannah's place was small and plain, just a large loft; three women worked with her, instead of the veritable army Mrs. van der Passe employed. Both of the starchers were from Flanders in the low, or Dutch, countries, but the older woman had come first and caught the queen's eye. Why, Dingen van der Passe claimed she could make a ruff from a spider's web, and she charged five pounds to teach others to starch their own neck and wrist ruffs at home if they didn't bring them in like the servants of the queen's courtiers did.

"Hannah!" Meg called up the narrow enclosed stairs, wishing the sprightly woman would come down to help her lug these sacks. Meg hoped she wasn't still upset over the way they'd contended over the price of the herbs last time. Gracious, that petite, pretty woman could screech and argue, and she was tight with the purse strings.

"Hannah, it's Meg Milligrew with your starch roots!"

Silence from above. Not even the usual echo of laughter or patter of quick feet. Was no one up there to help, even if Hannah had stepped out? Grunting, Meg trudged up the steps, bumping her sacks against the walls, half wishing she had let Ned come along. She really had been too hard on him.

Though amazed to find the loft deserted, she saw nothing amiss. Suspended from stretched cords, rows of newly starched ruffs of all shapes and sizes dried in the brisk air from a window set ajar. The neck-sized wooden forms that held ruffs while they were set with heated poking sticks bore finished ruffs.

Meg thumped her burden to the floor and noted that the low braziers that heated the poking sticks had burned down to silver ashes. She walked toward the long, open window overlooking the fields. Within the large, coffin-shaped dipping vat, the bath of milky white starch lay undisturbed—but for the stiff human hand that floated up from beneath to break the surface.

Chapter the Second

"ANNE," THOMAS GRESHAM CALLED TO HIS WIFE, "someone's moved my things all around on this shelf in here!"

She came to the door of his privy second-story chamber, which overlooked the central courtyard and gardens of their huge home.

"You surely didn't let little Marie play in here, did you?" he asked, glaring at the rearranged, neatly aligned items.

"At thirteen years of age, she's hardly little anymore. I've been out on an errand and just returned myself. Besides, you've ofttimes had her in here, our Marie-Anne."

Why did she always insist on using not the name the child had been born with, Marie, but the hyphenated one she had given the girl when she'd agreed to rear her? Bridling his temper, he said, "But she was only in here when I was with her."

"No, she wasn't in here lately."

"I told you the servants aren't needed here to clean, and only you have access besides me—"

"Whatever is wrong, then?" she demanded, bustling in with her household keys clanking. "Yes, I may have moved a thing or two, for I can't abide the jumbled way you keep things—bizarre things, as if you were yet a boy with your prizes from the woods or stables, like those strange brown pieces of soil dug from the earth of your beloved financial exchange."

"Hell's gates, woman, that's precisely the shelf that's been tampered with! It was right here," he said, banging his fist on the oaken length of it, now all dusted and tidied.

"But you already had plugs of soil you'd kept from the day the cornerstone of this house was laid. You even had doubles of them, so I assumed you have extras of the one that broke."

"Broke?" he echoed, raking his fingers through his hair. "Anne, just tell me where in hell are the pieces of my dried brown cake, the one that looked different from the others."

"Cake? That one did look and smell strange."

"About this big?" he demanded, circling together the thumbs and index fingers of both hands. "And—it broke?"

"When I moved it, it dropped and went to pieces and dust on the tiles, then dirtied the good Turkish carpet. It was a mess, and I swept it up, which I should never have to do in this huge house of servants, oh, no, not Sir Thomas Gresham's wife. But he doesn't want any servants in the great big room full of—of dirt in more ways than one!"

"I didn't ask or tell you to clean here—to tamper with my things!"

"But it was just soil, wasn't it? You look white as a sheet."

"Only because you managed to break and discard a gift for Her Majesty, a unique and expensive one at that!"

Anne sucked in a breath and clapped her hands over her mouth. She was still fair, his Anne, with her slender, erect form and piercing blue eyes that used to so enchant him. When their love was new-fledged, she could captivate him with a smile or a touch. Fire still danced in her eyes, even if now it oft heralded a spat and not a seduction. She might look fragile, but her physical stamina and strength were deceptive. Until Marie was nearly six years old, Anne had sometimes carted her about as if she were a toddler.

Once her passion had been for him; she'd been pregnant with their son when they'd married. But the flames slowly went out, and Anne never seemed happy again. Granted, she'd served as his hostess among the rich and powerful in Europe and much favored the new fashions and furnishings the Gresham wealth provided—yet, ever homesick, she'd carped about how much time he spent away, and she'd detested living abroad all those years. Even now, back in England with occasional visits to the queen's court, she was malcontent.

Besides a passion for power and possessions, Thomas felt he and Anne had little in common now. The tragedy of losing their only son and heir had not united them in grief but had augmented their alienation. Even their little girl, though beloved by both parents, managed to stand between them.

"Why," Anne demanded, as her fisted hands perched on her waist, "in all of God's creation would you give the queen a dirt cake? The pearls you found for her, the other things, including that fine Barbary horse you brought her back once, I can see, but—"

He collapsed into the nearest carved chair. His bad leg was losing its strength, and he was about to lose his temper. He felt sick, just sick. And here the queen had coerced him into visiting starch houses, one of which he'd vowed desperately to himself he'd never set foot in again, and to protect Anne, damn her.

"What was the little cake, then?" she wheedled, her voice

low as she propped herself up with both hands on the edge of his worktable. As if it were a dark mirror, the polished oaken surface reflected her image. Strangely, that recalled for him the painting of the twin girls he had hidden in a locked chest in this very room, one face in sunlight, the other more in shadow.

"That cake," he explained through gritted teeth, "was of a rare sort of dried paste the Spanish call *chocolata.* It is the source of a rich drink King Philip has had secretly imported from the New World. A royal drink among the Indian rulers there, good for health and worth a fortune—a perfect gift for a queen."

She had the decency to look shocked and sorry. He slumped back in the chair, gripping the arms of it so hard his fingers went white.

"I—you never tell me things anymore," she accused. "How was I to know? I never did know half the things you were up to. Can you get more? I know you have your sources. I know you have your secret imports, too."

He looked up at her; their narrowed gazes met and held. His eyes, not hers, were glassy with tears. The fact that he'd once taken a mistress and had loved her utterly—still did—was what truly always lay between them. It hadn't even helped that Anne knew the woman was dead, or that Anne deeply loved his illegitimate daughter she'd reared. She doted on the child she called Marie-Anne, as if she could pretend the child was truly hers and Gretta had never been. But she *had* been and seemed to stalk them yet, now not only as spirit but, lately, as flesh.

"Are you quite sure," he asked, trying to control his voice, "the cake of *chocolata* is destroyed?"

"Gone out with the rubbish two days ago," she said flatly—smugly, he thought, as if she were somehow now enjoying this. "My lord, I regret the mishap but cannot change it—like mistakes in life. Well, at least *I* admit and rue mistakes *I* have made."

He struggled to ignore that thrust. "Then I must ask you not to come in here again, even to tend or clean this chamber. And I'd best go see Marie to tell her the same, at least that she cannot enter unless I am here."

"Which you seldom are—never were," Anne muttered, and swept from the room.

He was surprised to find her waiting for him in the hall. Perhaps she wanted to be sure he did not speak sharply to Marie, but then she knew he cherished the child, too, for the girl's sake as well as for the lovely, lost woman who had borne her thirteen long years ago.

"Marie!" he called outside the girl's apartments. He heard no answer, no movement within.

"Isn't she about?" he asked Anne, who pushed the door open and went in. "It's nearly midday," he went on. "Don't you know where she is?"

They peeked into the bedchamber together. The bed was mussed but empty. "She was here, resting because she stayed up late last night, reading, she said," Anne explained, her voice rising. "I told her I would fetch her for midday meal when you came home. I told you we should find a young maid-companion for her, one to sleep in her room since her nurse is gone now."

"She's not feeling ill?"

"She said she was fine."

Fine or no, Marie was neither in her three rooms nor in the other thirty-eight on four floors of Gresham House. The parents and servants searched the central gardens, the stables, the street.

Thomas gripped Anne's arm when they met in their frenzy by the front entrance. Servants' voices calling for their daughter echoed through the mansion. "I'm going to the construction site to be sure she isn't there looking for me, though she knows better than to go out alone." He turned away, then added, "If she's not there, I'll raise a force of men. We'll search the area—the city if we must. The queen will help put out a hue and cry, I know she will."

"Godspeed, Thomas. Godspeed," Anne cried after him as he painfully climbed the mounting block he always used to get onto a horse with this damned leg. He blinked back tears. Those were the very words his dear Gretta had said to him before, still cradling their tiny baby, she'd closed her eyes and died.

In early afternoon, Queen Elizabeth walked in the walled privy palace gardens with her lord treasurer, William Paulet, the Marquess of Winchester. She'd chosen the fresh air because the old man always seemed to reek of the dust of the past. He'd served as comptroller of the royal household under her father and as lord treasurer under her brother and sister.

Widowed now, but looking for a wife even at age eighty-one, Paulet had entertained Elizabeth munificently at his country home in Hampshire on her royal progress last summer. She'd jested it was too bad he was so elderly or she would put him on Parliament's list of potential suitors. The wily old man seemed unwilling to retire or to depart this earth until he achieved his aims, several of which, she feared, ran counter to her interests. Politically, he was still helpful; personally, he was untrustworthy and Catholic to the core.

Worse, some of his closest friends were the northern lords she feared might rise in rebellion and support of her cousin, Queen Mary of Scots.

Of ruddy complexion, with thinning hair but thickening jowls, Will Paulet, as his friends called him, was hardly heeded these days by the monarch, and he knew it. Still, it did not keep him from lecturing her long and loud, for he was hard of hearing, too.

As ever today, he was accompanied by Hugh Dauntsey, one of his minions, who at least had the sense to stand on the other side of the large fountain to give them some privacy. Dauntsey was the charming, staunch Catholic her sister, Queen Mary Tudor, had brought in to replace Gresham in foreign finance, before she'd seen to her surprise and shame that he was all slick surface but wretched at his work. He had been summarily dismissed, and Elizabeth refused to employ the man in any position.

Though she hated to admit it, Hugh Dauntsey's very gaze unsettled her. His eyes were so pale blue and rimless that from a distance he seemed to have only white eyeballs with no irises at all. Of a pasty complexion and sporting a thin goatee, part blond and part white, the man almost seemed an albino. He was short and thin as a rail, with deliberate movements. Dauntsey was always finely attired, almost above his station, and it annoyed her that Paulet insisted on treating the forty-year-old hanger-on, who had never wed, more as a son than as his secretary.

"I observe, Your Majesty, the tasks of your government are overburdening the greatly reduced number of secretaries and comptrollers you keep on the rolls," Paulet lectured her in a loud voice as they took another turn on the gravel path, littered with autumn leaves from the fruit trees. He always turned the better of his two bad ears toward her and cupped it with his hand, despite how his stiff ruff got in the way. "The more subjects directly employed by the crown, the better for the country. Your father said that more than once. Keep them busy, keep them close."

"I see you keep your man Dauntsey close, my lord. But the bureaucracy was quite bloated," she told him, nearly shouting. She'd heard Paulet had a listening horn of some sort, but he never used it around her. "And feeding and feting so many people strained our finances. We've pared the government to a good level of efficiency. I expect my people not to cling to the past but to look toward new endeavors and enterprises."

"What surprises? You listen too much to Thomas Gresham, while he's obsessed with building that foreign exchange. It will just draw in more wily foreigners, I tell you."

"The influx of foreigners does not distress me as much as the behavior of my own countrymen, those who covertly keep to their Catholic ways. Be sure to share that with your northern friends, for they are being closely watched."

Despite his years of practicing a courtier's wiles, he looked momentarily like a fish out of water, gaping for air as she went on. "As for Sir Thomas Gresham's mercantile exchange, however much its style is inspired by the bourse in Antwerp, it is to benefit our people. He, at least, is loyal and valuable to me, though I know you do not approve of him or get along."

"Alone—that's exactly it. You listen to him alone these days. Why, I had advised the royal Tudors for years before Gresham was even born, Your Majesty."

As Elizabeth made the turn back toward the palace, she saw not only Hugh Dauntsey watching them—and probably hearing their raised voices, too—but Ned Topside, half behind a tree, no less, gesturing madly to her in a most rude way. She was briefly grateful that Paulet couldn't see well, either, these days. Whatever was the matter with her man to insist she come to him straightaway? More often than not, Ned Topside was saucy and needed his ears boxed, yet he seemed confident and almost commanding right now.

"I must leave you, my lord," she shouted at Paulet. "We will unfortunately continue this important discussion further." As the old man went into a creaky bow, she hurried toward Ned.

However much the buffoon Paulet sometimes seemed, she knew from privy reports he could wreak havoc and never forgot an insult. Then again, neither did she. He was fortunate she abided him at all. If he hadn't had one secret thing in his favor, the great mark against him she would never forgive would have had him in permanent rural retirement by now—and that leech Dauntsey with him.

"Ned, whatever is it?" she demanded when she reached him. "There will be hell to pay if Lord Paulet learns I left him for my principal player. I swear that if you—"

"It's Meg, Your Grace. I hustled her into a downstairs anteroom, as I didn't want her riling your maids or courtiers. She's come back nearly hysterical from the starcher's loft and says she has to see you, only you. I tried to comfort her, but she'll have none of me lately."

Elizabeth did not comment on that last remark but, with her heartbeat thudding like horses' hooves, hurried into the palace.

The queen found Meg crumpled onto a bench in a small, windowless room lit by a single lantern. The light was bright enough, though, to gild the tear tracks on her cheeks.

"Ned, step out and watch the door so we are not disturbed," Elizabeth ordered.

"But—" he began, then did as she said, quietly closing the heavy door she assumed he'd be trying to listen through.

"Tell me," the queen said only, and thrust the lacy handkerchief from up her sleeve into Meg's trembling hands.

"Someone's dead."

"In the streets? Who and where?"

"A woman. In the starch vat at Hannah's. I couldn't see a face, but a hand—attached to an arm, I'm sure—floated to the top of the milky stuff. No one else was there—deserted."

"That's dreadful," Elizabeth whispered, as her insides cartwheeled and her knees went weak. "Could it be Hannah or one of her workers?"

"I don't know, Your Grace! I didn't"—she blew her nose hard—"just couldn't bear to pull the body up and look. I dropped my bags of roots and ran back here."

"And well you did. But where were Hannah's women?"

Meg shook her head wildly. "Don't know. Don't know anything, if it was her or one of her women or a customer or that whitster friend of hers, Ursala something... No one with a wrist ruff, that's all I know."

"But you're certain," Elizabeth muttered more to herself, "it was not a man? I commanded Thomas Gresham to visit that shop, and if he arrives to find a corpse—or worse... He has enemies, but usually takes at least one guard with him."

She shuddered. Something had to be done about this now beyond summoning the constable and coroner. She hardly wanted Gresham walking in to find and report a body in a place she'd ordered him to visit. Perhaps it could be proved an accident or even a suicide, because the third alternative would open Pandora's box.

"Meg," she said, gripping the woman's shoulder, "you must go back. I'll send Ned, Jenks, and another guard with you. Put the guard on the door to seal the scene. Then see if you can discern who the dead woman is. Look for signs she might merely have slipped or tumbled in. I hear wet starch is slippery, so you never know. Then I will have Cecil speak to the local authorities to report the death. You are quite sure you saw no one suspicious fleeing the scene or lurking about?"

"No, but I can't bear to go back again, Your Grace," she insisted, twisting the handkerchief. "That hand just came floating up through that starch bath, probably made with my cuckoo-pint. And just think how red and raw starch makes skin . . . and a whole body steeping in there . . . bad enough to drown in water, but . . ."

"You must go back now," Elizabeth repeated, and pulled open the door only to have Ned nearly tumble into the room. Ordinarily she would have scolded him, but not now.

"Ned, help Meg settle herself, then fetch Jenks and a yeoman guard—take Adrian Bates, but tell him not to wear his livery—and the four of you head immediately for Hannah von Hoven's starch house, where there may have been a fatal accident."

"Hannah's dead?"

"Meg isn't sure. Hie yourselves there before someone else walks in, then report back to me forthwith. Leave the guard to watch the door. Tell him to just hang about there, not to look as if he's guarding it, but no one else must go in until we can look around. I must send a message to Thomas Gresham not to visit Hannah's today, for I fear I might have ordered him into a compromising situation. I only pray this will not turn out to be some sort of foul play, not only for Hannah's sake but for the stability of the starchers' booming trade here in London."

"You mean," Ned said, as he helped Meg to rise with his hand on her elbow, "that the insults and threats the van der Passes have made toward Hannah might make your chief starcher look guilty and, if Hannah's gone, you'd lose both of them?"

"What?" the queen cried, snagging Ned's arm so that he swung Meg back around and stood between the two women. "Ned, you jump far afield. I pray it isn't Hannah, and I have heard of none such threats from the van der Passes."

"Oh, yes, Your Grace," he insisted, "everybody knows it. Disparaging remarks about Hannah's work to customers, mostly from Dirck, Mrs. van der Passe's husband. A blowhard who towers over most men and flaunts that he was a knight in the service of the low countries before they came here to—"

"Oh, no," Meg blurted, gripping her hands together between her breasts. "He may be the man I bumped into in the street. Cursed me, he did, and said words odd, like *'ja'* instead of 'you,' but then so many folks in London talk strange these days, including Hannah."

"Get Jenks," Elizabeth insisted, as foreboding made her shiver. "And keep your eyes open, all of you. Go the back way. I fear the twists of this so far, and we don't even know who's in that vat of starch."

The queen pressed her royal insignia into the wax seal of her hasty note to Thomas Gresham and took it to the hall doorway herself. "Clifford," she ordered her big yeoman standing guard there with his ceremonial halberd, "this must go straightaway to Gresham House on Bishopsgate to Sir Thomas Gresham, or if he's not there, to the building site of the mercantile exchange."

But as she glanced beyond him at the clusters of her ladies, chatting with each other and the courtiers who stood about, she saw Thomas Gresham himself coming down the corridor with great speed, especially for one who limped so badly. His walking stick thumped out a quick beat on the oaken floor as if someone were pounding on a door. He looked frantic.

Thank God he was safe, but his haste boded nothing good. As she snatched the note back, she realized Gresham might have been to Hannah's loft and found the body. He'd probably already reported it, and a public inquiry might turn up that Dirck van der Passe had been in the vicinity—or that her servant Meg was.

"Your Majesty, may I have leave to speak?" Thomas cried out when he was yet twenty feet away.

"Enter first," she called to him, and gestured toward her withdrawing chamber.

She could tell he was loath not to shout to her from where he was, yet he followed her into the room and went down on his good knee. "My dear daughter's missing, Your Grace," he cried before she even gave him leave to speak. "I and my men have searched everywhere near Gresham House and the exchange site, but I beg your help to put out a hue and cry for any news of her."

"Yes, of course. She's twelve, I believe?"

"Thirteen, Your Grace, but seems to believe she is older and more responsible than that."

"Ah, yes, I remember. Thomas, you haven't been to either of the starch houses, have you?"

"Why, no. I planned to go today, but we discovered Marie was missing and . . ."

"I'll summon men to help you hunt for her. You must try to calm yourself and think of places she might be, places you haven't looked yet, or even admitted to yourself she might have gone. You must write a good description of her and perhaps what she was wearing for me to give my men."

"At once, Your Majesty. I warrant she had on her dark blue cloak on this windy day, a recent gift." As he spoke, he seemed to stare into space. "Very blonde like the mother who gave her birth," he went on, as if to himself. "Comely and fair, tall for her age, pert nose, graceful, delicate-looking, she is, but made of stiffer stuff than she seems . . ."

"Get up, Thomas," Elizabeth said, when his voice drifted off and it looked as if he would slump to the floor. She helped the trembling man to his feet and led him to a chair. "Sit here while I summon my yeomen guards, and do not fear."

The queen knew her words were bolder than her heart. She feared not only for a pretty female child of a rich and well-known man in big, busy London but for the female who floated, yet unidentified, in a vat of thickening starch not far from here.

Meg was relieved Jenks knew a back way to Hannah's loft through the vast royal mews and down a narrow, dim alley. At least their solemn assignment kept Ned and Jenks—and her, she admitted—from quarreling. They planted Bates, one of the queen's elite yeomen guards, now wearing daily garb, near the place. Jenks led the way up the dim stairs she'd climbed earlier today; they were much darker now. Ned brought up the rear, silent for once. The breeze had picked up even more. A blast of air swooped down the enclosed staircase from above, and Meg recalled that the large window overlooking the fields had been open.

"All clear," Jenks whispered, and motioned them up into the loft.

"Hardly all clear," she whispered. "Oh!"

"What?" Ned asked.

"My sacks of roots I dropped right here and left behind. Someone's dragged them off a bit—and two of them are missing! That's precious herb they've taken!"

"They who? And keep your voice down," Ned ordered. "But are you certain? I mean, in your panic to flee and fetch help—"

"Yes, I'm certain! You saw I had four sacks when you lifted two of them from my shoulders," she whispered. Jenks frowned at both of them, but she had no time to explain. Ignoring his rival's glare, Ned moved quietly but quickly to peer into the narrow rectangular vat she'd described to them. He squinted, trying in vain to see into the dense liquid.

"What if the body's been moved, too?" she whispered.

"Stuff and nonsense," Ned said. "I'd sooner say you imagined a hand floating beneath that viscous, opaque liquor."

"Stow the fancy words and dramatic speeches," Meg hissed at him. "You may live in a world of fancy, but not I!"

"Devil take it," Jenks said, also trying to peer in, "the vat is shaped like a coffin, but I don't see anything in it. Not hand nor hair nor hem of a gown."

"That can't be!" She leaned over the murky vat, which seemed not as full now. The liquid looked much grayer than she remembered. "It's just beneath the surface, that's all," she cried.

"Corpses in the river sink until they've partly rotted, then they float," Jenks put in.

"Hell's gates, would you stow it, man?" Ned demanded. "This isn't the river."

Meg watched as the breeze, through the open window over the starch bath, made the surface seem to shudder. Both Ned and Jenks were making her so overwrought she'd like to shove their thick heads into this thick stuff.

"Just find me a stirring stick or hand me one of those poking rods, and I'll show you," she ordered. "I know I saw part of a body in there, a dainty hand, graceful, too."

"Was it limp?" Jenks asked.

"Not," Ned said, "in a stiffening vat of starch."

"Leave off, both of you!" she demanded. As she took another step toward the vat, the soles of her shoes stuck slightly to the floor. She looked down and saw that they were standing in a half-dried, flaking puddle she was certain had not been there when she saw the hand. She knew she hadn't splashed anything out.

"Someone else has been here for sure," she whispered wide-eyed, as Jenks thrust the long wooden stirring stick into her hands. Suddenly even more scared, Meg stood still as a statue. Air through the large window moved loose tendrils of her hair against her sweating forehead and cheeks. Out the window, she could see the patchwork of drying linens and hear in the distance a woman's shouts. Shaking, she pushed the long stick down by inches into the starch bath and moved it slowly toward each of the sides of the vat, then the corners. Nothing. Nothing.

"God as my judge, I saw a human hand in here!" she wailed.

Ned took the stick from her and stirred to make slow

ripples swirl. "Could it have been some sort of apparition? Some twist of light in this strange brew, perhaps a reflection of your own hand?"

Almost ready to explode into sobs, she just shook her head wildly.

"Then," Ned went on, "the body's either been pilfered or it's taken itself for a walk. Maybe those were ghostly footprints on the stairs we came up."

"What?" Jenks challenged. His feet making light crunching sounds, he went over to stare down the steps. "Oh, those small spots of pale white? But they only go partway down and then seem to just fade into nothing."

"See what I mean—spirits abroad," Ned insisted.

Meg tried to speak calmly, rationally. "The queen will have our heads if we've been traipsing through footsteps and evidence and such and she decides to call a Privy Plot Council meeting to investigate."

Properly chastened, they searched the rest of the large, irregularly shaped loft and finally found six fat rolls of ruff fabric, two each of cambric, linen, and lawn, standing on end on a deep shelf in the farthest corner—a shelf that was dripping onto the shelf below and then onto the floor.

"That's just Hannah's rolls of patching pieces," Meg whispered. "They don't make ruffs here." She refused to go closer until Jenks took her arm and tugged her along.

Without another word, the men lifted the partially wet rolls of fabric away to reveal a wet, clothed corpse on the shelf. The three of them gasped in unison, then stood, shoulder to shoulder, staring as if they worshipped at a shiny marble effigy of a saint on an altar.

At first glance, the graceful, petite woman seemed asleep, but her slender body was glazed with a pearly film, drying from slick to crusty. It matted her pale eyelashes to her cheeks and her long, loose blond hair to her head and neck, at least where her tresses didn't stand straight out. Still sopped with starch, her sea-blue skirts formed fantastical shapes, but the edges, hems, and fringes—and her little neck ruff—had already gone sharply stiff.

Chapter the Third

"HEY, THERE—YOU, GIRL!"

The woman's voice meant nothing until she came close and stuck her face nearly nose to nose.

"You all right, then?" the woman asked. "You been standing there for hours, I seen you. And I can tell by your clothes you're not a street girl."

She hoped this woman would leave her alone. Strange, but she'd lost her voice, her thoughts. Lost herself. Desperately, she'd been trying to remember something—or was it to forget?

"Not 'scaped from a forced betrothal or some such, have you? You look frighted. Someone been bothering you? We're whitsters, see? We wash, bleach, and dry linens, that's our trade. You don't belong here. You just keep clear of trouble on the streets, hear?"

She nodded. Her head hurt, and her eyes ached from staring so long at the bright sheets in the wind and sun—and then at the high, open window across the way. Its slanted planes caught the sinking sun now and nearly blinded her, but she kept staring. She wanted to run from something, but her feet felt like lead, as in a nightmare. Was she dreaming? Something dreadful had happened. She'd seen it. But what?

"You hungry?" the woman asked, holding out a hunk of bread with a piece of yellow cheese.

She shook her head.

"Cat got your tongue, then?"

No, I'm fine, she tried to say, but she didn't hear her own words, her voice. She just kept hearing a muffled scream—and then nothing else.

But she did know one thing. The mere sight of food almost made her sick. She'd vomited in the hedges of this field earlier. She wanted to walk away from this place, this view, but she couldn't bear to go home. Not now. She was not even sure where home was.

"Here now, mistress," the same woman was saying, "you look peaked. Can I fetch someone for you, then? My name's Ursala Hemmings, so what's yours, eh? I've a friend near here, has a starch shop, and you could rest there out of the wind and sun while we find your folks."

A starch shop . . . starch shop.

Either she screamed *No!* at the woman or just thought she did. Some kind of sound like a shriek echoed, echoed, trapped in her head, trapped in a big attic. She gripped her laced fingers tighter as if she were praying. But she wasn't. She was just trying to make all the grief and horror stop.

Wending her way through the women with their linens, she turned away and started out of the busy field. Her shadow was long now, as if someone dark followed her. She didn't feel her feet. It was almost as if she floated, as if she had to swim through a thick, white haze. She gazed one last time at the high, open window, then forced her feet at a quicker pace away.

"You sent for the Reverend Hosea Cantwell, Your Majesty?" Cecil asked as he came in with a stack of bills and grants for her to sign. "He's been put in the corridor anteroom to await you and seems mad as a wet hen—a dour Puritan one."

The queen stopped walking so fast her skirts swayed. She'd been pacing, waiting for word about the body in the starch vat. Cecil knew naught of that yet, though he'd been a key member of her Privy Plot Council. Over the last eight years, a small group of trusted friends and servants had helped her solve several murders that had struck close to the crown.

Besides that distress, she'd been praying her men who had fanned out over the city with Thomas Gresham's staff would find his daughter. Never had her little band searched for a missing person who was not a murderer, but she had silently vowed the Gresham girl would be found.

"'S blood, yes, I sent for Cantwell, but it slipped my mind," she admitted, and smacked the heel of her hand against her forehead so hard she rattled her pearl eardrops. "My lord, I cannot abide Cantwell's public pulpit rantings against me. Or against current fashions, as he's likely to damage the ruff-making industry or the starch market. That, in turn, would affect the dyers, the seamstresses, and the tailors," she plunged on, flinging gestures.

"I completely agree, Your Grace. Indeed, one man could affect the balance of crafts and trades, and just now while the mercantile exchange is being built."

"Exactly. Hosea Cantwell makes far too much out of little things, not to mention he's one of the most vocal agitators in the Commons about my marital status."

"It's not just you he harangues, Your Grace, I assure you."

"But it's I who mean to have it out with him," she declared, and headed for the door.

His arms still full of papers, Cecil leaped to open it for her. "Then should I accompany you?"

"I need you to stay here and inform me if Meg Milligrew, Ned Topside, or Steven Jenks returns." She stepped back into the room and closed the door. "There's been a strange death at Hannah von Hoven's starch house. 'S blood, just wait until Cantwell gets wind of that. Oh," she said, opening the door again despite his stunned expression, "and let me know at once if there is word of Thomas Gresham's young daughter being found."

"What? All that when I've been gone but three hours?"

"I'll explain the moment I have dealt with Cantwell. I have never met with him privily, but it needs to be done," she concluded, and left him sputtering.

If Hosea Cantwell had been, as Cecil had said, angry, that was not the case now, Elizabeth noted as he bowed before her and they exchanged proprieties. Rather, he seemed sure of himself, almost smug, not the wet hen but the cock of the walk. The man was much too handsome to be a Puritan cleric, or lay preacher, as he was often called. His hair shone like polished ebony; dark lashes fringed large brown eyes in a well-chiseled face. He had a Roman nose, which balanced a strong mouth. His manly form bespoke more of riding and sweating than of reading and sermonizing. No wonder more people than Puritans filled his pews lately. Elizabeth thought all that made him more, not less, dangerous.

"Let me cut directly to the topic at hand," the queen said as Cantwell began to comment on the windy weather. "Do you not have better things—more important things—to speak of from your pulpit and in the halls of Parliament than styles and starch?"

"Ah, and I thought I was summoned for my stance on your marital state, Your Majesty."

"It goes without saying that I resent your trying to coerce your queen to that. But starch, man? Would you have us return to the old-fashioned days of paste wives with laces steeped in egg white or made rigid with beeswax and wire supportasses, which go all limp and poke one in the neck or wrist to boot? Is it true you have ranted that starch is 'the devil's liquor'?"

"I pray I have not ranted. Counseled, perhaps. Pleaded. I plead guilty to that, at least, Your Gracious Majesty."

Somehow this man kept defusing her fury. With his wit and puns, she might think she was verbally sparring with Ned Topside. Was this the same person who had glared at her when she defied Parliament? Though she'd pictured him up close as stiff-faced with a stiffer backbone, his lips curled into a smile and his eyes twinkled. His voice was smooth and modulated, not piercing, as someone had told her it was when he preached.

"May I explain, Your Most Gracious Majesty?"

"You may try."

"While courtiers and the Londoners who ape them and the English who then ape the Londoners spend small fortunes and large amounts of precious time on what is on their backs—around their wrists and necks in this instance—they are being ensnared by the world of the flesh and the devil. The ruffs, like other personal tomfooleries, grow larger and larger. Forgive me, Your Majesty, but any fashion you set, all will follow. Starch is but one foreshadowing, no doubt, of a curse on our nation—a curse that can spread. You already favor black and white, not so far a reach from plain Puritan garb, so why not simple collars and cuffs?"

She'd like to cuff him, the queen thought. Yet, though she was ready to explode at his presumptions and his dire prophecy, he'd said that last with a little disparaging flourish of his hand toward his own garments. She felt entirely pent up about the Gresham girl and the death at the starch house. She had fully expected to berate this man, but his demeanor and delivery were not what she had expected. Was he one who could change his leopard's spots quickly and at will, like Satan himself?

This man bore watching, she decided, and not just because he was quite clever. She didn't trust those whom she knew opposed her yet tried to get in her good graces. The man had criticized her garments, her judgment, and her morals, yet done it so cunningly she had found no sure footing to scold him in turn.

"That is all for now, as I have much to do," she told him, and waited until he bowed himself out. No good if he'd be hanging about to hear there could have been a murder in a starch house today—and in a vat of the very thing he had labeled "the devil's liquor."

Elizabeth barely had time to tell Cecil that Hosea Cantwell was not only a critic of morals but a chameleon of moods when her trio of servants trooped back in via the privy staircase that faced the river. Her lady-in-waiting Rosie Radcliffe, now her most trusted confidante since her dear friend Kat Ashley had died, had opened the door for them behind the arras when they knocked.

"We decided to come by this entrance, for you told us to go the back way, Your Grace," Ned explained.

"Good, but never mind all that. Was there a dead woman in the vat?"

"No—and yes," Meg said, out of breath. "Someone had lifted Hannah out—"

"It *was* Hannah von Hoven?"

"Yes, I regret to say so, Your Grace. Between the time I fled and the time we got back, someone, perhaps her murderer, had pulled her from the starch bath and laid her out on a shelf."

"She looked—Hannah looked, not Meg," Jenks put in, "like she'd been dipped and set out to stiffen. And she was starting to, in more ways than one."

Ned rolled his eyes and shook his head at Jenks's dull-witted rendition of things. Cecil and Rosie moved to stand on either side of their queen as she sank into a chair at the head of the long table where her paperwork awaited in Cecil's neat piles.

But life wasn't neat, wasn't fair, Elizabeth thought. Hannah had been young, ambitious, and comely, just setting out on a great endeavor in England. Even before promoting her to Thomas Gresham, the queen had hoped to champion the young woman as a symbol of competition in the kingdom. Like Elizabeth Tudor, Hannah von Hoven was a woman making her own way despite the odds against her. After all, Hanna's rival starcher had a husband, one who perhaps really ruled the roost.

"Even if we might think she slipped into the starch by accident," Elizabeth said with a half-groan, half-sigh, "we can hardly tell ourselves she got herself out and onto a shelf as if she were her own starched goods for sale. Yes, I wager we have a murder on our hands, unless, like Meg, someone else just stumbled on her, chose to pull her out, then panicked and fled."

She thought again of Cantwell's prediction of a curse caused by starch and the results rippling through her kingdom. Pure coincidence, she thought, that one of the royal starchers now seemed to have been fatally punished.

"Your Grace," Cecil said, "are you quite all right? Shall I send for something, or do you need one of Meg's calming potions?"

"If so, I should share it with her for being the one who found Hannah drowned—or however she died. Were there marks on her throat or any other discernible bruises?" she asked the three of them.

"I—she's so slippery and sticky with starch," Meg said, "we didn't wash her off to look closely, but ran back here to tell you."

"Your Grace," Cecil put in quickly, "do you mean to pursue this and not just turn it over to the constable and coroner?"

"The men of my city's criminal law enforcement will be informed in the morning, after we've had a good look around the place and at the body."

"We?" Cecil repeated. "But, Your Grace, surely you don't intend to go there yourself to—"

"The weather is cool," she interrupted him, "and the body will keep a few more hours. Bates is still there, standing guard, is he not?"

"Aye," Jenks said, "and standing a ways off, like you said."

"Then we will go together at nightfall the back way and tarry but briefly. I can think of one or two who might fall under suspicion for this terrible deed, and I mean to look into it."

"Surely not Meg, Your Grace!" Jenks blurted. "And why then? Just because she and Hannah been arguing sore about prices for the roots?"

The queen saw Meg shoot Jenks a look that could indeed kill. Jenks's talents had always been for dealing with horses, not the intricacies of human reason. Still, Elizabeth knew he was utterly faithful, not only to Meg but to her.

"No, of course, Meg is no more under suspicion than any of you. I mean Dirck van der Passe, my other starcher's husband—and who knows who else," she added, thinking again of Hosea Cantwell's probable desire to make his curse come true.

"Are we to have a meeting of the Privy Plot Council to solve a murder, then, Your Grace?" Meg asked, wringing her hands.

"I warrant we are having one now, so all of you are sworn to secrecy on this. As soon as darkness falls, all but Cecil are off for Hannah's. Then first thing tomorrow morning, here is how we will proceed. Ned," she said, looking at him, "will ask Hannah's neighbors if they saw anyone suspicious lurking about today. Meg, you will speak with the women Hannah employed, if they arrive for work, and if not, you must try to track them down. Why was she evidently alone when they all should have been there, with the demands on their time?"

"I can also talk to the laundresses and whitsters who frequent that area to ask if they noted anything amiss," Meg said. "Hannah had that friend Ursala who might know if the poor woman had been courted by anyone—or more than one, fair as she was."

"Yes, of course," Cecil said, folding his arms. "That sort of passion possibly gone awry could be a motive for murder, too."

"Jenks," Elizabeth went on, regarding him now, "you will stick close to me when I venture out tonight to visit Hannah's. Then, from when we arrive at the starch house until the time we summon the authorities and they arrive, you will help Bates guard the door to Hannah's rooms so that no one else enters or leaves."

"Which reminds me, Your Grace," Meg put in, "I'm sure the intruder—mayhap the murderer—took some of my roots with him. Two sacks of them were missing, and one of those emptied out. The thing is, if cuckoo-pint roots are ingested, they are deadly poison."

"Hell's gates, that's all we need," Cecil said. "Poison starch, a unique weapon, I'll say that. One murder's bad enough, let alone the means for more at large somewhere in London."

"Which is another reason we must look into this, and quickly," the queen said. "Later tomorrow, Meg, you and Clifford will go with me when I visit Hannah's rival, Dingen van der Passe, and speak with her husband, too. But Rosie, first thing in the morning, you will take two guards and ride to Gresham House to inquire how the search for their child goes and to keep me well informed of any progress."

"And I, Your Grace?" Cecil asked.

"You, my advisor and friend, will remain here lest decisions need to be made—or the fact the queen is going out dressed as a market woman on the streets needs to be hidden from my courtiers. And, as usual, my lord, you will fret for all these dire and dangerous doings, but I wager you will help me to think them all through, too."

The girl stood staring up at the blood-red windows set in the tall brick walls of yet another building. The sun was setting, gilding the already russet bricks and reflecting its face in the glass. The palace of the queen, she'd heard someone say, pointing it out to his companion. Whitehall Palace of the queen.

She knew she wanted to get through a tall window like that. To get past the stonework and wood and brick. To remember. But all she could recall was a surprised face staring up at her, the mouth open in a silent scream filled with gray . . . a face with open glassy eyes, a lovely face marred by swirling white, floating, then sinking into the depths of memory . . .

In her dreams she saw her mother's face, a mother she could not recall . . .

A face in the shadow of a hood floated into her vision. A scarred face. Under the pox marks, perhaps pretty. And yet young. She stared into that puckered visage, and it stared back at her. Was this girl a part of herself, her reflection in the glass? Did this other self know what must be remembered?

"Hello," the girl, younger and shorter than herself, said. "I come from the country, but my mother lives here, and I needs find her." She pulled her deep hood closer about her face, as if to hide. Perhaps they could hide together. The girl was speaking again.

"But they told me to get 'way from this gate."

Get away, get away. Yes, those words sounded like ones she had to remember. She reached out and took the younger girl's hand. They were both trembling.

"Could you please tell them for me?" the scarred girl went on in her slow country drawl. "Tell them my mother's the queen's herbal woman? My name's Sally Downs, really Sarah Milligrew. Her name's Mother Meg, Meg Milligrew. My other mother said Mother Meg told them to tell me the truth 'bout my poxed face, but they didn't 'til now. Ten whole years, so I ran 'way. Why did they have to hide it all from me? They told me years ago I wasn't their daughter but 'dopted."

That, too, struck a chord. *Adopted.* And something was hidden. They should have told her, told her, but she went to find out for herself . . .

This girl had said she ran away. Those words echoed. *I ran away . . . get away, get away . . . No, no, don't!* screamed in her head. She wanted to hold Sally's hand and run away, but again her feet wouldn't move. Why hadn't she called for help when someone screamed, *Get away, get away*?

She couldn't swallow the jagged pieces of fear in her throat that choked her voice, even her breath. Her knees shook, and she crumpled against Sally and slid down her to the cobbled street, but she did not let go of her hand.

"Help!" she heard Sally scream. "Help, this lady's ill! Stand 'way! Give her some air, then!"

The small crowd near the palace entry shifted slightly, but not, she could see, to give her air. They backed away from a thunder of hoofbeats, the thud-thud as a skull struck the wooden tub. No, there was no wooden tub here. Men, at least six of them on horseback, and one of them gaping down at her and Sally.

He reined in and shouted, pointing right at her. "My lord, hold there! Look, that girl with the other!"

The party of riders reined in, strung out toward the guarded entrance of the palace. She felt Sally start to tug free of her, but then she felt the younger girl's arm go around her shoulders to prop her up.

"Badger, I owe you my life, my life!" a man was shouting. He sounded as if he were crying—a man, crying. "Yes, it looks like her . . ."

Sights and sounds swirled around her as she held hard to

Sally and stared straight up. The sky, the tall palace walls sinking into shadows . . . the wooden, slanted walls of a loft somewhere . . . a woman, sinking.

"Marie!" the second man cried. "Thank God, Marie!"

He managed to slide off his high horse, but he almost crumpled when he hit the ground. The man who had seen her first helped him, a short, quick man with eyebrows that came together like a dark stroke of a pen. The taller man who nearly fell took a long stick from the one he'd called Badger.

She went still as death as the stranger fell to his knees and grasped her to him, breathing hard, choking back sobs that shook him. She wanted to scream, *Get away, no, please don't . . . stop,* but she was too weak.

"Men, haste to the queen and say we've found my daughter!" the man cried. "One of you, ride to tell my wife that Marie has been found. Dearest girl," he said, bending back over her, "your mother is beside herself—I, too . . . whatever happened?" He tried to free her hand from Sally's, tried to lift her to break their grasp.

"No, don't!" she cried, with great effort. Had he said her name was Marie? "She is—with me!"

She saw the man who was her father turn to Sally. He saw the girl's face and shuddered slightly.

"Yes, yes, of course," he muttered. "She will come with us. You're tired, sweetling, hurt, too, or hit your head."

Had she hit her head? Was that why she could not swim up through the slippery, suffocating press of stairs and windowpanes? Was that why she kept hiding, so afraid to scream or flee?

Still holding tightly to Sally's hand as her father held to hers, the girl he had called Marie surrendered in his arms to sudden, drowning sleep.

Chapter the Fourth

"YOUR MAJESTY, THEY HAVE FOUND GRESHAM'S daughter, just outside the palace!" Ned Topside called to her. With the others, he had just left her to prepare for their foray this night, but he'd darted back in even before the door was closed behind Cecil.

"Here? Had someone taken her?"

"I know naught else, but she's being carried in, quite dazed."

"Fetch Doctor Forrest—but first tell them I said to put her in Mary Sidney's rooms, as they are empty now. And that I want someone to bring Lady Gresham to the palace. Where is Sir Thomas?"

"I heard he's the one found her, so I assume—"

She waved him away and hurried out into the hall herself. Ned was already running toward the stairs. With two guards falling in behind, Elizabeth went down the central staircase. Leaning over the bannister, she could hear the hubbub coming from the entry by the Kings Street courtyard.

Ned must have done as commanded, for she saw Sir Thomas coming up the staircase, laboriously limping, though he would hand over the child to no one else. Flanked by three of the queen's men and two of his own, his awkward progress rocked his daughter to and fro as if they had set sail upon a windy sea.

Marie Gresham, the queen saw now, was hardly a child, but a young lady. Ned said she looked dazed; her eyes were open and fixed on nothing. Pale and pretty, she did not cling to her adoptive father but rather to another child whose hand she held, pulling the smaller girl along. Marie's blue cloak would have dragged on the stairs and tripped her father had not her companion, in a mud-splattered brown cape and large hood, lifted Marie's hems with her free hand as if she carried her train. Perhaps Marie Gresham had run off with a servant girl. The queen paid the smaller child no more heed as she waited for the men to reach her around the turn of the stairs.

"Your Majesty!" Thomas cried, perspiring and panting. "The lost sheep is found, but frightened or stunned. Your man said we could tend her here, so—"

"Yes, follow me. I've sent for one of my physicians."

The queen led Gresham down the corridor away from the royal apartments toward the wing overlooking the kitchens. With the court in residence here, it provided the only empty rooms she could think of, though the area made her uneasy. Not only was this hallway supposedly haunted by the ghost of one of her stepmothers, but memories of her dear friend Mary Sidney, who had been so ill here, seemed to cling to the place. Now another patient, Marie instead of Mary, would be cared for in the same chamber and bed.

Elizabeth hesitated at the door, then opened it herself to usher them in. She motioned Thomas through the first chamber, where his entourage waited, into the bedchamber within.

"Put her on the bed," she said, her voice wavering. Before she banished the image, she could yet imagine her friend lying ill here.

Mary Sidney was the sister of Elizabeth's dear Robin, Earl of Leicester. How the queen missed her at court, her laughter, her loyalty—and the way she used to serve as go-between with their love letters.

But after tending Elizabeth when she nearly died of the pox four years ago, Mary had been ravaged by the disease. The queen had escaped with a few permanent pocks on her face and arms—and with the burden of guilt for infecting her friend. For beautiful Mary became horribly disfigured, and now kept mostly to her husband's seat at Pembroke Castle. The queen could seldom entice her to court or get away to visit her, and she missed her sorely.

Elizabeth turned toward the bed and gasped. All shadowed, Mary's face peered at her from within the mystery child's hood! It was as if her friend yet stood here, poxed and scarred, desperate to hide her ruined visage.

Those in the room turned to the queen as she stared at the companion of Marie. But before anyone glimpsed her face, the child curtsied as low as she could with Marie still gripping her hand.

"Your Majesty, whatever is it?" Gresham asked. Two yeomen were instantly at her side. For one moment, Elizabeth thought she might faint.

The child in the hood rose from her shaky curtsy and exploded in tears, murmuring something about her mother, or was it two mothers?

"Is this Marie's maid?" the queen asked Thomas, though her voice still shook.

"I never saw her before I found Marie outside. Sally

something, but they seem most devoted," he muttered, as Dr. Forrest bustled into the room so quickly his black gown flapped and the strings of his cap fluttered.

As most attention turned toward the doctor, Elizabeth reached over the corner of the big bed and touched the hooded girl's shoulder. "It's all right," she whispered. "You simply surprised me by reminding me of a dear friend. Who are you, then?"

"Your Maj'sty," the child choked out between sobs, "I met you once—on the heath years ago—with Mother Meg."

"Meg Milligrew's Sally? But how you have grown! And to find you here in London . . . I'll take you to your mother in a moment, if your friend Marie will let you go."

"But she won't," Sally said with a sniff. "She's holding on so tight it hurts, but I'd best not leave her."

Elizabeth stepped to the doorway of the bedchamber and spoke quietly to her yeoman guard. "Clifford, find and fetch my herb mistress, Meg Milligrew. Say her daughter has come for a visit." As she turned back toward the bed, she saw Dr. Forrest lean over his patient and put his hand on the girl's forehead.

"Forgive my wretched tears, Maj'sty," Sally whispered when the queen returned to the bedside. "I'm so mighty joyous to be here. Ran 'way from home, I did. And I know I caused much grief, but I was so o'erturned."

Countrified or not, Elizabeth thought, the child had natural wit, grace, and much heart. She had questions for both girls, but Marie's health—and Hannah's death—must be seen to first. The doctor was running his hands over Marie's scalp.

To clear the crowded outer chamber, the queen sent Gresham's party down to the great hall for food and ale, though she saw that one man hung behind, peering through the doorway. She recognized him as the fellow who had stayed close to Gresham when she toured the exchange, the quick, wiry watchman with the solid slash of eyebrow across his sun-browned face. For all she knew, the man was Gresham's bodyguard. Once again, she smelled that acrid scent about him, which she'd once thought was from construction supplies.

Thomas must have seen her staring. "Your Majesty," he said, "that is Nash Badger, the man who noted Marie in the crowd. I owe him much."

"Then I do, too," she said with a nod at Badger as he bent to a quick bow, then backed away. "At least perhaps the quiet here will help Marie—"

As if to mock those words, Meg came running in so fast she nearly skidded into Badger. "Where, Your Grace?" she cried, out of breath. "She can't be here. Did they bring her clear from the heath?"

Elizabeth motioned for Meg to hush and come closer. At the sight of her mother, Sally threw her hood back and finally tugged her hand free of Marie's grip. "Mother Meg, I know I done wrong to hurt them, but they hurt me, too, aye, they did! I hid in a hay wain and rode into London town, then asked where the palace was to find you."

Meg bent over to hug Sally hard. "Loose on the road and in London—you—you could have been hurt—been killed," Meg said through her own sobs.

Suddenly Marie Gresham was shrieking, "No! No, don't hurt me! Please don't hurt me! Unhand me!"

Raising his voice, Dr. Forrest asked Thomas, "Is she fearful of physicians?" Both men fought to restrain the screaming girl as she thrashed and hit against them. "I find no nodules or lesions on her skull under that thick hair," the doctor went on, "so I haven't hit a tender spot to set her off so."

"She wouldn't even talk before," Thomas cried. "Mistress Sally, will you come back here?"

Meg and Sally moved together; Marie grabbed Sally's hand. Sally flinched at the ferocity of the grip.

"I can't breathe, can't breathe!" Marie cried as her eyes darted wildly around the room. But it was obvious to all that she was indeed inhaling, even gasping in huge, heavy breaths.

"A soothing potion, that's what she needs," Meg said to Elizabeth.

Dr. Forrest glared at the herbalist. "I am here to tend her with proper medical treatments, Mistress Milligrew," he pronounced over the girl's shouts. "If my patient needs a soporific, I shall see to it."

Elizabeth felt on the verge of hysteria herself. She didn't hold out much hope that visiting a dead woman in her starch shop after dark would be much better.

As darkness fell, Elizabeth felt even more on edge. Marie Gresham appeared to have no injury or physical ailment, not even a fever. Dr. Forrest had deduced that her humors were severely unbalanced from the malady of melancholia and that she was suffering from fantasies of the brain. Nearly incoherent, the girl could tell them nothing of how or why she left Gresham House or how she had come to stand in the crowd outside the palace gates.

Nor could Sally Downs, Meg's daughter, offer anything about Marie that would help, though her mere presence by the ill girl's bed finally allowed the doctor to get a sleeping potion down the distraught young woman. Marie's mother had arrived, but that had hardly calmed the child. Both parents hovered over her as the queen slipped away to join her covert detectors for their stealthy visit to Hannah's starch house.

Elizabeth was taking no chances of running into a marauding murderer who might have returned to the scene of his crime in the dead of night. Though she had ordered a guard posted at Hannah's door, she had the men in her party arm themselves with swords and knives, while her yeoman Clifford also carried his halberd. She added two more guards at the last minute, planning to leave them behind in the nearby royal mews while the Privy Plot Council members went on from there.

The stomping and snorting of the horses in their stalls in the vast, dim royal mews made her even more nervous. Ordinarily she loved proximity to these big beasts, but tonight they were acting as if a storm were lurking just off the black horizon.

"Bit jumpy tonight, every rogue one of them," Jenks said from behind her, as if, for once, he'd read her mind. "Maybe it's just this fitful wind outside." His sword clanked in its scabbard until he put his hand down to still it.

"Never mind that," the queen said. "They've got their grooms nearby. Where are the lanterns you said we could take? Two will suffice. And don't forget the horse blankets. Do you think four of them will be enough, Meg?"

"We better take five, Your Grace. The window over the starch vat is quite large, so it will take two to blacken it against our lanterns, I warrant. There are two smaller windows over the street. And none," she added more quietly, "over the back alley or on the side running along the stairs."

As her cohorts gathered blankets and lights, the queen

noted that all straw and feed near the few lanterns had been raked away for safety's sake. *Thank God,* she thought, for ever since she'd solved the mystery of the fire-mirror murders, she had been even more wary of possible conflagrations.

The queen carried both lanterns, and the others bore the blankets as they made their way from the stables. Leaving the two extra guards behind at the edge of the mews just four buildings from Hannah's house, they plunged into the darkness of the brisk October night. Ned now led the way, with the queen, Jenks, Rosie, Meg, and then Clifford in his wake.

As they approached the covered stairwell, the queen's guard Bates emerged from the shadows.

"Hold there!" he said, and blocked Ned's path with a staff.

"We been sent by the queen, Bates," Jenks said. "I'm to stay down here with you while the others go on up for a look round."

"Has anyone else tried to use these stairs?" the queen asked Bates. She could see in their lantern light that he nearly fell over at her voice and, no doubt, from the fact that it came from a plainly garbed and hooded woman.

Bates cleared his throat and shifted on his big feet. "Only one. A friend of Mistress von Hoven's named Ursala Hemmings been by. I told her not to go up, that her friend was ill. That all right, Your Maj—my lady?"

"Yes. Ill. Very ill," Elizabeth said, and turned away to head upstairs. She'd chosen well, she thought, to trust Bates. The trouble was, had she known or trusted someone else who had done this terrible deed, or was poor Hannah's slaying merely tragic happenstance? A robbery gone awry? Meg, who had evidently haggled with Hannah over the price of cuckoopint, had said Hannah was tight with her money, so perhaps she kept some on the premises and word had gotten out. Or, since she was so fetching, had she played some man false, or more than one, and paid the ultimate penalty? But why, evidently, in broad day had her workwomen not been with her? There was, Elizabeth prayed, always safety in numbers.

Thomas Gresham's heart had finally settled to a slower thud in his thin chest. Sally, who had turned out to be the daughter of the queen's strewing woman, had agreed to stay with Marie, and both girls had fallen asleep. Neither had so much as moved, as if they shared the sleep of the dead. He thought again of the precious portrait he had hidden at home of the two girls, so close and yet so different.

Marie is safe, she's safe, he kept repeating to himself. And, in a sort of frenzied litany, *My dearly beloved Gretta, she's safe, she's safe.* He still couldn't fathom why Marie had gone out alone, and why to this area of the city a goodly ways from their home. The possibilities of that terrified him almost as much as the looming loss of her had, almost as much as the queen's sending him to see Hannah von Hoven's starch shop had. He'd feared Her Majesty would suggest he sponsor Hannah's fledgling endeavor. What then if Anne found out?

He forced himself to put his arm around Anne's shoulders. She did not settle into his embrace but leaned stiffly toward the bed again. "My poor, dear Marie-Anne," she mouthed for the hundredth time since the queen's doctor had left. "Thomas, I can't believe our daughter clings to this girl and not to us." Biting her lower lip, she wiped her eyes again.

"You heard Dr. Forrest," he whispered. "Given time, rest, and quiet, she may come out of this on her own and retrieve her memory."

Another thing Thomas could not fathom was what this other child meant to Marie, especially since she must just have met her, not to mention the sad fact that Sally was so heavily poxed. Most children sheltered like Marie, who had not seen such horror, would be repulsed, but his dear child was like the mother who bore her—calm, at least usually, and tenderhearted.

He pictured Marie's mother again, his Gretta, fine and fair. Desperately, he summoned up the memory of her laughing, not crying as she'd been those last few days when the childbed fever racked her and she feared that she would die. Not sobbing as she'd been when she'd entrusted to him the portrait of herself as a child—so much like Marie now—with her twin sister. Yes, now he saw Gretta laughing like that time she had introduced him to Hannah, her near image, not only in the painting but in the flesh.

Two of you? he had teased, kissing each one on the cheek. *Double the delight of such beauty in the world?*

"Thomas," Anne hissed in his ear, "what in all creation are you smiling for at a time like this?"

The smile and the memory faded. "Hasn't our dear girl always brought us joy?" he countered. "And we have her back safe."

"Safe in body, perhaps, but something dire and dreadful has happened to her—something she must recover to tell us. Let's offer to keep this Sally as her companion and maid, if the queen and the herbalist will allow it. With Sally's help, Marie-Anne must recover to tell us the truth!"

In Hannah's chill and breezy loft, they closed the windows, then draped the horse blankets over them to hide their lights.

Meg pointed out the dipping vat, still full of thickening, settling starch, and then the shelf where the body lay. The six fat bolts of cloth hid all but the top of Hannah's head, with hair so stiff it stuck out in all directions.

Elizabeth observed everything in silence, then glanced back toward the starch vat. "That large window overlooking the street and St. Martin's fields was open even now, so we might assume it was open during the murder. Ned, be sure to ask those you question tomorrow if they heard a scream or a fray—or glanced in to note a stranger inside, and I don't mean Meg."

"Yes, Your Grace."

"And try to discern if there's a way to escape through the window without being seen from the street or the fields, which I doubt."

"It looks l-large enough for someone to c-creep in or out," Rosie whispered. Not only had the woman gone to stammering, but her eyes kept darting everywhere in the dim room with its shadows shifting from their lanterns. She looked as if she were certain something was going to leap out at them, and it didn't help Elizabeth's pluck to have her companion so knock-kneed.

"But now," Elizabeth plunged on, "to the terrible tasks at hand. Are these bolts of fabric placed, do you recall, Meg and Ned, much the way you and Jenks found them—and her?"

"Quite sure that's the way they were when the men put them back in place before we ran to the palace," Meg assured her, "though I think her head was more hidden when we found her. Do you—want us to take the bolts away?"

"Yes, in a minute. What are these bluish blurs on the linen roll? Let me have more lantern light here."

"I saw that before," Meg murmured, "but just thought it

was damp seeping into it from her body or garments. Her skirt is blue, so maybe the dye—it bled. I think it's on more than one of the rolls."

"Yes, two others, only more faded. Perhaps all these rolls were defective or stained, so they were just left on the shelf and not used. The blue tinge is probably not from the murderer but from someone who simply mishandled them earlier. Now, we must study the way she's been set on the shelf. Then we will lift her out onto the worktable over there. Rosie, note carefully what is on it, and if there is naught suspicious, clear things away and spread this last blanket there."

Giving Rosie a lantern and holding their other one high, the queen watched as Meg and Ned removed the six wide rolls of fabric. Stiff as a stone effigy—body, garments, and hair—Hannah von Hoven lay as if encased in crystal.

"Now that it's gone dark, even in our lantern light, she seems to glow," Meg whispered, sounding awed. "You know, the pollen from the cuckoo-pint herbs the starch is made from glows in the dark."

"She is not glowing in the dark," Elizabeth insisted. "She just looks pearl-coated because of our lights on that sheen of starch. Men, lift her over here and carefully."

Ned grimaced as he helped Clifford, and not, she suspected, from the weight of the corpse. "Never felt anything quite like this," he muttered. "She's slick but sticky, too. And she looks like—like she's flying with her hems and hair like this."

"Or been caught in the big breezes outside," Clifford put in.

Elizabeth nodded. In the starch vat, Hannah's hair must have drifted or floated, then set into this bizarre shape, which made it look as if her tresses were wings sprouting from the sides of her head. Her skirts—she wore a brown work gown with only one petticoat—also had assumed a strange shape, perhaps that of the coffin-like vat.

Elizabeth jumped as Meg broke the solemn silence. "She looks peaceful with her eyes and mouth closed, not like she's met a violent end, but gone to sleep."

"Or has been arranged in death to look so," Elizabeth surmised, "just as someone might close the eyes of a corpse and compose the features before burial. Men, stand away for propriety's sake and search the loft for anything you deem unusual. We women will examine the corpse."

Wiping their hands off, Ned and Clifford seemed only too eager to obey. They took one lantern, and Rosie held the other over the body.

"I only met Hannah once," Elizabeth said, "but she was so bright, in more ways than one. This is foul play, I fear, and I mean for us to discover what happened here. I will not have unwed women who strive to make their own way in my kingdom become victims of brutal men."

Elizabeth's own words to Parliament danced through her brain again: *Fatal fashions are treasons, greed and lust, adultery and murder, in my kingdom . . .*

Both Rosie and Meg looked at her wide-eyed, as if they had caught on to another reason—besides affordable, fashionable ruffs—the queen had favored Hannah von Hoven.

"I see," Rosie said, and Meg nodded solemnly.

"Then let us see what we can discover here. Untie that little neck ruff of hers, if you please. It looks crushed in places, yet seems to have sprung back in others."

"Mayhap," Meg murmured, "in its starch bath, it popped back."

But they had to find scissors and cut the stiff, S-shaped curves of the four-inch-deep ruff carefully away. Discolored bruises lay not under it but lower on her neck, like a mottled necklace against Hannah's alabaster throat.

"Choked or strangled," Elizabeth whispered, "but that does not mean for certain it was the cause of her death. Pin that ruff back on, and let's see if we can find other marks on her."

Pulling up sleeves so stiff they crackled, they scanned her white flesh and found blue and brown bruises on both wrists.

"She struggled," Meg whispered, tears in her eyes, "but someone bigger and stronger held her down in that starch. A killer strong enough or tall enough to lift her up into the vat's liquid, either to drown her or hide her."

"Yes," Elizabeth agreed, "strong enough to lift her high so the vat did not tip and, evidently, not that much of the liquid starch sloshed out. Men," she called over to them, "see how stable that long vat is and what holds it."

They moved immediately to peer under it and tried to move it.

"Seems solid," Ned called to her. "It's set in a sturdy wooden base, kind of like a wooden cradle, but one that doesn't rock."

"There was some starch spilled on the floor," Meg put in. "Not the first time I saw her floating hand, I think, but when Jenks, Ned, and I came back."

"Then it was spilled when he—surely it was a man—lifted her out to hide her on the shelf," the queen pronounced. "Why didn't he just leave her in the vat? His garments must have become sodden with that starch. Perhaps that is what we are looking for—a man with dried starch slopped upon his doublet or cape. But what would that look like?"

"And he could easily change or destroy that garb. But I just remembered something," Meg added. "Jenks noted sticky footsteps on the stairs, but they had mostly dried when I saw them."

"Which would mean," Rosie whispered, "the murderer left by the stairs and not the window."

"We shall examine all possibilities," the queen declared, "and any person we even slightly suspect."

She turned back to the corpse again. "Rosie and Meg, stand firm, for we are almost finished here. Before we summon the authorities of this ward, we must see if she has marks on her backside. I've seen dead bodies where the blood settles and so reveals what position they were in when they died—and this poor, strangled woman . . ."

But as they rolled her on her side, white starch water gushed from her nose and dribbled from her mouth.

" 'S blood, or *was* she drowned?" Elizabeth cried as her skirts took the stream of what Hosea Cantwell had called the devil's liquor. "If she were dead when she was put in the vat, would she have that stuff inside of her?"

"I guess some could seep in, but that much?" Rosie cried, dabbing at the queen's skirts with a corner of the blanket.

"No, don't," Elizabeth insisted. "Leave it be so we can see what we might be looking for on the murderer's garments. But I warrant, then, she was still breathing when she went into the vat and took several gasps of that stuff as she died."

She braced her hands on the edge of the worktable and shuddered at the image that brought to mind. She prayed poor Hannah had not been ravished, too, but she could not bear to examine her private parts for bruising. That would somehow be the final insult, especially with the men in the room, and whether Hannah had been raped or not, she was still dead. Elizabeth meant to find the murderer, and then he would confess all the how and why, she swore it.

Besides, the body had gone as solid as the wooden vat itself, not only in the starch but in what doctors called *rigor mortis.* Elizabeth had noted that even Hannah's face was stiff, so she must have swallowed much starch for it to seep out through clenched jaw muscles, teeth, and lips.

"Meg, you said that the cuckoo-pint herb is poison," the queen said. "But mixed with water for starch, it would be diluted from being fatal, wouldn't it? I mean, if she somehow toppled in, hit her head to knock herself out, then imbibed a huge draft of the starch by mistake—"

"I think so much water mixed in would weaken the power of the herb. I warrant it does not poison instantly. Yet it's strong enough to chafe skin and turn it red, like a laundresses's hands."

"Yet Hannah's hands and skin look as smooth and white as carved ivory under that glaze of starch," Rosie observed. "Maybe it's because she was already dead when put in there, and dead skin won't chap."

"I don't know for certain how fast it even works on a living person's skin," Meg admitted. "I can ask a laundress or a whitster about that. This area teems with them, and I'm sure I could find you one who—"

They all jolted at the muted yet shrill sound of a woman's voice. The queen's stomach cartwheeled. For one wild moment, she thought the corpse could be exhaling one last breath to produce the sound.

"Sounds like much ado downstairs," Meg muttered as

they laid Hannah on her back again. "Jenks's voice, too." Ned and Clifford rushed toward the steps, but the queen motioned them back. Below, at the bottom of the dark staircase, she could barely make out Jenks with his arms around a struggling woman.

Chapter the Fifth

"WHAT GOES?" ELIZABETH CALLED DOWN TO JENKS.

"Caught this one trying to sneak up the stairs."

"Hold her, and we will come down."

"I just had a thought," Meg whispered behind Elizabeth. "Hannah was real tight with her money. What if her work-women rebelled at their wages or some such, and an accident happened? More than one woman could manage to lift her. Then they felt guilty about leaving her in the vat because they knew what it would do to her skin."

"Hold all that for later," Elizabeth said. "For now, we must speak with that woman. Men, put the body back on the shelf, then continue your search for anything unusual. Rosie and Meg, with me, for I will speak with Jenks's captive."

Meg took the second lantern and, as the queen ordered, preceded Her Majesty down the staircase, lighting their way. Lady Rosie, who seemed only too relieved to depart the loft, hurried behind them.

"Unhand me, you great oaf!" the struggling woman cried, and landed an elbow in Jenks's solid midriff.

Meg noted she was nearly as shapely a blonde as Hannah. With one arm around the woman's narrow waist and the other over her bouncing breasts as she tried to wriggle free, Jenks looked as if he were actually enjoying himself.

"I'll not loose you. Hold there!" he ordered. Bates hovered a short distance off, scanning the alley.

The wench was hardly a goodwife but a laborer in brown homespun with a well-worn apron. She looked ready to cry. Her long hair spilled from her cap in such disarray it reminded Meg of poor Hannah's.

"Stop struggling!" the queen ordered, though she kept her voice low. "I would but ask you a few questions, mistress, and my man will not harm you."

Evidently at the sound of a woman's cultured voice and tone of command, Jenks's prisoner went still in his arms. Reluctantly, Meg could tell, he released her but for one hand on her forearm.

"Who are you, then?" the queen asked the disheveled woman.

"Ursala Hemmings, whitster, that's me, and live nearby, a friend to the starcher what works here," she said in one long, ragged breath. "Thought you be night thieves or anglers breaking in and these your spotters, that's what. I meant to send out a hue and cry for the night watch, but this base-court codpiece grabbed me—"

"Hold your tongue!" the queen ordered. "We came to see the starcher ourselves, for we do business with her."

Ursala gasped, then blurted, "Hey then, you ladies from the queen's court come to fetch the royal starched goods? But where's Hannah? Heard she's ill. Or she been hurt?"

"Yes, I regret to tell you she's been hurt."

Ursala broke into tears. "That one, there," she accused,

pointing past Jenks at Bates, "been guarding her door and wouldn't let me pass to see or help her earlier. Thought I'd sneak in at night, 'cause Hannah's not in her room near mine, and—something else gone amiss, hasn't it? Something's dreadful wrong!"

Meg could always tell when Her Majesty had decided on someone, that is, whether to trust the person or not. She could see the queen was going to take this plucky woman into her confidence, at least to get out of her anything she could.

"Yes, I regret to tell you, Mistress Hemmings," the queen said quietly, "that Hannah has died, and not of her own hand."

"Murder?" Ursala screeched before Jenks clapped his hand over her mouth and held her tight again.

"Meg," the queen said, "run upstairs to tell the men to douse their lantern, uncover the windows, and follow us to the mews forthwith. Jenks, bring Mistress Hemmings along where we can talk more privily and quietly than shouting bloody murder in the night streets. Hie yourself now, before someone summons the night watch and we must explain more than just a whitster's skulking about."

"I can't believe it's come to this," Cecil told Elizabeth as they sat in the royal withdrawing room the next morning over mulled wine and partridge pie that had long gone cold. "A young woman, a starcher, of all things, murdered," he went on, taking some sort of notes—Cecil was always writing something. "A great tragedy and a mighty mystery, I admit, Your Grace, but why not allow the ward constable and the coroner to deal with it?"

"Because they might *not* be able to deal with it." She

pushed back her chair and went to look out the window. "Sad to say, some of this country's constables reason things out on a level with my dear Jenks—'s blood, you know what I mean. Oh, for certain, they inquire of neighbors if anything was noted amiss, but if no one saw the murder directly, they close the books on it. Besides, I just have an inkling that this death might have ramifications."

"Are you worried, as Ned suggested, that clues and suspicions might lead straight to your master starcher and her husband?"

"I don't know, but I intend to find out. Meg and Jenks may have gotten something out of the hysterical Mistress Hemmings by now, but I intend to pay a visit to the van der Passes' starch house this morning. At the least, I will observe closely how they react when I give them the news of Hannah's tragic death."

"You could summon them here."

"That might alarm them and give them time to hide something. Now that I've seen Hannah's shop, I want a good look at theirs."

"Do you intend to search their residence as you did Hannah's?"

"A lot of good that did us," she muttered. On the way back to the palace last night, the queen and Clifford had gone one street behind Hannah's shop to her small single room, which Ursala had described. They'd found it stripped of whatever garments, personal effects, or money she might have had there. Someone had been in a big rush but had, once again, been clever enough not to leave clues to his or her own identity behind, besides the fact they were dealing with someone obviously dangerous and desperate. Elizabeth meant to have Ned inquire if those neighbors heard or saw anything strange, too.

"If the van der Passes are to blame," Cecil said, "I doubt you'd find one thing in their starch house or privy chambers to cast guilt on them."

"Yet I keep hoping," she told him, her voice trembling, "that if we turn over enough rocks—or, in this case, stir up enough starch—a clue will turn up."

Frowning, she gazed over the broad Thames as it sprang to life with horse ferries, barges, and wherries plying the white-capped waves. The dawn sky tinted the water a pewter hue, and she thought again of the starch bath that had held poor Hannah.

Elizabeth knew that she herself could have been killed in her youth, her future obliterated by her Catholic sister, Queen Mary, when she sent her to the Tower for her supposed part in a Protestant rebellion. Through a slit of window, she'd glimpsed the Thames and wished she could escape on it. Mary had wanted to execute—to murder—her. For more than justice's sake in her realm, Elizabeth felt compelled to discover and punish whoever was guilty of Hannah's horrible death. Murder was always an immoral act, but murder of a clever, ambitious young woman in her prime was intolerable.

She turned back and walked toward Cecil, who had become as silent as she. Neither of them had gone to bed last night; he looked normal, but exhaustion drained her. As she glanced down, she saw that, as if from a bird's-eye view, he'd sketched a huge neck ruff with an open circle in the center, the outer part in sections like a pie cut in wedges.

"I was fearful I'd see starched ruffs in my sleep," she admitted, "but they obsess you, too? And why only six sections in it instead of many?"

"Because, Your Majesty," he said as he scribbled something else in, "that has oft been the number of guilty parties we must investigate when your privy plot counselors probe a murder."

She steadied herself with her hand on the back of his chair and leaned over his shoulder. As she watched, he made a big question mark in the center of the ruff where the wearer's neck would go. He'd left three sections of the ruff itself blank, but he'd written in three others: *Competitors Dirck and Dingen v. d. Passe? Lover? Disgruntled worker?*

"It bolsters me to know, Cecil, that your mind is already at work on this, too. I warrant we shall have additions to that chart, and hopefully deletions, for, yes, it could lead to economic chaos with our tailoring and textile commerce if our fledgling starch industry collapsed. If, that is, the van der Passes are somehow involved with the murder, so that I would lose Dingen as well as Hannah."

"Please, Your Grace," Cecil said, jumping to his feet, evidently when he realized she stood while he sat, "just see that in all this, in addition to your regular royal duties, *you* don't collapse."

"As dreadful as this is, I've been through worse," she assured him. "I just pray God this investigation will not come near the throne or those I must rely on to rule and reign. Who would have known," she added under her breath as she turned away to call for her coach and cloak, "that starch could become a fatal fashion?"

"Can't thank your lady and you both enough for your help," Ursala Hemmings told Meg and Jenks for the fourth time since they'd awakened.

Last night the woman had become nearly incoherent when she'd learned her friend had been murdered, so Her

Majesty had asked the two of them to take her home and stay the night with her. As of yet, Meg realized, Ursala did not know the one she called "your lady" was England's queen.

Ursala Hemmings lived in two back rooms near St. Martin's fields with her sister and sister's husband, whom they had not roused. When Meg, Jenks, and Ursala finally became exhausted, they curled up for fitful sleep in big baskets of sheets amid washtubs and smaller soaking vats and barrels. As daylight crept into London's narrow streets, only now, Meg judged, did Ursala Hemmings seem calm enough to question.

Meg herself didn't feel calm, though, and not only because she was anxious to get back to her daughter. Meg feared that if she hadn't been sent along to watch him, Jenks might have comforted Ursala in more ways than one. The man was obviously smitten with this—this laundress, when Meg had never known him to be one bit fond of any woman but the queen and herself.

And what if it turned out that Ursala was racked by guilt instead of grief? More than one woman—even purported friends—had murdered another over something or other, usually a man, which reminded Meg that she'd have to ask Ned privily if he had ever tried to entice Hannah with his charms. That's all she'd need, Ned involved personally with the dead woman when the queen was hell-bent on solving this crime.

As light seeped into the room to replace the glow of two tallow candles, Meg realized the laundry room's vats and barrels of liquids reminded her of the starch tub in Hannah's loft. Shelves lined two walls here, and Ursala had long wooden stirring sticks.

"What's all this liquid besides wash water?" she asked as

the woman started to open the two small front street shutters. Though he wasn't needed, Jenks scurried over to help. Meg glared at him behind Ursala's back.

"That first tub's for soaking stubborn stains," she explained, pointing. "Got alkaline water of lye in it. We buy wood ash from ovens, strain and mix it here. Real good to take out grease, tallow, and fat stains, sure is."

"And this?" Meg asked.

"Oh, that's just powder from ground sheep's hooves for treating grease spots. Lots of those on tablecloths. Lemon juice takes out iron stains, and we rub fruit stains with butter, then wash them quick in hot milk. Fur pieces like those hanging over there just get brushed through with bran."

"Sounds like," Jenks put in, "you've got everything in store we'd need for breakfast. But what are those big hooks on the wall?"

"Oh, those," she said with a slight smile his way. "Twisting hooks to wring water out 'fore drying things outside. We reuse as much water as we can, 'cause it's such a burden, hauling it from city cisterns."

Meg hoped Ursala would answer questions about Hannah with the ease and equanimity with which she was talking now. "And this barrel is hard cider?" Meg asked, staring down into a potent-smelling vat.

"Oh, that's just sheep urine for soaking sweat-stained shirts. Then we wash them in hot water."

"That would cover up the sweat smell, all right," Jenks said in a wry comment worthy of Ned. Meg jumped away from the vat, but the hint of another wan smile at Jenks lit Ursala's tear-streaked face and tilted her blue eyes.

"Mistress Hemmings," Meg said, trying as much as she could to sound like the queen as she steered the woman over toward the big worktable, "I must ask you several questions about your friend Hannah. Do you know why her workers weren't with her yesterday after midmorn?"

"Oh, sure," she said, nodding vigorously as she sat and gripped her hands on the table. "Saw one of them, Dorothy, in the drying fields, said Hannah gave them a holiday after they came in. Surprised they were, every one of them."

"So that was unusual?" Meg prompted as Jenks came over to sit silently by Ursala on the plank bench.

"You think the likes of us can afford giving our girls time off?" Ursala cried. "She promised them pay, and Hannah was close with money, too."

"But she didn't give her women a reason for their impromptu holiday?"

"Their what holiday? Was yesterday some saint's day?" Ursala demanded. Jenks patted her shoulder. Meg reminded herself to ask the queen *not* to send him back to Ursala, but then, the queen should never have sent Ned to visit Hannah, either.

"No, not a saint's day," Meg explained. "But you were in the fields across the way after Hannah let her women go?"

"With my sister and our workers," she said, nodding. "In that stiff wind, things dried fast, but we have to guard them. Lose a sheet or tablecloth sets us back a pretty penny."

"I can imagine. So you saw nothing at all unusual that day?"

"Nary a thing. But—I just 'membered a young lady what got lost, kept standing 'bout, was mayhap mute or simple. Come to think of it, she kept looking up toward Hannah's windows, she did."

Meg's and Jenks's gazes met.

"So, mistress," he said, "how was this young lady attired?"

Propping her elbows on the table, Ursala put both hands

over her eyes. "Keep only seeing her scairt face. Ah . . . she wore a blue cloak, had fine shoes on, with soles not worn much, neither." She looked at Jenks, then Meg, in turn. "I tried to feed her, but she warn't hungry. Can I get something then for the both of you?" she said, popping up as if her interrogation were over.

The idea of having breakfast in a room with vats of lye and urine didn't appeal to Meg, though Jenks looked as if he'd happily jump in one of them if he could please this woman.

"We need to go speak with the lady that sent us," Meg said, and stood before Jenks could answer.

"But we'll be back to be certain you're well," Jenks assured her, and reached over to squeeze her shoulder. As Meg took Jenks's arm to propel him along, the door at the back of the workroom opened. Another woman, the very image of Ursala, stood there with an older man behind her.

"Who's these folks, Lally?" the woman called out, but Ursala just followed them to the door.

"My sister Pamela," she explained as they stepped out into the street. For the first time, Meg saw that Ursala's sweet face was dusted with light freckles. "Born the same day," she went on, "but I'm older by a bit, and people always mistake us. We're not close, though," she whispered, "not since she wed. That's Peter, her husband, what owns this place and her now, too. Hannah and I"—her blue eyes clouded with tears again and she sniffed hard—"she took my sister's place when I kind of lost her, but now—she's gone . . . Hannah had a twin sister, too—we had that in common . . ."

Sensing Jenks was tempted to take Ursala, alias Lally, into his arms and wipe away her tears, Meg gripped his iron-muscled arm hard with her fingernails and steered him down the street. As they passed Hannah's starch house, they saw Bates in front of it, earnestly speaking to the red-coated constable the queen or Secretary Cecil must have sent for.

Dingen van der Passe's starch establishment was at a similar distance from the palace as Hannah's, but, considering what Elizabeth hoped to accomplish, she knew it was no good trying to sneak there in disguise. Simply informing her servants that she wanted to see the van der Passe starch house, she went in her coach with Lady Rosie out the main palace gate and down the broad Strand toward Holywell Street. As ever, when she appeared with an entourage, townfolk, especially children, followed along or huzzahed as she passed.

"I'll never become used to the jolting of my coaches," Elizabeth groused to Rosie. "They may be the new thing in transport, but someone surely must find a way for us to have a smoother ride. This damned thing is likely to shake my teeth out of my head! 'S blood, I just bit my tongue!"

"I must say, they are beautifully painted and carved, Your Majesty."

"I'd hang all that for a gentle ride," Elizabeth insisted, swallowing the tart taste of blood, then dabbing at the bite mark with a handkerchief. "For once, I think those with less wealth and position have the better way, to simply walk," she went on with a bit of a lisp. "But it does keep the dust and rain off—and shelters me from anyone who would dare harm."

"I know you prefer to ride ahorse, Your Grace."

"But that can be dangerous, too. Thomas Gresham's crushed leg came, you know, when he was ahorse on an errand for me on the Continent. A loud bang afrighted his mount, it reared, and that was that. He well-nigh died from his injuries, and the leg pain nearly cripples him yet."

She thought again of Gresham's pain over his daughter's mental state. The parents had been relieved their child was not injured, yet was not the child's malady worse than one that could be physically categorized and treated? At least, the queen had heard, Meg's little Sally was well and being fed and bathed.

Both the queen and Rosie jolted and jerked as a wheel bounced through what must have been a hole as big as a pot. "Hell's gates, Boonen," the queen called to her coachman, and rapped on the ceiling, "keep a better eye out for those!" She would have slapped the leather curtain down over the window, but people were waving and cheering along the way between the Savoy and Somerset House, so she smiled and waved despite the jostling ride.

"At least a coach journey is usually smoother in the countryside," the ever cheerful Rose said. "There the streets don't have these modern cobbles, so is progress indeed better? But, Your Grace, is there anything special I should do when we arrive at Mrs. van der Passe's starch house?"

"Do not let on that Hannah is dead until I inform them, and keep your eyes on their shop and on their faces. I'm sure Dingen will not appreciate an unannounced early-morning royal visit, but that is just too bad."

The small scattering of Londoners from all walks of life cheered their queen as she emerged from the coach, smiling, nodding, surrounded by six guards who had dismounted. She waved at her people before she swept through the starch-shop door Clifford held open for her. Inside, there was much stir even before the twenty or so women bent over their tasks looked up to see—for all they knew—a grand lady with a small entourage cross their threshold.

Then, from the back, someone whispered, "Laws! 'Tis the queen herself!"

Those closest curtsied, and the others followed; everyone gaped. One woman at the back of the room turned away and pounded up the back stairs.

Lady Rosie followed the queen in, and then came Clifford, who had ridden with Boonen. Clifford, Elizabeth noted as the van der Passes rushed down from their living quarters above the shop, was exactly the height and girth of Dingen's brawny husband, Dirck.

"Oh, Your Majesty, a surprise and honor, *ja,* it is!" Dingen cried as she hurried through her women and curtsied low.

Her handsome attire indicated she might plan to oversee her shop, but not labor in it herself, for she wore both neck and wrist ruffs. Dirck was another story. Elizabeth noted he had hastily pulled on his black leather jerkin and a flat red-and-blue-striped taffeta cap. Sweeping off the cap, he sank into a bow just behind his wife.

The van der Passes were sturdy people of big frames and ample flesh with light brown hair, pale skin, broad faces with cheeks polished like pippins, and bright blue eyes. Elizabeth judged them to be nearly fifty years of age. It had always seemed to her that husbands and wives who had lived long together, especially if they oft worked side by side, began to resemble each other, and this couple attested to that belief. Both spoke with pronounced Dutch accents. Despite all the workers toiling here and her own fine attire, Dingen's hands were rough and red, much more than Hannah's had been.

"To vat do ve owe the honor of this visit, Your Majesty?" Dirck asked as he stood erect again.

"For one thing, I wanted to see this busy hive of activity. I have been proud to employ both you and Hannah von Hoven, so surely a visit is in order."

"Oh, *ja*," Dingen said, "but ve are bigger and better here dan her place."

"Do you know that from mere hearsay or have you seen it?"

Though he had not been addressed directly, Dirck answered. "Got to know about one's competition, eh, vife?"

"Oh, *ja*, and Hannah's most welcome here in turn. Dat young voman trespass for sure, taking some of our London business," she said, shaking a finger as if Hannah were here to be lectured, "but ve not call it trespass if she visit here. Perhaps she vould learn something to see a proper new mangle and our stirring stools instead of sticks."

Dingen gestured to the three-legged stools that her women dipped in two big barrels to stir the thick, pasty starch mixture. That, too, looked different from what Hannah had been soaking in.

"May ve show you around, den, Your Majesty?" Dingen asked.

"I would count it a favor."

At a flick of Dingen's wrist, her women moved back against the walls to give them access to the array of tables, drying racks, and troughs of gray, thick starch a woman had been ladling out. But where was the large dipping vat?

The queen's gaze snagged Rosie's surprised stare; she gave her a barely perceptible shake of her head. She had planned to surprise the van der Passes immediately with news of Hannah's death and then observe them, but she needed to see how this starch shop was different. That alone could have fostered competition and hard feelings between the two rival starchers.

"You see, Your Majesty," Dingen said, holding up a thick-bristled brush, "ve brush dis stiff starch paste in each fold of each ruff and dry it vell." She gestured to rows of racks and shelves stacked with tiers of ruffs on wooden forms in the shape and size of necks and wrists. "Poor Hannah, she still use dat vat'ry starch—so I been told. Next ve dampen and set de ruff, de most difficult process. I tell you, it takes great patience—even teaching my vorkers takes great patience.

"Den, vit heated rods called poking sticks—ve are the only starch shop in all England can do it—ve set up to six hundred tiny pleats or S-curves of vide or small sizes and add a tiny dab of vax—one of my secrets, but I share it vit you—to fix the curves together so it not collapse like a ruined French egg *soufflé, ja.*"

It annoyed Elizabeth not only that Dingen kept subtly denigrating Hannah but that this Dutchwoman must enjoy French food. Even foreigners were now preferring things foreign.

"Oh, Your Majesty," Dingen plunged on, her hands clasped before her ample breasts and her face nearly enraptured, "just vait til the next new ruffle fashions sweep your court!"

"If they sweep my court, I shall set the fashions while you set the ruffs, Mrs. van der Passe."

"Oh, *ja,* of course, but it shall be dis starch house, not da small von Hoven's place works vit you. I vill introduce—vith your approval, of course—colored starches, not just the ivory ones ve see now but yellows, pale reds, and lilacs, and encourage ruffs vit lace, tiny jewels, embroidery. I intended to beg for your permission, but since you are here—Your Majesty, I vould ask one boon."

Elizabeth was becoming even more disturbed. What if these people—or even just Dirck—were actually guilty of harming Hannah? If the queen could prove that, what if, as Ned had mentioned and Cecil had suggested, this starch house collapsed in a flurry of suspicion and accusations over Hannah's death? The queen knew she must indeed tread carefully here.

"Would both of you please step out into my coach with me?" she said, and, used to her merest hint being a command, started for the door.

She looked back to see the couple exchanging dire glances. Dingen wrung her hands while Dirck whispered to her, and they both nodded. Looking as if they were going to their doom, they followed her out and up the steps of the coach. Rosie climbed up, too, and, as a last thought, since Dirck looked large enough to harm a woman of any size, the queen gestured for Clifford to climb in as well. At her nod, Boonen closed the door on the five of them.

"Ask your boon, then," Elizabeth told the nervous couple.

"That you keep," Dirck spoke this time, "that Puritan cleric from our shop. He's come more than vonce unbidden—to preach and threaten us vit fire and brimstone from heaven and a place in the very bowels of hell."

"Hosea Cantwell?" Elizabeth gasped. "He has intruded and threatened you?"

"Twice," Dingen put in, "and said he vould return."

Then, the queen reasoned, he could have been to Hannah's, too. Had he found her alone, threatened her, they'd argued and things got out of hand? No doubt many homicides began as arguments, which led to accidents, and then the murderer panicked and tried to cover things up.

"I assure you I will speak to Hosea Cantwell," she said.

"Ve only bothered you vit this," Dirck said, leaning forward on the leather seat, "since he's a member of your own Parliament."

"Hardly *my own* Parliament, but I will see to it. However, I have come for another reason besides seeing your thriving establishment or hearing your hopes for future fashions. I regret to tell you that Hannah von Hoven was murdered yesterday by a person or persons unknown."

Both of them looked speechless—and scared stiff. Dingen tried to say something but only sputtered. Dirck turned beet red. Elizabeth was surprised but suspicious when neither of them asked for details of the murder. Were they just too shocked, or did they truly not care—or did they already know?

"And," the queen plunged on, pressing her advantage, "I have it on good authority that you, man, were seen near Hannah's house the day she died."

"But," Dingen cracked out, "my husband could have nothing to do vit that! He oft goes about to buy goods or to deliver dem, dat's all."

"I asked your husband why he was there, not you, Mrs. van der Passe."

"Vell, I vas taking a constitutional," Dirck said, sitting up even straighter. "A valk, and the air in St. Martin's fields is fresh, that's all. *Ja,* I varrant I vas near the poor voman's place, but hardly vent to see her—vouldn't. Dere vas no need, for our starch house is far better than hers . . ."

He must have realized he might be digging himself a deeper hole, for he suddenly stopped in midthought.

"Ve regret the death of one so young and promising," Dingen said, her voice wavering. "How did she die? Vat really happened?"

"That," Elizabeth said, "is what the constable and coroner intend to discover. And since Hannah is gone, can your shop rise to the increased demands you will now face?"

As they both effusively assured her of that, she felt again they might indeed have arranged Hannah's demise. Why, then, had Hannah sent her workers away? That smacked of preparation for some sort of lovers' tryst, not a visit from the husband of her rival.

As the couple disembarked the royal coach, the queen looked past them and saw William Paulet's lackey, Hugh Dauntsey, standing well back in the crowd. She refused to believe it mere circumstance—like Dirck just happening to be in Hannah's neighborhood the day she died.

If Dauntsey didn't live in this immediate area, she'd summon him to find out why he happened to be lurking here. She didn't trust his puppetmaster Paulet not to try to upset her plans for England's economic growth without him at the helm. Both he and his underlings needed watching.

Dauntsey's icy gaze chilled her, so she sent Clifford to fetch Dingen back to the coach again. She came, this time, with her round, rosy face dour and her lips pressed so tightly together her mouth looked like a purse drawn in by strings.

The moment the coach door was closed again, the queen asked, "Are you familiar with a man named Hugh Dauntsey?"

"Hugh? *Ja*, he's our money man, helps us good vit sums and figures, knows English taxes ve didn't at first. He been seen near Hannah's, too?"

"He's in the crowd outside your door, that's all."

"Your Majesty, just 'cause a starcher got herself killed, don't mean me or my family involved. Just 'cause Hugh Dauntsey outside our door or vorks for us, don't mean a thing. If—if my Dirck loses the fine reputation ve got here—a reputation he long built as a Flemish knight, and ve left our homeland to come here . . . I just not go on. I just close my starch house and not go on."

"Stay calm, Mrs. van der Passe. I simply wanted to bring the sad news to you myself and clear up a few things. There is no need for such fears and dire predictions. You may go now, as I'm sure you and your starchers have much to do."

The woman scuttled out of the coach as if she had been burned. Elizabeth leaned back against the tapestried seat as the door closed yet again, and the coach bounced into motion. After all, she also had much to do.

Chapter the Sixth

"SO, NED, TO SUMMARIZE," ELIZABETH CUT IN AS HE continued his extended, dramatized report to the assembled Privy Plot Council, "none of the neighbors you interviewed saw aught amiss at or near Hannah's place the day she died, including anyone climbing out or in that large open window."

Everyone seemed to take a breath when she interrupted Ned. It was nearly ten o'clock that night, and they were all exhausted.

"God's truth, Your Grace, I thought you needed ample details about those I asked. All claim they were going on about their business. So it seems that Ursala Hemmings is the only one who saw anything suspicious, that being the Gresham girl hanging about—"

"Yes, I will deal with that later. It seems, then, we either have a murderer who did not seem out of place, even if seen, or one who is so wily that, even if a stranger, he convinced Hannah to send her women away so she would be alone in the loft."

"Indeed, our prey seems coldly calculating," Cecil said, "though we must not discount a possible crime of passion, a planned meeting that escalated to emotions. But whether it was an intentional murder by someone she knew or a spontaneous one by a stranger, we have a difficult and dangerous task ahead."

"Exactly, my lord," Elizabeth agreed. "Since Hannah sent her workers away, I yet wonder if she did agree to a tryst, though that starch loft is hardly a romantic bower. Jenks and Meg," she said, leaning forward to see them on the other side of Ned, "is there anything else odd you can recall except the fact that Hannah gave her women an unexpected holiday?"

"Not that I can think of," Meg said, and Jenks shook his head to back her up. For some reason, their visages both reminded her of thunderclouds.

"Ned," the queen went on, "then I charge you to learn from Ursala who Hannah's women were so that you may question them, each alone. One of them might have heard a hint, at least, of why they were released early that day. Or they might have seen or overheard something earlier about a liaison Hannah had planned, or have discovered someone who seemed sweet on her. Jenks, whatever is it?" she asked when she saw his expression turn even more grim.

"I can fetch Ursala 'stead of Ned," he said gruffly. "Then I can escort her to talk to Ned or just get the names from her, too, seeing I know where she lives."

The queen caught the exaggerated way Meg rolled her eyes. Something strange was afoot here.

"Meg and Jenks, why the theatrics I usually expect from Ned? What is going on behind my back?"

"Nothing, Your Grace," Meg murmured, not daring to look her in the eye.

"I just thought," Jenks said, "you'd rather have Ursala here to talk to, 'stead of letting the other whitsters and her sister know all about these doings, like if Ned goes there."

The queen smacked her hand flat on the table. Everyone jumped. The nib of Cecil's feather pen splattered ink on his paper.

"Yes—'know all about these doings,'" Elizabeth repeated. "Here I am, relying on all of you to keep me informed about these doings, and something is going on I either need to know or at least need *not* to have bandied about covertly in my presence. Jenks, tell me."

The big man shifted in his seat as if he'd been caught at something dire. "It's just Ursala's real delicate right now, Your Grace, and Ned might upset her," he mumbled.

"Might poach in your territory," Meg muttered.

"Meg," the queen cried, "I hope you have something to add to that, something spoken clearly that makes sense and contributes to my question."

"I just think Jenks favors her—Ursala. So he might try to protect her when mayhap she shouldn't be protected any more than any other person we suspect."

Jenks turned toward Meg in his chair so fast it squeaked under his big body. "We don't suspect her any more than the man in the moon!" he exploded. "The poor girl's completely o'erturned by her friend's death!"

Ordinarily, the queen would have demanded silence or tossed them out for arguing before her, but she—like Cecil, scowling across the table—chose to let them rail on.

"Ursala was out guarding the laundry in the fields," Jenks insisted. "Otherwise, she wouldn't have seen the Gresham girl there."

"But maybe she wasn't in the fields all day," Meg countered. "With the others about, they could take turns slipping away. I do agree with Jenks, though, Your Grace, that it's best not to let Ned squire her about. Ursala's as fetching as poor Hannah was, and we don't need his special attention to—to her, too."

"Too? Ned?" Elizabeth said before Jenks and Meg could go at it again.

"Yes, Your Grace?"

"Don't try to bluff or cozen me! I thought perhaps you'd best head off what Meg implies before I ask her to explain."

Her principal player managed to look completely calm and even innocent, which made the queen think there was, indeed, something amiss.

"I assume, Your Majesty," Ned said in his smoothest tone, "that Meg still has her dander up over the fact I visited Hannah von Hoven, weeks ago and only once, after that day you ordered me to take Meg's starch roots to her, the day Meg was sick, and she's still acting sick right now—lovesick, if you ask me, so—"

"I didn't ask you," Elizabeth interrupted, "at least not that. Jenks, is it true that you are sweet on Ursala Hemmings?"

"I feel sorry for her, Your Grace, and just want—to help her," the big man said, but he squirmed in his seat again.

Meg snorted; the queen sighed. It never took much to read Jenks's heart, which was one reason Elizabeth knew how loyal and honest he was. 'S blood, why didn't Cecil step in to help with this? Right now, she had no inkling what her brilliant secretary of state was thinking, though he kept scribbling at that damned sketch of a ruff with the names of the possibly guilty in it.

"Let me say this," Elizabeth told all of them, pointing like a schoolmaster, "and just once. Whatever frictions—or friendships—are among any of you, I need them to be subjugated for a time so that we, pulling as a team, can solve this murder. Is there anyone at this table who cannot swear to me that he or she can discipline himself or herself to that cause?"

She stared at each in turn. No one so much as blinked. "Then," the queen added, "is there anything else for the good of the order before I tell you how I think we should proceed?"

"One thing Meg and I forgot, Your Grace," Jenks said.

"Say on."

"Ursala said one reason she missed Hannah so much was 'cause Ursala used to be close to her twin sister—Pamela, married now, the one she lives with, along with Pamela's husband. Ursala said that Hannah also has a twin sister. Both being twins brought Ursala and Hannah closer, I take it."

"Or *had* a twin sister," Meg put in, frowning. "Ursala might have said Hannah *had* a twin sister, not *has*."

"Thank you, Jenks and Meg. I don't see how that figures into this thick brew of possibilities, but anything we learn may help when we get more of the pieces put together. My lord Cecil, whose names are you filling in on your chart of suspicious persons?" she asked, leaning closer to him. "Ursala Hemmings?"

She noted that Jenks tensed as if he would spring across the table at Cecil. "Not specifically Ursala, Your Grace," Cecil said, squinting swiftly over at Jenks, then back down to his parchment. "I have simply added to the section marked 'disgruntled workers' the words 'or one of Hannah's friends.' But after what you and Lady Rosie have reported to us of your visit to the van der Passes, I have also included Hosea Cantwell's name in another section of the diagram."

Elizabeth nodded. "A wild card, indeed, and one I intend

to keep face up by speaking with him again, on the morrow to be exact. And there's one more possibility, though a vague one, by the name of Hugh Dauntsey, though I won't have you add him to our list until I hire and question him."

"Hire him? Hugh Dauntsey?" Cecil demanded. He never raised his voice when others were about, but she had always promoted a good give-and-take in these Privy Plot Council meetings. "When we're trying to cut back that spider's web of a bureaucracy your royal forbearers managed to let everyone spin around them?" Cecil plunged on. "That rabidly Catholic lackbrain Dauntsey?"

"My lord Cecil, he may have ruined his opportunity to take over Thomas Gresham's role as chief Tudor financial advisor and foreign agent, and he may be rabidly Catholic—which is another reason he needs watching—but he's no lackbrain."

"He's Will Paulet's lackey, at least, and has been ingratiating himself with him. For all I know, he thinks he has a large bequest coming when the old man finally dies."

"My point precisely—no lackbrain," she argued. "Rather, a clever man with, no doubt, fettered and frustrated ambitions and a hatred of the Tudors for dismissing him and of me for never hiring him to do so much as count coins. And he must detest the fact he was replaced with Thomas Gresham, whom I yet favor."

"But hire him?" he repeated. "He'll babble everything you tell him to Paulet, and it will upset Gresham mightily if you start to trust Hugh Dauntsey."

"Perhaps even more than it has upset you," she admitted. "But I said hire him, not trust him, my lord. I learned just before this meeting that the ward constable you summoned about Hannah's death has handed the investigation over to the chief constable at his request. And though I can't recall his name, the chief constable—"

"It's Nigel Whitcomb," Cecil said, shaking his head. "He was previously chief steward of the Skinners' Guild. He's that new member of the Commons in your rebellious Parliament, though he was wily enough to hide in the back row that day you took them to task for urging you to wed. The man's a stickler for detail and has a much inflated opinion of himself. And he's as pushy as a North Sea wind."

"He has moved quickly. He's met with the coroner who examined Hannah's body and ruled it a murder, and he's convinced the coroner that since Hannah had no known heirs and was a royal starcher, part of the worth of her goods should come to the crown. Of course, Whitcomb's trying to curry favor with me, but this plays right into our hands, as it will allow me to keep a better eye on Dauntsey."

"It's usually a percentage of the goods of the murderers, not the murdered, that comes to the crown," Cecil said, frowning. "But what does Whitcomb have to do with Dauntsey?"

"I intend to hire Hugh Dauntsey to survey Hannah's goods and reckon their worth, pretending I simply want to be sure the crown is allotted its proper share. 'S blood, my lord, stop staring at me as if I've taken leave of my senses. You know if there is someone I do not trust, I oft bind him to me, to observe him all the better."

"According to Gresham," Cecil said, while everyone else hung on each word, "Dauntsey's always got one hand in the till—someone's till."

"If he crosses me, it will be a way to permanently rid myself of him, and perhaps Paulet, too. But I will use his reports to me as opportunities to discern if he could be more than what Dingen van der Passe called her money man—a mere accountant, who just happened to be watching me from the crowd when I came calling there. What if he was doing more to help the master starcher and her husband compete with poor Hannah than tend their books and teach them how to cheat at taxes? I just plain don't trust the man, though I am trying to overlook the fact that his appearance is so—unsettling."

"What if, you mean," Rosie said in a near whisper, "Dauntsey was also hired to rid the older starcher of her younger competition?"

Elizabeth nodded. "Besides, through Dauntsey, I'll be able to keep an eye on what Paulet and this chief constable and pushy parliamentarian Whitcomb are doing and perhaps thinking. Now, let's see—what else was I going to say?"

More than once at this meeting, her mind had wandered. Swimming in exhaustion, she intended to sleep well at least this night. She needed her strength to speak tomorrow with Dauntsey and Hosea Cantwell.

"Your Grace," Rosie said, "there is something I, too, forgot to tell you in the hubbub of all that happened at the van der Passes' starch shop. I—I regret I'm not much help on all this thinking and planning, but I just can't get the memory of that poor woman's starched corpse out of my mind."

"Nor I," Elizabeth said. "I warrant we are all on edge. Tell us, then."

"Meg said that some of her starch roots seem to be missing from Hannah's loft—at least one sack of them."

Meg nodded, wide-eyed. Elizabeth saw Ned lean protectively toward Meg while Jenks just frowned.

"You see," Rosie went on, "you told me to keep my mouth more or less shut but my eyes open at the van der Passes'.

Well, I saw a big bag of roots there like the ones scattered on the floor of Hannah's loft that I assume were Meg's cuckoo-pints. I noted that several had rolled under the worktable where we—we examined the body . . . Of course, I realize the van der Passes must use the same roots for that thick, gray starch paste of theirs, but what if those were Meg's roots, taken from Hannah the day she was killed?"

"There would be no way to prove they were mine," Meg put in.

"But Rosie is right. What if?" Elizabeth echoed, hitting a fist on the table. "Until the murderer gives himself—or herself—away, that must be our battle cry as we delve deeper and turn up more evidence.

"Jenks, you will go tomorrow morning and escort Ursala here so that she can assure us Marie Gresham is indeed the young woman she saw in the drying fields, staring up at Hannah's window. Then, if so, with Meg and her daughter Sally's help, I shall try to assist Marie to recall what she saw.

"Because," she said, standing to dismiss them, as they all rose hastily, scraping their chairs back, "the what-ifs become even more dangerous if the Gresham girl witnessed such horror."

More than once that night, Elizabeth wished that Rosie had not mentioned she couldn't get the memory of Hannah's starched corpse out of her mind. Though the queen was overtired, she slept fitfully, tossing about and slogging between nightmares that dragged her from agonizing over the present murder into the past.

The thought came to her clearly: Her father had murdered her mother as surely as if he had struck off her head himself.

Riding off to wed his new wife, he had not even thought to order a coffin for the woman who had once been his passion and who had borne him a red-haired daughter instead of the desired son.

So the executioners had hastily placed Queen Anne Boleyn's slender body in an empty arrow chest, her legs bent and her head by her feet. They had quickly interred her under the paving stones of St. Peter in Chains Church in the Tower, where she had been beheaded for unspeakable crimes of which she was surely innocent.

Now, even now, in the dead of night, Elizabeth entered the cold, gray, lofty place where her mother's corpse was laid out. But why had they put her body, wet with sticky, white blood, upon a shelf? Elizabeth looked around but found herself alone with the body. Was she a small child again, like the day she'd lost her mother, or was she now queen? Was she safe or still at great risk?

She screamed so loudly in the dim church that all the dead must hear her. "I am your anointed queen! Do not try to force me to wed and bed! Do not dare to murder me!"

Her voice stopped echoing, for the cold night air sucked the sounds out the window in the loft where her mother lay, not on a shelf now but in an open coffin filled with swirling mist. No arrows in it, only dense, drowning whiteness, thick as starch.

Elizabeth struggled to close the window, but it stayed open, with a stiff breeze blowing into her face. She leaned all her weight into it but kept slipping, slipping in the thick blood, then sliding backward into the black Thames, drowning with her father's hands about her throat . . .

Drenched with sweat, Elizabeth sat straight up in bed with the sheets wrapped around her. Stunned that her hands gripped her own throat, she thrust them in her lap and bent over, trying to seize control.

Slowly, the horror faded, but her mother had been too young to die, only thirty-four, almost exactly Elizabeth's age now, and . . . Hannah . . . even younger . . .

Sheltered in the curtains of the vast royal bed, the queen of England pressed her face into her hands and wept.

The Puritan cleric Hosea Cantwell surprised the queen yet again when he was escorted in by Clifford, who remained at the back of the anteroom. This time the man wore not the strict black and white he had argued for last time but a blue so dark it looked black, until the shaft of window light sliced across his body.

"Not practicing what you preach?" she challenged after proprieties had passed. "You seen quite the sport today, Mr. Cantwell, in that deep blue hue."

"I should have realized your hawk's eye would find me out, Your Majesty. 'Tis only that I do not pay richly for my garb, and the merchant must have sold me a shoddy doublet that would fade. Not yet, I assure you, have I gone to sporting, as you say, the frills and ruffles your followers call ruffs today."

"So you are not a follower of mine?"

"Of course, though not in fashions," he parried, "for you are the nation's monarch, to whom I owe a certain allegiance."

Damn this man of the cloth, supposedly a man of peace, she fumed. Why did she always feel she was dueling with him and he knew the thrusts and feints as well as she?

"Then, if you spend none of your hard-earned money from the church offerings on ruffs, Hosea Cantwell, why do

I have it on good authority that you have visited starch shops?"

For the first time, she felt she'd struck a hit. The slick-tongued man looked at a loss for words, though he quickly recovered.

"Surely you do not have me followed, Your Majesty. Or have your starchers tat-taled that I have urged them to mend and stiffen their ways instead of their flimsy fashions?"

"Then you admit you *have* been to see the van der Passes and Hannah von Hoven?"

"I owed it to the Maker of Mankind to challenge the makers of mere fripperies."

"Tell me your version of how each reacted to your intrusions."

Again, after the initial look of surprise flitted across the man's handsome face, he gave no other indication he had been caught at anything. Surely, if he'd known Hannah was dead, he would be more panicked now, though she had come to think of him as the chameleon cleric. Today, whether he wanted to admit it or not, he had even changed his colors.

"I saw the young von Hoven woman only once," he explained, "but returned to the master starcher's twice. The first time I visited the van der Passes, that big husband of hers declared he was still a Flemish knight and threatened me with bodily harm," he added with a dismissive sniff and a tug at his cuffless sleeves.

"Did he lay hands on you?"

"He did, and as good as threw me out."

So, she thought, Hosea Cantwell was physically courageous, for he went back a second time. She was anxious to know how he would describe his encounter with Hannah, who had no such watchdog to ward him off.

"And my other starcher, Hannah von Hoven?" she asked, trying to rein in her impatience.

"She did not throw me out but threw starch on the front of my breeches," he admitted with a little shrug. "Imagine, Your Majesty, she claimed I was too rigid, and then threw starch on me to make me more so."

She stared at him. Surely this man was not making a bawdy joke as well as a pun. He must have naught to do with Hannah's demise or he would not be so flippant.

"When did you visit her starch house?" she asked. "And did her ladies see you there?"

"Your Majesty," he said, drawing himself up to his full height, though he stood below her level and had to look up to where she sat upon a dais, "does this interrogation have aught to do with the poor girl's dreadful death? Word is that she fell in her starch vat, hit her crown, and drowned, so I've said more than one prayer that she *did* regret her craft but *did not* decide to take her own life."

"I—" Elizabeth got out, then shut her mouth. This man knew all along that Hannah was dead and had not let on. Still, he was only answering her questions. But she noted well he used the old word for head, "crown." Another pun on who he'd really like to see fall and drown—the one who wears the crown?

"From whom did you hear of her death?" she demanded.

"From one of my parishioners. Word of the tragedy is probably all over London by now, an especially tasty bit of gossip, I don't doubt, because she was a royal starcher as well as a common one."

"Your view of the world is quite jaded," she accused.

"Perhaps that is only because I see the world through ancient eyes," he countered, "the eyes of the Almighty. As to your query: Did her ladies see me there?" he said, adroitly picking up on a question she'd forgotten she'd asked him. "Of course, for I went in full daylight to visit such a place."

Such a place, the queen thought, feeling more distraught. As if poor Hannah had been running a house with strumpets instead of starchers. Furious at herself for mishandling this interview as well as at him for his presumptions, she added, "Then I shall discover from her women when you were there and what passed between you."

"Passed between us? My words of counsel, which ruffled her composure, and her words of petulance and willfulness, Your Majesty."

"Which then ruffled your composure?" she challenged.

"Not at all. I offered to pray for her, and she threw starch at me from that big vat of it that I told her was a bath for the devil's liquor. I'll not lie about that or aught else, so you have but to ask in what must be your own investigation of this sad event. I shall pray for your success in the endeavor," he added with a nod and a sigh, "for now, alas, I shall not be able to pray for Hannah's changed ways, but only for her immortal soul."

Elizabeth silently scolded herself for letting this man irk her so. She'd let slip that she was interested in solving the puzzle of Hannah's death. Was he merely the pompous if witty prig he seemed, or would he stoop to harm Hannah? Surely she would never have sent her women away so that she could speak with this man, however handsome and glib.

This surprising interview had convinced the queen of one thing. She was going to tell Cecil to keep Cantwell's name on his chart of possible murderers.

Thomas Gresham was feeling a bit better today about Marie's state of mind, though she was yet not responding to questions or suggestions. At least she was not hysterical or contentious, as she had been yesterday. As long as she had Sally in sight, she was not insisting she hold to her, either. Marie lay in bed, awake but restful.

He and Anne, as well as Sally, stood when the queen entered the bedchamber at midmorning. As the door had opened, he'd glimpsed Nash Badger still in the next room, keeping guard, and again vowed to richly reward the man.

They had not seen the queen since last evening, though one of her ladies-in-waiting had visited to assure Her Majesty that Marie was resting well.

"Has Dr. Forrest returned?" the queen asked as they rose from their bow and curtseys.

"Yes, with more soothing tonic, which, as you can see, may be helping," Thomas told her, gesturing toward the bed. He was deeply moved and honored by her concern.

"She's told you nothing of why she left your home or where she went?" the queen pursued, keeping her voice low.

"Nothing, Your Majesty," Anne answered. "We are grateful for your hospitality here, but feel we should take her home. And we are wondering," she said, speaking even more quietly now, "if we could hire the girl Sally to go with us as a lady's maid for Marie-Anne. We'd pay her well, and, of course, her mother could visit her whenever—"

"I think it best you not move her yet and keep her near Dr. Forrest," the queen said. "But first, I have someone who can perhaps help us discover where Marie was before she was found dazed outside the palace. If you will allow me to bring someone in—"

"Who is it?" Thomas asked. He realized Anne had

spoken those very words in unison with him. His heart started to pound. What if his worst fears were realized and Marie had discovered who had come to town? And had gone there to learn all he had tried so hard to hide? Anne looked totally distraught, too, though she'd said earlier she wanted to learn where Marie had gone when she was missing.

"It is just a woman I know," Elizabeth explained, "who lives not far from the palace, near the royal mews. Ursala!"

At first he saw only Sally's mother, the queen's strewing woman, in the doorway, but then another, a comely but unkempt young woman behind her. The queen motioned again, and the stranger came into the room, to the foot of Marie's bed, and stared a silent moment at her.

"That's the one for sure," she whispered before the queen's strewing woman whisked her out as fast as she had come. Sally ran after her mother, and Marie started to stir and fuss again.

"Who was that?" Thomas asked the queen. "And where was Marie seen? Anne, won't you go and fetch Sally back?" he added, turning toward his wife. "We can't have Marie distressed again."

"In a minute," Anne said, standing her ground. It was no surprise that his wife gainsayed him, but that she did it before the queen astonished him.

"I don't understand the how or why yet," the queen told them, "but that woman observed your daughter standing in St. Martin's fields, staring up at a window of a loft near the royal mews."

"She's been asking for a horse of her own," Anne said, sounding entirely rattled. "Perhaps she simply wandered to the royal mews—to look at the horses."

"She told me nothing of wanting a horse, and she knows

she can ask me for things," Thomas blurted. He realized he should just listen, but he was so fearful of what he might hear.

"She appeared," the queen went on, "to be looking up at the window of the starch house of a woman who worked for me, a Hannah von Hoven."

Thomas fought to keep from falling to his knees. He felt as if he'd been poleaxed. To his amazement, Anne leaned against the high bed, holding the carved post as if the name meant something to her, too. How had it come to this?

"And I regret to inform you," the queen said, "that was the very day Hannah was found dead, evidently murdered."

"B-but," Anne stammered, "mere happen—happenstance. That woman is mistaken at what Marie-Anne was staring at, especially in her state of m-mind. We don't know either that woman you say saw our daughter or that Hannah von something-or-other who died. This misidentification must be straightened out. Thomas," she demanded, and tapped his shoulder, "do or say something."

"I assure you," the queen went on, "it all will be straightened out as soon as possible, so do not fear for your daughter's involvement or safety. But what if she happened to see through that window the one who harmed Hannah? I know it is a wild possibility, but we must protect her so that we can discover . . ."

Discover . . . discover. I might be discovered, Thomas thought. The queen went on speaking. Anne was insisting they take Marie home, for she would also be well protected there. Thomas was sure that he had said something, too, but he was sick to death that what he had done would be discovered.

Chapter the Seventh

AS THE QUEEN FACED HUGH DAUNTSEY IN THE SAME chamber in which she'd interrogated Cantwell that morning, she prayed this encounter would go better. She was still distressed by how shaken the Greshams had been that their child had been in the vicinity of a murder. They had insisted on taking her home. The queen had acquiesced but told them she would call on them at Gresham House on the morrow to see how Marie was doing. And, for now, Meg had agreed Sally could go with them; the child was pleased she could earn some wages. That Sally was safe and chose to stay a while in London had been conveyed to her adoptive parents by royal courier.

The queen tried to buck herself up as Dauntsey rose from a smooth, deep bow. *A daunting task*, she thought, and almost giggled at her pun. 'S blood, she was exhausted—and at midmorn, she scolded herself—if she found amusement in any of this mess. Had she caught this dreadful punning malady from Hosea Cantwell?

"I have had good report of your skills from Lord Paulet," she told Dauntsey. "Whatever has passed between you and my royal family in the past, I have need of your service now."

His face lit so it nearly reflected the rosy silk of his slashed and jeweled doublet. The man always overdressed for someone of his rank; he could nearly challenge her favorite court peacock, her dear Robin Dudley.

"I would be utterly honored, Your Gracious Majesty, whatever the task."

Looking directly into Dauntsey's eyes immediately cured her exhaustion. The hair on the nape of her neck rose, and her pulse pounded. His gaze was unnerving with those pale, rimless eyes, as if he had no irises, but rather vacant eyeballs, at least from this distance and in this light. With his pale skin, blond hair, and close-cropped beard, the man looked as if he had a tight white sheet wrapped about his head—as if he were some sort of specter. No wonder Dauntsey had failed not only at finance but at earning the trust of foreign moneylenders, for merely looking at him set her teeth on edge.

"As I have cut my number of bookkeepers to the bone," she told him, "I shall hire you to oversee a brief project, which, of course, could lead to other things."

"I am all ears, Your Majesty, though I do advise Lord Paulet on personal finances and have my investments in the stock market—"

"The what? I know all the major markets in my capital city, but the *stock* market?"

"The new name for meat on the hoof at Smithfield Market, Your Majesty. Investments are booming there. It's not horses sold on that spot anymore, but mostly cattle—a bull market, as we say. I keep a place of business at Smithfield and bid and sell on stock, sheep, too, that are driven from the countryside into Smithfield. A few of us are doing quite well, running our own stock exchange."

Her ignorance on the matter annoyed the queen, and

she hated so much as the mention of Smithfield, where she hadn't set foot once during her reign. Years ago knights had jousted there, horses were kept and traded, even duels of honor fought. Then her Catholic sister, Queen Mary Tudor, whom Dauntsey once served, had ordered Protestants, many of them hardworking Londoners who would not renounce their faith, burned to death at Smithfield. It had sickened the nation and turned thousands against her cause. As an ardent Catholic himself, perhaps Dauntsey valued the site as much as Elizabeth detested it.

"I was about to say," she went on, fighting to keep her voice under control, "that I need a man with financial experience to account for a deceased person's goods, then to see that the allotments of such property are correctly dispersed."

"I would be honored," he said, sweeping both arms gracefully to his sides. "May I inquire what courtier or ward has died?"

"Have you heard of the death of my starcher, Hannah von Hoven?"

"Your starcher? Yes, but I thought a person of some import—"

"She was of import to me. She leaves no heirs, for I have just learned from a friend of hers that her twin sister died in childbirth in Antwerp years ago, and evidently there was no one else. At any rate, I need a man I can trust to oversee this task, especially since Chief Constable Nigel Whitcomb has declared the crown shall have a share—twenty percent. The rest will go to initial investors and, of course, to her clients who had already paid her for work not completed. In short, it will take more than simply looking over her books."

"Then Master Whitcomb will oversee this dreadful death inquiry, but you need a financial representative you can trust—and, of course, Thomas Gresham is busy with his building project and other, grander investments."

"Yes. You will work with Whitcomb on this, reporting to him as well as to me."

"I understand, Your Majesty."

"I take it Lord Paulet—and the van der Passes—can spare you?"

He looked taken aback. "Lord Paulet will be honored to do so. As for my other clients, how appropriate you have chosen me, for I am honored to keep your other starcher's accountings."

That was, she thought a few too many "honoreds," but at least she had this man right where she wanted him for now. Too, she had well noted one fascinating fact. From excitement, or some other emotion she could not name, Hugh Dauntsey had begun to sweat profusely through his fine attire.

The next morning the queen called for her coach to visit Gresham House. At the last minute, she told Boonen to drive her past Smithfield first. Both Rosie and Meg, who were with her in the coach, looked as surprised as Boonen sounded.

"Smithfield Market, Your Majesty?" he asked, speaking through the open window before he mounted his perch. "Where all the animals are driven in and then taken off to butcher shops?"

"The same, Boonen," she replied, holding up the leather flap.

"But it's noisy and smelly there—could be dangerous, too, as the drivers of the herds can't keep them all in check."

"Then go as near as you can, my man, without getting us in some sort of wild melee of hoofs and horns. This," Elizabeth said to Rosie and Meg as she settled back in her seat, "will give Jenks and Clifford some new scenery atop this rocky ride."

"Why Smithfield, Your Grace?" Rosie inquired.

"Because I was annoyed to discover yesterday that some of my subjects have places of business there to wager and bid on what they call stocks, and I need to see the place myself. Which reminds me—Boonen!" she cried, and rapped her knuckles on the ceiling. "After Smithfield, take us round to see the progress that Gresham's new merchant exchange is making. And watch out for those holes in the street so big we may fall through to Muscovy or China!"

Rosie thought that quite amusing, but Meg looked only nervous. No doubt, she was ruffled about seeing how Sally was doing in her new position as Marie Gresham's maid. Or perhaps it was that lovers' triangle with Jenks and Ned again. Meg had nearly wed Jenks two years ago but had always been more taken with Ned—any lunatic could see that. Now Ursala Hemmings had been added as new thickening in the stew, but it was Meg who seemed to be nearly ready to boil over.

With four riders before and four following, the coach clattered out of the cobbled courtyard. The queen recalled that when this grand conveyance was new, people had run from it and children had screamed as if it were a monster from the gates of fiery hell instead of Whitehall. Now, a moving attraction of high style, it made its way along the busy strand to Ludgate Hill and then turned north with the three women looking out from beneath the partly covered windows.

They smelled Smithfield before they saw it—and heard it, too.

"See if you can find a place to stop with a view of the meadows!" Elizabeth shouted out the window at Boonen.

"No meadows anymore, Your Majesty," Jenks cried, leaning

down to call in at her from his place as footman at the rear of the coach. "Just dirt pounded flat by bellowing beasts."

Holding a handkerchief over her nose to stem the stench and dust, Elizabeth gazed out over the pentagonal expanse of Smithfield. No longer the tilting field full of knights, tents, and gay banners she recalled, the place was indeed packed with beasts of both the animal and human kinds. Long, deep wooden drinking troughs radiated from the center, not only watering the stock but keeping them penned into pie-shaped areas.

In the very center of the expanse, she could see the rough wooden monument erected to the martyrs who had died here during her sister's rampage to return England to the Popish religion. As many of those arrested were local commoners, the trinkets of their trades, everything from kettles to horseshoes, were nailed to a huge tree trunk, meant to resemble the stakes at which they had died. Rust from the items had wept down the tree, like brown bloodstains.

A wave of nausea swept Elizabeth, but she fought it back, trying to concentrate only on the animals. Cattle still streaming in from the countryside—beef on the hoof—shoved together those already herded at the stock market. She saw sheep for mutton, even pigs. Dogs yipping at the heels of the animals helped their drovers cut some out for purchase. Those were driven down different lanes, no doubt headed to butcher shops or to the large slaughterhouses near Eastcheap. Protesting sheep flowed past the coach, with their new owners shouting at them, trying so hard to keep the flock together that they barely gave the big coach a second glance.

Despite the past horrors and current reeking ruckus, the queen thought, it was all somehow new and vital. She could see how men could make a fortune off this living lake of beasts and the rivers of flesh that flowed away from it to various parts of the town, including, no doubt, her own palace. She'd try to speak more about this stock exchange later with Hugh Dauntsey.

As the coach rolled away and passed the site of Gresham's expanding mercantile exchange, she noted well how it had changed in the four days since she had first seen it. A skeleton of wooden scaffolding clasped the lower building blocks; masons stood on it to help hoist the stones in place as they were winched upward. This time, neither Gresham nor his man Nash Badger was in sight, though the place crawled with workmen and builders. She saw four men, perhaps Gresham's masterminds, glancing at their papers and pointing here and there.

"On to Gresham House," Elizabeth called to Boonen, and the coach jerked away again.

Marie woke to find the thin red-haired woman speaking with her parents again. They were in the bedchamber they had said was hers. Yes, she remembered it now. She was grateful to be hidden away here with her other self, for Sally was nearby and had slept on a trundle bed last night. Sally no longer wore her hood to hide her face, and Marie knew it was now just herself who was hiding something. Or was she hiding *from* something—or someone?

She remembered then that this woman who asked all the questions was the queen.

"Marie, how are you feeling today, now that you are resting at home?" the queen asked, leaning over the bed to take her hand.

"Better, I thank you."

"And speaking so much more. Are you remembering better, too?"

Marie darted a glance at Sally, who smiled. "I don't know what I'm to remember," she whispered. "They—Mother and Father—have asked me, too, but I don't know what I'm to recall."

"Then do not disturb yourself. I am going to speak with your parents in another room and then come back to see you again, so I will leave you here with Sally. Is that all right?"

Marie nodded. She wished she could shake things up inside her head, so she could recall enough to make them all leave her alone. Why couldn't she just go on from here? Why did she have to recall things she didn't want to?

When the queen went out with her parents, Sally brought a basin of water over to the bed. "How 'bout let me wash your face," she said. "You got all that sleepy stuff round your eyes, thick white stuff I'll just get rid of."

Marie wasn't sure why she did it, but she knocked the bowl from Sally's hands, splashing water on the bed and both of them. She gasped as a picture came back to her of someone's face and head going under, under the water with white stuff in it...

Sally looked shocked, but when she saw the look on Marie's face, she held her hard.

"What is it?" Sally cried. "Did you 'member something?"

Marie nodded wildly, her forehead against Sally's shoulder. But the picture in her mind faded again, into half light, half dark, like a painted picture she remembered from her father's privy chamber. Yes, she was remembering that, so was she better now? A portrait of two girls, like her and Sally, one in light and one in darkness, like some woman who had been in the light and then been plunged into death.

Marie began to gasp and heave huge sobs.

"I'll fetch your parents or the queen," Sally cried, and tried to pull away.

"No, don't leave me! I have to tell you about the painting—of two girls like us. It all means something I can't recall, but I saw it."

"Saw what painting? Where is it, then?"

"I'll tell you," Marie said, still holding tight. "And then you can tell them so everyone will leave me alone, because I can't—just can't—remember more."

It seemed to the queen as she conversed with Thomas and Anne Gresham that, though they might be falling all over themselves with hospitality to her, they were hardly speaking to each other. Thomas held his walking stick under his arm and kept twisting his grasshopper signet ring as if he could unscrew his finger itself. Anne seemed ill at ease in this room, which was obviously Thomas's inner sanctum, filled with unique items he was most eager to explain, though it irked Elizabeth that his tour of the chamber kept them from the topic of his own daughter.

A knock on the door startled them, and Anne darted away to answer it. Nash Badger stood there, holding a tray with three small bowls and an engraved silver pot as if he were now a server instead of a bodyguard. Another man, a fat, nervous-looking one, stood behind him.

"You found some?" Thomas called to Badger, who, rather begrudgingly, Elizabeth thought, let Anne take the tray from him. Perhaps, she thought, he had wanted to bring it in himself. Recalling all he had done to help find Marie, she went to the door herself. Thomas followed, his walking stick tapping on the floor. Anne, holding the tray, looked as if she were caught at something.

"I believe much thanks is owed you, Master Badger," Elizabeth told him, "for your help to this family, and so, indirectly, to me."

He bowed, as did the man behind him, one garbed like a cook fresh out of the kitchens. As Badger stood straight again, an acrid aroma floated to her nostrils; she sneezed and stepped away.

"Anything I can ever do to help—" Badger was saying as Anne closed the door with her foot.

"He was letting in a draft," she said as she carried the tray to the table before the hearth. "Or it was that dreadful smell from his drinking tobacco that made you sneeze so, Your Majesty? If he hadn't found Marie, he'd be back just guarding the building site, if I had my way."

"He is useful to me," Thomas said only, gesturing that Elizabeth should come sit on the largest chair of the three grouped around the hearth. "The tobacco drinking is an annoyance, though."

"I have heard of this new practice, especially that sailors inhale fumes of the burned stuff," the queen said. "Since it reeks so, what is the good of it?"

"It evidently tempers one's moods, Your Majesty," Thomas explained, "so perhaps we could all use a whiff of it. The user inhales it into the mouth and throat and blows out smoke, as if a smoldering fire burned within the belly or brain. But I have here a new drink that will please you mightily and smells and tastes delicious—"

"I can't recommend it, as I haven't had it yet," Anne put in.

"—because it is laced with sugar to balance the flavor perfectly." Thomas finished his thought while ignoring his wife. Again, the queen felt her hosts were at great odds and wondered why. Had they argued over whether to bring Marie home or not? She had thought they agreed on that.

"Where did you obtain this new drink?" Elizabeth asked Thomas.

"I am hesitant to tell you, because of certain inimical international relations, Your Grace." He smiled as if he had made a jest, but twisted his signet ring again. "Actually, it's from Spain, though it has been imported from the New World, where it was the drink of royalty."

"The rulers of the indigenous folk there, the ones with all the gold their explorers have found?"

"I warrant that is so, and some say this liquid is as dear as their gold to them. It's a sacred and magical drink to those New World natives, and King Philip and the Catholic Spanish are guarding it practically on pain of death."

"Then if it is a Spanish secret, I shall try it."

"It's called," Anne put in as she poured three bowls of it, "*chocolata* and comes in little cakes, round, brown ones, dry as dust and likely to break into dust, too, and bitter as can be without sugar. We had such a cake of it lost but found a way to get another one."

"Badger did," Thomas muttered, leaning forward to watch his wife pour the precious stuff as if he thought she'd spill it.

Elizabeth sipped the dark drink. Both tart and sweet. Rich. It was as if merely tasting it could convey the exotic nature of the place from which it had come. If starch was, as Hosea Cantwell had said, the devil's liquor, this was surely the drink of angels.

"*Chocolata,*" the queen said, "is quite lovely and soothing, though I don't suppose it will catch on with the common people. Sugar alone is expensive, and to import the *chocolata* in little cakes from the New World will drive the price up even more. But now we must talk about how we can best help your Marie to remem—"

The three of them turned toward the door as it creaked open without a knock, swung inward, and banged into the wall. With Sally just behind, Marie herself stood there. As if she were sleepwalking, she looked at none of them but headed straight for the corner of the room.

"I remembered something," she said, quite clearly, though she still did not look their way. Anne put her drink down and stared as if she'd seen a ghost. Thomas rose to go to Marie, but Elizabeth seized his arm to stay him. Sally trailed behind Marie, bobbing a curtsy at the queen as she passed.

Marie approached a large coffer, made from a hollowed tree trunk, and opened it. She bent over it, then knelt, digging down under papers and who knows what else like a dog after a bone. Elizabeth stood to see better. From the dark depths of the big hump-backed trunk she pulled a small framed painting, two hands wide and slightly narrower in height, though a painting of what, the queen could not tell at that distance.

Holding up her other hand to stop the Greshams' rush toward their child, Elizabeth asked softly, "What is it you recall, Marie?"

The girl cradled the front of the picture to her, then turned it around so Sally could see. Elizabeth rose and walked slowly forward to look at it, too.

The portrait was of two young girls, no doubt sisters, perhaps even twins. They looked to be near ten years old. One was in light, the other more in shade. Except for the open window with blue sky behind them, the painting had no background.

"It reminds me of us," Marie told Sally. "Or, if I am not

this girl," she said, pointing to the one in the light, "I am part of her."

Anne gasped, and Thomas cut in, "Marie, you must return to bed. You are not yet well, sweetling." Elizabeth thought he would pick his daughter up as he had the day she was found. To her surprise, it was Anne who lifted her, as easily as if she were still small. Marie still cradled the painting until Thomas took it from her.

"I pray you will forgive us for one moment, Your Majesty," he said and, leaning heavily on his walking stick, hurried from the room after them.

"Sally!" the queen called as she, too, started out. "Your mother is waiting to speak with you downstairs with Lady Rosie. But I need to talk to you first."

The girl came back and curtsied yet again.

"What else did Marie say about that painting? What else has she recalled?"

"She doesn't want to 'member more, Your Majesty, that's what I think. She saw something terrible that's unhinged her. Sometimes she thinks I'm part of her—or her twin sister, like in that picture."

Hannah was a twin, the queen thought. And Ursala Hemmings, too, but what did that all add up to? Thomas Gresham had some questioning coming, and not with his angry wife hanging on.

"Go down to see your mother," the queen told the girl. "The Greshams will tend to Marie until you return. And, Sally, I am absolutely relying on you to tell your mother Meg or me immediately if Marie says anything else about what she saw that could have rattled her so. Promise?"

"Oh, 'course. Should I send Badger with the news then, like Marie done?"

"Marie sent Badger to someone? To whom and about what?"

"Don't know. She just said he took privy messages for her."

"Thank you, Sally. No, do not use Badger, for I will send a man named Ned from the palace every day to ask you personally how you are doing, as well as Marie. If you need to send a message to me or your mother—especially about anything Marie recalls—you tell Ned. He has curly hair and green eyes, and you will like him immensely. Off with you now."

'S blood, Elizabeth thought, starting to pace in Gresham's sollar, she'd told Cecil if they just stirred the starch long enough something else would float to the top. Now she not only had to corner Thomas alone but also had to discover from the smoke drinker Nash Badger what privy messages he'd carried for the coddled and sheltered Marie Gresham.

Chapter the Eighth

AS THE QUEEN PEERED OUT INTO THE LONG SECOND-floor corridor of Gresham House, she saw Nash Badger standing by a distant door, through which she assumed the Greshams had gone. She stepped out and motioned him to her. Though he seemed reluctant to leave his post, he obeyed.

"I would ask you a question or two, Master Badger," she called to him as he came closer. He bowed, then kept his gaze cast down as if he were pondering the hems of her gown. Again, the acrid scent of tobacco floated to her like an invisible mist around the man.

"Anything I can do, Your Majesty."

"I have observed that is your service to Sir Thomas—anything you can do."

"I admit that I have hitched my future to his rising star. He is a man much to be admired."

"And protected from his enemies, evidently. You are primarily his bodyguard?"

"I do whatever needs to be done."

"That includes acting as courier for Marie Gresham's secret messages to . . ." She left the question hanging. He looked up at last—wide-eyed, before he narrowed his gaze.

"Mistress Marie told you, then, or her new companion did?" he asked.

"Do you deny you have done such for Marie?"

"I promised her I would tell no one."

"Not even your lord Thomas? And your queen, who is asking you directly and for good purpose?"

He opened his mouth to speak, closed it, then said, "I'd rue the day I caused the child trouble, Your Majesty. With her parents, I mean. Harmless fun, I thought, her sending letters to a friend, though doing it round Robin's barn. 'Fore she found little Sally she was too often alone, I wager. She was ofttimes with her mother and servants, that is, but no friends."

"I believe you have an avid eye and kind heart, Badger, but back to the question at hand. If the child has had no opportunity to make friends, to whom would she send these epistles? I, too, am trying to help Marie. Tell me quickly all you know about your errands of kindness."

"Four times, Your Majesty. The letters were sealed, and I didn't look within, God's truth, I didn't, so I can't tell you more."

"You delivered them to . . ."

"A glover's shop on Eastcheap just at the edge of the shambles—you know, the butchers' district."

Elizabeth shuddered at the memory of Smithfield's livestock milling about, soon to be executed, like the many martyrs who had died there. "Yes. Say on."

"That's it," he said with a shrug. "As a favor to the girl, I took the notes to the glover's hard by Abchurch Lane. Left them with a young woman named Celia who perfumes gloves, rough-looking though she is. Doubt if that's Marie's friend, but didn't ask. This Celia's little corner in that shop was 'bout the only sweet-smelling place with the shambles nearby, if you get my drift."

"So you took no notes back to Marie in turn?"

"If she had a return from her friend, it was by someone else's hand."

"You know nothing else about this friend?"

He shook his head. "I just dropped the letters off in a roundabout way, heading for my duties on the site of the exchange."

"Then who was guarding Sir Thomas during those times?"

"He hadn't left this house yet."

"But you then went ahead to the exchange, so he was unprotected during his short journey there?"

A flash of frustration swept his face before he could control it again. "He has other men with him."

"I believe," she went on, "he never rides anywhere alone since that strange accident that nearly took his life six years ago. Were you with him then?"

"No, Your Majesty. He took me on shortly after."

"What were you doing before that?"

She noted well Badger had begun to shift his weight from one foot to the other and flex his fists at his side. "The same, but for lesser men," he said. "Anything that needs to be done."

Though she meant to question him more, the queen saw Anne Gresham rush out the door down the hall. Without a glance their way, she hurried downstairs as Thomas, again leaning heavily on his walking stick, came toward them.

"Your Majesty, forgive us for rushing off like that," he said, sounding out of breath. Badger bowed and stepped out of their way. Each time he moved, the tobacco smell emanated from his person.

"I completely understand, Thomas. Is she resting, then?"

"Better than we could have hoped, though the nonsense about the painting shows she is not yet back in her right mind."

"I must be going, but I will bid her farewell first," the queen declared. She walked quickly toward the girl's room, with Thomas thumping along behind and Badger trailing them.

"So kind of you, Your Majesty," Thomas cried, "but perhaps another day when she is more herself."

"Sir Thomas Gresham," she said, stopping before Marie's door so fast her skirts swayed, "you know I lost my dear companion Kat Ashley not long ago. In her last years she was quite delusional and yet in such spells always revealed aspects of her deepest self. I will bid a swift farewell to Marie, alone," she added pointedly, went in, and closed the door in his face.

She rushed across the outer room, for she knew that Anne would be back soon, probably with Sally or a servant in tow. She found Marie in her bedchamber, though not in bed as she'd expected. The girl was sitting in a deep window seat, propped against pillows with a coverlet over her legs. The room was warm and stuffy with the sun pouring in and no windows open.

"Your Majesty!" she said, looking surprised. She started to scoot to the edge of the seat, but the queen raised her hand and sat down facing her. The view was of the sheltered central courtyard and gardens gone to riot with leggy autumn blooms.

"Marie, since that double portrait of the sisters is not really of you and Sally, who do you think it is?"

Her composure crumbled. Her eyes filled with tears; her

chin and lower lip trembled. "I don't know," she whispered, "but I'm sure it's important. My parents just say it's no one I know. Yet if it isn't me in that painting, it's something about me."

"How long have you known it was there?"

"I found it several months ago—I recall that. But then I—I just thought it was pretty, but now—there is something else about it now."

"All right. Who did you send the four secret letters to, the ones Badger delivered for you to the glover's shop on Abchurch Lane in Eastcheap?"

She blinked. Tears matted her lashes and trickled from her eyes. "I remember writing them, but not why or to whom," she said, swiping at her cheeks. She propped her elbows on her knees, bent over, and covered her eyes with both hands. "But I—I think I have a copy of one of them, an epistle I started but put away . . ."

She got up and went to a corner of the room to a drop-leaf table and opened its single small drawer. Elizabeth heard Anne in the hall, talking to Thomas in urgent tones. This time the queen felt they might be hostile not only to each other but to her. Though she had not meant to unhinge Marie more, she, too, rose and went closer to the desk and peered in the drawer.

The girl was scrabbling through pieces of parchment. "Here," she said as the queen heard the door to the outer room open, "it might be this."

Elizabeth took the note from the girl, folded it once, and thrust it in the folds of her skirt. "Let me worry about it. Don't even fret your parents over this," she urged, and shoved the drawer closed with her knee as Anne, pulling Sally, burst into the bedchamber with Thomas behind. Elizabeth watched as Anne gazed first at the window seat and was startled to see it empty. She looked even more distressed when she saw them standing by the table together.

"Your Majesty, we are so grateful for your care and support in all this," Anne cried, rushing to them, "and we will surely send you news of Marie's continued recovery, but we believe she needs her rest now."

"I do indeed expect to be kept informed," she told both Greshams as Thomas entered the bedchamber. They looked, she thought, distraught yet defiant. "Sally," Elizabeth said, turning to the girl, "your mother Meg will visit from time to time as well, but my man Ned Topside will see you each day, should you wish to send your mother news of your stay here. Marie," she said, turning to take the girl's hand, "do not worry yourself, and perhaps what we need to know of your difficulties will solve themselves some other way.

"Thomas," she said. He stood leaning against the door now, as if he had need to prop himself up. "Attend me at Whitehall tomorrow afternoon. It may be the Lord's Day, but your queen needs some advice."

"About the mercantile exchange, Your Majesty?" he asked, looking as if he were about to be put on the rack.

Still clutching the draft of Marie's letter, the queen realized the girl must surely have traded it with someone forbidden to her. "Yes," she said, "about the exchange."

"Boonen," Elizabeth said as she climbed into her coach and looked back out at him, "to Eastcheap. To be exact, the edge of the shambles hard by Abchurch Lane, to a glover's shop."

After their detour to Smithfield, evidently nothing surprised the man, for he merely nodded and closed the door.

Elizabeth kept the rolled window flap halfway up, not for air or a view but to read Marie's letter in decent daylight.

"What is that, Your Grace?" Rosie asked.

"Maybe nothing, maybe everything," Elizabeth told her, and bent over the small, ornate script.

Dearest Friend,

I pray you let me visit, for I can manage it without their knowing, I vow I can. Please, for I would know so much more of her, more than just seeing her in your lovely face. Or could you not come here again and I will slip out where we spoke before? I hope you will wear these sweet gloves, my gift to you, in exchange for any sweet memories you can give, and if you still need money to

Here the last words about the money were crossed out, and below was scribbled in: *and if you would accept from me money as you asked others for earlier*

That, too, was crossed out, even more heavily with big *X*'s. What appeared to be teardrops blurred some of the words. Elizabeth gazed out the window without speaking.

"Did Sir Thomas or Lady Anne recommend a good glover, Your Grace?" Meg asked, breaking the silence.

"No, but Marie did."

Thomas didn't even try to comfort Anne as she lay facedown across their bed, sobbing. "What if she never gets her memory back?" she wailed. Finally she sat up to blow her nose into her handkerchief. "But I'm more fearful she will. Something dreadful happened to her that day."

"Anne, for all we know, she might have just felt too cooped up here and dared to go out for a walk. I'll talk to her about that, explain about rogues who would prey on young women from wealthy families. Perhaps she simply darted in front of a horse and was temporarily knocked witless. Her gazing up at that window could be pure happenstance, as you said before."

"Yes, yes, I know," she said, dabbing under her eyes. "Of course, that's it, but it's so . . . tawdry, that she could have seen something of a starcher's murder—and that the queen obviously suspects that or more."

"The dead woman was not just any starcher but a royal starcher."

"I don't care what she was. It's Marie-Anne's reputation we must safeguard. Good young women from important families in service to the queen do not simply go about the streets by themselves! But then, neither do good husbands keep portraits of their mistress and her twin sister! They are the ones in the portrait—I know it!"

"It was just a charming painting to me, that's all," he said, but he felt like the low liar he was.

"And that's why you never showed it to me? Why you display it only in your privy chest in your privy chamber? You lied to me years ago when you said you were oft away on business, but you were meeting—to put it prettily—with her!" she shrieked, her face contorting into an angry mask. "And if the great and mighty Sir Thomas Gresham can lie with impunity to his wife, is he not lying to others, even his queen?"

He cracked his walking stick so hard on the carved bedpost that his signet ring bit into his flesh and the stick splintered. At the sudden explosion of violence, she rolled off the other side of the wide bed. God help him, he felt the reins of his control slipping again.

"You got Marie in the bargain," he shouted, "so you'd best take better care of her—and my reputation, too!" He pulled the Gresham grasshopper ring off his bruised finger and threw it at her. It missed and rolled off the bed onto the floor. "And I don't mean keeping her a virtual prisoner here as you do, so she has to flee to find friends of her own!"

"That's not fair! And you'd best calm yourself before that leech Badger overhears you," she hissed at him as she edged toward the door. "You may have sent him down to the kitchen, but I wouldn't put it past him to be hovering just outside even this door, at your behest and with your blessing! I can't abide his foul smell, I tell you, nor the way his hands are all stained—dirty hands from drinking tobacco."

He felt so pent up he was ready to explode again. "I'll not have you judging my staff when it's Marie who is your concern. At least she is making progress daily," he said softly, slowly, hoping she would accept his quieter voice and calmer temper as a peace offering. The last thing in the world he needed was his wife openly hostile to him.

But, he thought, Anne was right. What if Marie's progress led her to recall what he most feared? That she'd seen a murderer. If she wanted to face and accuse him, that could put her—put them all—in grave danger.

He swore under his breath as Anne fled the room, slamming the door behind her. He limped over to a chair and slumped in it, flexing his painful ring finger. It might hurt, but his bad leg—like his conscience—was killing him.

At least, Elizabeth thought, the stench in the long, broad street called Eastcheap was not as potent as that of Smithfield Market. Unlike many of her subjects, she had a very sharp sense of smell. She always insisted the court change palaces more than the other Tudors had, for she smelled the too-full jakes before anyone else. Without a personal strewing herb woman to scent her clothing and linens daily and to fill the pomanders she always carried with sweet herbs, she would have nearly died of the scents of her own city. Unlike others, too, she both washed and bathed often—so often that, more than once, Robin had called her "his mermaid."

The sounds here jolted her, too, as the coach jerked to a stop. Shoppers shouted, hawkers cried out their wares, and the undercurrent bellows of beef and the shriller sheep awaiting their fates nearby thrummed beneath all that.

"Eastcheap at Abchurch, Your Majesty," Boonen announced from outside the coach.

Holding her pomander to her nose, Elizabeth peered out under the leather window flap. "Do you see a glover's shop nearby?" she asked.

"One on this very corner, other side of the coach," Boonen said, pointing as both Jenks and Clifford joined him beneath her window. Elizabeth slid over on her seat, opened the opposite flap, and squinted out into the afternoon sun. Yes, a large wooden glove painted bright yellow hung above a narrow shop entrance to identify the goods within.

"Meg, you go in so as not to startle the girl who perfumes gloves there. Her name is Celia. Give her a groat from the pouch of coins I gave you and ask her to come out to the coach to speak with the queen, as I would like to order some gloves. Boonen, you and Clifford remain here, and Jenks, go with Meg but wait for her outside. If this Celia is not there now," she called to Meg as she climbed down from the coach, "be sure to discover where she lives."

Once people in the street discerned the queen herself was in the grand coach, they began to gather around it. Elizabeth took to waving out the street side, then sliding across the seat to watch how things were going for Meg. When she disappeared inside, Jenks lingered near the door of the shop, then began pacing back and forth across it, craning his neck to look in each time he passed.

"Should I go in, too, Your Grace?" Rosie asked, peering out her window.

"It should not be taking this long. Something's amiss."

"Perhaps the woman needed to ask the shop owner for permission to leave."

"No, I shouldn't have sent Meg. We'll both go in."

"But—"

The queen opened the door facing the shop and stepped out onto the step; instantly Clifford ran around to offer his hand. As she appeared, the crowd rushed around to her side and cheered.

"Make way!" Clifford shouted. "Make way for the queen's majesty!"

When the crowd noise swelled, Jenks came running.

"Where is she?" Elizabeth shouted to him.

"Went into a back room, I think. Guess the shop owner's not there right now, 'cause I didn't see anyone but Meg and a woman. Hard to see well when the shop's dark and I'm in the sun. I figure the woman had to fetch a cloak, and Meg went with her to keep an eye on her or something."

Or something. Elizabeth's stomach cartwheeled. She rushed inside with both big men behind her. "Close the street door and open that back one!" she ordered, glancing around. In the corner nearest the window, through which the perfumer could have seen the coach coming, was a worktable with leather and glove linings and pots of rich ambergris and sweet-scent unguents.

Jenks banged the back door open. It revealed not a dim room but a narrow, dim alley. "Gone!" he shouted as the queen pushed past him and Jenks to peer out.

"'S blood!" she spit out, and hit her fist on the door frame.

She strode into the alley and looked both ways, then up. Nothing, as if two women could have vanished into the ether. She scanned the dirt for tracks and saw something bright nearly at their feet.

She bent herself to retrieve it. A groat.

"It could be a coin Meg dropped, either on purpose or accidentally," she said. "She had a pouch of them."

"Look—another farther down!" Jenks cried, bending to pick it up.

"She's leaving us a trail," Elizabeth said. "We must go now, before others find them and pick them up. Rosie, return to the coach and tell Boonen to wait there. Jenks and Clifford, with me."

"Just the two of us can follow these, lest there be danger," Jenks protested, but she had already hefted her skirts and was running down the alley, not bothering to pick up the next coins she saw. She heard her guards pounding behind her; one, then both, scraped their swords from their scabbards.

Crossing the next crowded thoroughfare, they lost the trail, but Clifford picked it up again on the other side. Elizabeth spotted the first drops of blood, following the same path as the coins.

"She could be wounded," she muttered. "Dear God in heaven, what if I sent her to question a murderer who attacked her and forced or dragged her out?"

The coins became sparser and the blood heavier. Gobbets of pink flesh now dotted the path of coins. The queen's heart was thudding, and she was out of breath, but her mind was racing faster. Could Marie Gresham somehow be the connection to the person who murdered Hannah and now had attacked Meg when she was cornered? But a glove perfumer named Celia in Eastcheap? Too many links were missing. Something was so very wrong.

"There!" Jenks shouted, and pointed.

Elizabeth looked farther ahead. Meg's body was slumped in the alley, her shoulders and head against the wall. Everyone ran, though Jenks got there first.

"No!" the queen cried when she saw Meg's face and chest blood-splattered—but she did have good color for a corpse.

"You found me," Meg gasped out, opening her eyes. "I just got so exhausted. I—she ran and I lost her. I'm sorry, Your Grace."

Elizabeth knelt in the dirt and looked Meg over. Until that moment when she thought Meg might be dead, she'd forgotten how much she meant to her. Though a servant, Meg had spirit and spunk and could look so much like her queen that they could have had a painting done as sisters.

"Thank God you are all right, my Meg. I should not have sent you in, but this investigation keeps surprising me. Though it was the hard way, we have learned the perfumer had something serious to hide, or she surely would not have fled."

"I can describe her," Meg said. "Rough-looking with a scar on her chin. And I'm sure we can find where she lives when the glover gets back. Then we can go there and sneak up on her."

"If she fled like that, she might be too afraid to go home, though we'll send someone to find out. Let me help you up. Meg, when I saw that trail of blood and worse—"

"I know," she said as Jenks and the queen helped her to her feet. "Well, she did hit me in the face. I got a bloody nose, but the blood in the alley isn't mine. I just thought if I dropped the coins near it, you'd be more likely to find them. Bet someone just carried a carcass down this way, since we're so near the slaughterhouses."

"Do you want Jenks to carry you?" Elizabeth asked.

"No," Meg muttered, shaking his hand from her arm and not so much as looking his way as she brushed herself off. "He happily carried Ursala partway home the other night when she was so distraught, but I'll be fine without him."

Elizabeth watched the look that flashed between Meg and Jenks. It lacked the bitterness and anger they had shown at the Privy Plot Council meeting the other night. Now the queen herself was feeling bitter and angry. *Since we're so near the slaughterhouses,* Meg had said. Elizabeth knew she was not anywhere near solving the slaughter of Hannah von Hoven in her starch house.

Chapter the Ninth

MEG NEARLY JUMPED OUT OF HER SKIN AS A shadow plunged the inside of her herb-drying shed into darkness. "Is there no rest, even on a lovely Sabbath afternoon?" said the mellow voice behind her.

Ned!

She spun to face him, standing in the doorway, looking jaunty and charming. "I'm not really working," she told him. "I just wanted to take a walk and thought I'd see if these herbs are dry yet."

"They look fine to me." He stepped inside the little shed, set among the jumble of outbuildings behind the palace. Touching one of the suspended bunches of lavender and harebell, he sent them swinging. "Mmm, sweet-smelling, too. Anything here to make a poultice for that black eye of yours?"

"I'm afraid that glove perfumer who hit me wasn't sweet at all."

Though her jest was a lame one, he chuckled and stepped closer, tipping her face up with his hand on her chin and shifting his big body slightly to get better light. "The bruise looks more green and yellow to me—very pretty, Mistress Starch."

"You're not to call me that. And the bruise looks dreadful. I saw it in the queen's mirror."

"If it's really bothering you—the look of it, not the soreness—I have just the thing to cover it in my actor's bag of tricks."

"You have more than skin paint in your actor's bag of tricks, Ned Topside, and always have."

At least she was giving as good as she got today. She was determined not to let her feelings for this man turn her to a babbler, a scold, nor a mere melted hunk of butter in his hands ever again.

"I came to find you not for that, though," he said. As he took a small step back, his green eyes swept her down, then up. The impact was delicious; she felt as if he'd caressed her right through her cloak and gown. "You still look fine to me," he went on, with a slight tilt of the corners of his mouth. Then he turned more sober. "Meg, Her Grace is sending me daily to Gresham House to ascertain your daughter's well-being—and, of course, pick up any information Sally gets from the Gresham girl. Sometimes, I hear, we're to go together, and I want us to get on."

"I'm glad Her Grace chose you," she admitted, skirting his implication. "Sally will like you. You'll take my messages to her, too?"

"Of course, when I'm not taking you with me."

"Ned, I know you fancy pretty faces, so please don't let her think you find her odd or ugly."

"Of course I won't. She has the same spunk and inner beauty her mother has, and nothing will ever change that."

So much, Meg thought, for not wanting to melt at his feet. All along she'd known why women adored Edward

Thompson, alias Ned Topside, and it wasn't just for his face and form. She'd loved him from the first, despite his flaws—but then, he was a man.

They stared into each other's eyes. He came closer again and reached up to gently stroke the puffy area around her eye. Not only did it not hurt, but she wondered if he had some healing touch—at least on that single spot, because the rest of her was on fire.

He smoothed tendrils of her wayward hair back behind her ears, then placed his cheek against her right temple, slowly, as if afraid she'd balk. He turned his head and nibbled her earlobe. "Such lovely seashell ears and satin skin," he whispered.

She had to remind herself to breathe and wondered if he could hear the pounding of her pulse. Evidently not yet daring to take her lips, he puckered his and brushed them across her forehead, then pecked the tip of her nose, working his way down much too slowly.

She thought it probably surprised him when she threw her arms around his neck and kissed him hard.

Thomas Gresham was usually too busy with worldly duties to spend much time in prayer, but this Sabbath afternoon, even as he entered Whitehall Palace and was shown into the presence of his queen in her withdrawing room, he prayed harder than he ever had. He feared she would question him about more than the building of the exchange or financial matters. Worse, she had Secretary of State Cecil with her, who kept taking some sort of notes.

"First of all," the queen said as he stood before them, for

they were both seated, "I want to inform you that I have hired Hugh Dauntsey to oversee the accounting and dispersing of Hannah von Hoven's worldly goods, as it seems she has no heir."

That alone knocked him back. Did she already know more than she let on? To cover his shock, he began, "But Hugh Daunt—"

"Ordinarily I might have consulted you, but you are busy overseeing your building project and, of course, tending to the needs of your daughter and your wife."

"I have it on good authority that Dauntsey is head over heels in risky investments, Your Majesty," he said, fighting to keep his voice in check. "I've heard he's making what they call a killing in the stock market from illegal practices such as forestalling and engrossing, and, as you know, he has ties to Paulet. I can't advise trusting him and—"

"Sadly, Thomas, there are many I can't trust." Her dark stare bored into him. His heartbeat kicked up, and he began to sweat. He twisted his grasshopper signet ring around his still-sore finger. He hadn't been able to find the one he'd thrown at his wife, but he had several of them.

"I am not asking for advice on this," she went on in a cold tone, "but merely informing you of his special appointment. What I do need from you concerns the double portrait of two young girls that is in your possession and disturbed your daughter so. I am hoping you can tell me why."

He wanted to lie, but he couldn't. Not to Elizabeth Tudor, who had saved the country from the financial excesses of her father and sister. Not to this queen who had trusted him so, and on whom the good of the realm rested. He decided to tell the truth, but as little of it as he could get away with.

"It's a work I acquired in Antwerp years ago, Your Majesty."

"It's quite charming, so why not display it?"

"My wife doesn't like it."

"Really? You seem to be lord and master of that inner sanctum and what is displayed there. Besides, I had the distinct impression Anne hadn't even seen the portrait. Then, when she did, I agree that she seemed to dislike it instantly and immensely, however much she tried to cloak her reaction."

He saw he'd have to give her something more, to make an offer, like giving someone a small loan at low interest hoping he'd be appeased and not ask for more capital.

"You look ill, man," she said. "You may sit down while you tell us all."

He nodded and gladly got off his bad leg as he sat across the narrow width of table. The two of them had known each other well enough over these years he'd helped her. She'd often taken his advice, but now he must take hers, even if it meant revealing things about himself that might mean the end of his service to her, one way or the other.

"I shall start at the beginning," he said, his voice catching.

"Do that. And don't mind my lord Cecil. Anything that is said here will be safe with him, for all England is safe in his hands. Say on."

As he began to speak, he held to the fact that she needed him. Surely she needed him, despite what he was going to confess.

Elizabeth tried to appear calm but she gripped the arms of her chair so hard her fingers went numb. Thomas Gresham was terrified, and that terrified her. She could not lose him, but what was he going to say that shook him so?

"A long time ago in Antwerp, before you were queen," he began, then paused.

"It sounds like the beginning of a fairy tale, but I warrant it is not, is it, Thomas?"

He cleared his throat. "No, Your Majesty. Fourteen years ago, to be exact, though I was wed, I took a Flemish mistress, and she bore a child the next year, a daughter."

Click went one of the pieces of the puzzle, the queen thought. At least that could be the reason for the terrible tension between the Greshams.

When he hesitated again, she prompted, "And that child is Marie?" An admission of marital infidelity from even one of her closest friends used to send her into a ranting fury over another man betraying another wife. Hell's gates, at this rate, she feared even Cecil kept a string of women, when she knew he was entirely too busy with his royal mistress and the kingdom.

"Yes—Marie," Thomas nearly whispered. "Anne does dote on her, though."

"I've seen that. She hovers over her and can yet carry her about as if she were still in leading strings. Go on, then. I know there is more."

"My lord Cecil, are you recording what I say?" he asked, craning his neck to see what the queen's chief advisor wrote. "Oh, you are just drawing—a large ruff?"

"Say on, Thomas!" the queen cried. "Since you came in you have hopped about like the grasshopper emblem your family claims. My lord Cecil is merely here to help me think all this through. And that, my man, is why you are going to tell me more."

"Anne insists on calling Marie—the name her real mother gave her—Marie-Anne after herself. Marie's mother, Gretta, died of childbed fever six days after the birth. I was distraught. I adored Gretta. God forgive me, she was the love of my life."

"My royal father once told my mother that—before he went merrily on to other women and other wives," she cried, and smacked her palm flat on the table.

Thomas jumped. Cecil merely shifted in his seat.

"Anne and I," Thomas went on when she said no more, "well, she hasn't been happy for years, and nor have I."

"And who is in the painting?" Elizabeth demanded. "I want more matter with less cunning."

The man's facade crumbled; he looked as if he would put his head in his hands on the table and sob the rest of his story. "In the double portrait, the girl in the window light is Gretta, actually, about the age Marie is now. And the one in shadow, evidently because her temperament was darker, is her twin sister—Hannah von Hoven."

Elizabeth sat back in her chair. Finally she held a trump card, but if she played it—if she lost her financial genius Gresham—could she still lose the game?

"You knew Hannah back in Antwerp also?"

"Not well, but yes. Hannah was lighthearted on the surface but resented me." Words seemed to pour from him in a great torrent. "I met her again when I—we—buried Gretta. Hannah was struggling financially. It seemed she always was. I promised her that my wife and I would rear the child as our own. Hannah wanted her, too, but she could ill afford to rear her. You see, Anne had a difficult birth with our son, and we knew there would be no more children, which she—we—longed for. I gave Hannah some money to start her starch business in Antwerp and didn't see her again."

"Not even when she came to England, sir?"

He looked taken aback, perhaps at her formal address to him but more likely because he saw where this was going. "Yes, I saw her here—just once, when she came to the house for money again."

"Which you gave her?"

"I did. I asked her to wait in the courtyard while I got it for her right then, so I would not have to see her another time. Badger saw her, but I told him she was the widow of someone I'd known abroad who needed financial help. I swear, I didn't see her again after that. Anne was out of the house at the time and never saw her, not that she would have known who she was anyway."

"Even if not, Thomas, perhaps someone else did see her. Was Marie home?"

"But she knew nothing about her real mother or Gretta's twin sister. She's never asked Anne, for fear, I think, of hurting her."

"You do realize Marie has a clear view of most of the large courtyard from her windows, do you not? Young women are so curious, especially one who is watched so closely. Let me have the letter, Cecil," she went on, holding out her hand. "Thomas, I have a note here your daughter wrote surreptitiously to an unnamed friend, but I believe we can guess the intended recipient. Listen to this,

"I pray you let me visit, for I can manage it without their knowing, I vow I can. Please, for I would know so much more of her, more than just seeing her in your lovely face . . ."

"No!" he cried. "God as my judge, I had no idea."

"There is more. *Or could you not come here again and I will slip out where we spoke before? I hope you will wear these sweet gloves, my gift to you, in exchange for any sweet memories you can give, and if you still need money to . . .* There she stops."

"You received that from Marie?"

"Do you doubt it? I would let you see it closer, but, sadly, this is evidence as to why she, though now senseless of the reason, was near Hannah's starch shop that sad day."

"You think she went to see her? But saw something else, something terrible?"

"Don't you, Thomas?" she demanded, flourishing the note before she returned it to Cecil, who slipped it back into his papers.

"You aren't saying they had some s-sort of argument?" he stammered. "That little Marie h-harmed Hannah?"

"I am saying that if Hannah knew her niece was coming to visit and realized that niece was Thomas Gresham's natural daughter—perhaps even an heiress—she might send her ladies home for the day. That's what she did, and I could not fathom why."

"Marie wouldn't harm Hannah—wouldn't harm anyone."

"Thomas, someone has harmed Hannah, and if it's not Marie, we must work together to discover who it was."

"As always, Your Majesty, absolutely anything I can do to advise and help you, I will do."

She nodded, but she felt afraid to trust him now. Besides, she could see from the corner of her eye that Cecil was scribbling on his diagram exactly what she was thinking. In separate sections, he'd added to his list of possible killers not Marie's name but those of Thomas Gresham and his wife,

Anne. And Thomas's name had gone in the place where Cecil had previously written *Lover?*

Monday morning, Hugh Dauntsey requested an early audience with the queen, so she summoned him to the privy gardens, where she was taking her morning constitutional with her ladies trailing behind. The brisk breeze tugged at their clothes, and everyone's feet crunched gravel on the angular paths.

Besides hearing what he had to say, Elizabeth hoped to learn more from him about his ties to her other starcher. Now that the Greshams had a motive to silence Hannah—to keep her from perhaps extorting funds from them, embarrassing them, or even alienating them from their daughter's affections—the queen was desperate to prove someone else had murdered her. Even if she lost her master starcher and the entire ruff market crashed to ruins, she could not lose Thomas Gresham.

"Your findings so far?" she asked, looking not into Dauntsey's rimless eyes but straight ahead as she walked.

"I simply wish to give you a preliminary inventory, Your Majesty," he said, walking briskly to keep up with her. He wore a doublet and matching cape of canary yellow, but at least it was not adorned with jewels or slashings. Did the man actually visit that dirty, smelly stock market in such garb? The stranger thing was that each time they took a turn onto the path facing eastward, between the sun in her eyes and his pale clothes and coloring, he almost seemed to disappear.

"But," he went on, "I have a question, too. Although Hannah von Hoven's starch shop seemed quite untouched, but for her body being found there, of course, her earthly personal goods in her privy chamber nearby were obviously picked over, to say the least."

"I cannot account for that," she told him, not mentioning she'd taken a look at the place the night she'd seen the body. "Whether someone heard that she had died and broke in to pilfer her things, or the murderer himself went through looking for something that might implicate him, I know not."

She forced from her mind the image of Thomas ransacking Hannah's room, looking for something that would link him to her. *No,* she told herself for the hundredth time, *it cannot be Thomas.*

"You assume the murderer and pilferer was a man, Your Majesty," Dauntsey went on. "But in speaking yesterday with Chief Constable Nigel Whitcomb, he mentioned the murderer could well be a woman. That is, I'm quite sure he said 'she,' not 'he.' "

Elizabeth nearly stumbled. "He has told me no such thing," she declared. Could Whitcomb have found a link to Anne Gresham so soon?

"He mentioned he was coming here with particular proofs and even a warrant for you to sign—to question someone under duress, I think he said. Here are the separate inventories of the shop and house of the deceased," he went on, handing her two folded lists from the soft leather pouch at his waist. She noted for the first time that his fingers were stained with black ink. "I also have quite a list of those who must have ruffs or fees returned, so that will cut into her estate a bit. But you see how short the household list of goods is."

She skimmed it quickly. The accounting amounted to large items that could not easily be moved, such as a bed, washstand, chair, and table. Very few garments—but for four shifts, a night rail, and a pair of perfumed gloves! It could mean the notes from Marie went through the perfumer to Hannah—or it could be mere coincidence. Perfumed gloves were expensive, but they were all the rage. Would a starcher who had evidently borrowed money more than once own a pair that wasn't a gift?

"This pair of perfumed gloves," she said, pointing to the item in his bold, slanted writing. "I would like to have them to give to a woman who was Hannah's close friend, a whitster who lived nearby and has been of great assistance to me. I know they would mean a great deal to her."

"Ursala Hemmings, Your Majesty? She came round today while I was working in the loft, but I sent her scurrying. No good to have her in the way or trying to make off with something, but I didn't know you favored her. I'll see that the gloves are included with the reckoning that comes to you, along with the worth of each item, when I find fair market value for the things."

"That would be fine. How long will it take, do you think?"

"I am making it my first priority, though some of the starching items I'll have to price by speaking with the van der Passes or perhaps your own herbalist. She evidently sold Mistress von Hoven the starch herbs—ah, here," he said, pointing to the longer list. "Cuckoo-pint herbs with the name Meg Milligrew, queen's herbalist. Strange name, cuckoo-pint, isn't it? Do you know what it means?"

He was glib and ingratiating today, while she felt simply stunned. Could her chief constable have solved this crime? If Anne Gresham had discovered Marie was entranced by Hannah, could she have followed the girl that day but found Hannah alone? After all, Hannah could have dismissed her women so she could meet secretly with Marie—or even with Anne herself.

Then Anne's argument with Hannah might have turned violent. If Anne could yet carry Marie about so easily, she could surely choke Hannah, then heft her into a tub of starch to finish her by drowning. So, did she return hastily home to join the search when Marie was discovered missing?

No. If Anne were so protective of their child, surely she would not have left her out on the streets—unless she had no idea Marie had seen her kill Hannah. Such a terrible thing could be what caused the girl to lose her senses. But then, who took Hannah out of her starch-water coffin and put her on that shelf?

"Your Majesty?" Dauntsey prompted when she did not answer whatever he had just asked. "Are you quite well?"

"Of course, and pleased with your progress so far. I shall see you again when your sums of the goods are ready for me."

Though the queen had a full agenda planned that day, she ordered Nigel Whitcomb to be brought to her forthwith when his request for a hearing was announced. "Cecil," she said, "send someone ahead to the council chamber to delay the meeting with my advisors, but come back to hear this. I think the chief constable of London may have some interesting news for us. Perhaps our local law enforcement is not as impotent as I believed."

Nigel Whitcomb was built like a tree trunk, straight up and down and sturdy. Somewhere between thirty and forty years old, he was balding and, no doubt, had grown a long beard to make up for that. Elizabeth barely recalled seeing him, but Cecil had said he had more or less cowered in the back row the day the delegation from Parliament visited to urge her to wed. Cecil had also said the man was pushy, picky, and vain. She was reminded that he had been head of the Skinners' Guild when she saw the fine fur trim on the cape and cap he held in his nervous hands.

"Your Majesty, I bring good news—and sad news, too," he told her as he produced an official-looking parchment, sealed with a big blob of wax, and proffered it to her. "My immediate and thorough investigation of the starcher's untimely demise indeed shows murder, and the coroner has agreed. I have petitioned here to question the chief possible perpetrator of this heinous crime."

In uneasy anticipation, Elizabeth shifted forward in her seat, took the warrant, and handed it to Cecil, who stood behind her.

"Why is this sad news?" she asked Whitcomb as she heard Cecil break the seal. She steadied herself to hear the chief constable or even Cecil pronounce Anne Gresham's name. She would have to deal with it, she thought. At least suppress Anne's being examined until she could break the news to Thomas and assure him that his wife was merely being questioned to provide information.

"Because the person I must accuse and examine is in your charge, Your Majesty."

"All my subjects are ultimately in my charge, Master Whitcomb."

"I have it on good authority from several witnesses that jealousy was part of the motive," he went on.

"Yes, I understand that."

So he had somehow ferreted out that Anne Gresham was still jealous over the fact that Hannah's twin sister had been the love of her husband's life. Surely Hannah's resemblance to Gretta had not lured Thomas to desire her, too? Could Anne have yet been so incensed about Gretta that she took her fury out on the dead woman's living image, or had Hannah been blackmailing Anne? And how did this man uncover all of that so swiftly?

Whitcomb was still speaking. "I also have the sworn statements of several women who overheard an argument over prices for supplies between the deceased and the accused herein."

"What?" Elizabeth demanded.

"Your Grace," Cecil said quietly behind her, "best brace yourself. This warrant for interrogation and arrest names Meg Milligrew and no other."

Chapter the Tenth

AS MEG SAT WITH NED AND SALLY ON A BENCH IN the corner of the courtyard gardens at Gresham House, she had never been happier. Marie was to join them soon, but for now it was just the three of them, so Meg could pretend that they were a family with a fine home of their own. Ned was attentive to her and so very kind to Sally.

"I still love my other mother and father," Sally told them, "though they let me down something dreadful, not telling me 'bout how I was poxed and all."

"They wanted to protect you," Meg said, reaching for her hand. "Just as Marie's parents have tried to shelter her, they didn't want you to be hurt."

"And now look what it got my folks and the Greshams! 'Sides, just like Marie, I think this place is so fine—the city, I mean, not just Gresham House." Though no one was nearby, Sally lowered her voice. "It's kind of a pretty prison here, Marie says, and I know what she means. It's lots more of a lark to go out and 'bout. Bet her real mother'd never take her out for a day picking herbs with fairy lights," she added with a pert smile and a squeeze of Meg's hand.

Meg gaze snagged Ned's. He, too, must be thinking not only of Sally's two mothers but of Marie's. At the Privy Plot Council meeting last night, the queen had explained about the von Hoven connection to the Greshams and how neither Sir Thomas nor Lady Anne had really gotten over it.

But Ned asked only, "Fairy lights? It sounds like something I could use to present a fantasy at court."

"You know, you could," Meg said, "but you'd better use them for a tragedy. We could dust one of your ghosts with cuckoo-pint pollen—I've a box of it saved—because it would give an eerie glow in the dark."

"I believe both you ladies are going to come in very handy to me," Ned said, and bathed them both in his brightest smile. "Sally, is there anything you have to tell the queen? Has Marie remembered anything else?"

Sally darted a glance up toward Marie's second-story rooms. "Don't look now," she whispered, "but Lady Gresham's staring down at us."

"That's all right," Meg assured her. "Tell us if there's aught else before Marie comes down to join us."

"Don't know if she really will, 'specially with Lady Gresham nearby." She hunched forward, gripping her hands on her knees. "Each time Marie looks down into this garden, she says it 'minds her of something bad, something lost. I know her mother don't really want her to talk to you each day, Master Topside, or to you either, Mother Meg, but Marie don't, either, not here anyway."

"Because of something she's lost in this garden?" Ned repeated, frowning. "A trinket or another letter like she gave the queen or—"

"I think it's 'bout someone she saw here, or argued with here—a woman."

"She told you that?" Meg asked.

"No, but she said it in her sleep last night, over and over. I'm in a trundle bed next to her tall one, and she kept saying she looked like the woman she met in the garden. I thought she meant like the girl in the painting, but she was saying 'woman' and 'garden' and then that she lost her, lost her and can't find her anymore. And then crying for her lost mother, too, not Lady Gresham, 'cause she's 'dopted like me. Honest, I heard her aright, e'en if she was all upset in her nightmare."

"Listen, lovey," Meg told her, reaching into the girl's hood to stroke her rough cheek, "if she has a nightmare again like that, wake her up, won't you?"

"So she won't keep having it so bad?"

"Yes, but also because when you're waked from a nightmare, you might remember things from it you can't recall the next morning."

"Marie would like to remember. Last night she said she's afraid, but she wants to recall things and doesn't know how. Lady Gresham told me never wake her, but should I do it and ask her who's the woman in the garden?"

"Ask her anything she can remember about anything," Ned put in, nodding at Meg. "If she can't recall what happened in waking life, maybe her dreams will give the answers."

"Yes," Meg said, looking now only at him. "Sometimes you have to just trust your dreams."

"What?" the queen cracked out so loud that Nigel Whitcomb scurried back several steps. "You accuse my herbalist, Meg Milligrew, of this foul murder?"

She seized the parchment from Cecil's hands and skimmed

it. The document listed the names of four women—evidently some of Hannah's workers—who claimed to have overheard an argument about the prices of starch herbs between *said victim* and *said accused.* Worse, it listed the names of several *servants of the queen* who had witnessed an argument between Ned Topside and Meg Milligrew in the *public place of Kings Street on Wednesday, the 23rd day of October, hard by Whitehall Palace.* This concerned how Meg was jealous that *a person who went by the name of Ned Topside had visited the victim privily after the queen had sent the same Ned Topside once to see her publicly.*

" 'S blood," Elizabeth swore, and followed that with a string of curses.

"Of course, I would be willing to question her here on these premises," Whitcomb said, his voice at first a mere squeak, "Your Majesty, if you would just sign the document, since she's your—"

"I know these people intimately," the queen interrupted, waving the parchment. "I can attest to their character, especially Mistress Milligrew, and she did *not* murder Hannah von Hoven! She's the one who stumbled on the body and first reported the crime."

"More than once in my experience, Your Majesty," Whitcomb said, "the one who supposedly discovers the deceased has been the one who killed said person. It is a wonder to me how they can be attracted to the site of their crime and the victim's corpse, too. Why, I once heard of a murderer who not only attended the funeral but kept visiting his victim's burial site."

"This is outrageous!" she insisted, brandishing the warrant again. "Chief Constable, I will look into this, but it is entirely beyond the pale. You are dismissed now, and I shall summon you again if you are needed."

"Pardon, Your Gracious Majesty, but I must ask that this woman be handed over for questioning at the least. My inquiries have determined that she is the only possible—"

"You do not know whereof you speak," Elizabeth went on, her voice steady and quieter now. "My lord Cecil and I have knowledge of several persons who might have wanted to kill Hannah von Hoven."

"You—but . . . *I*, Your Majesty," he said, drawing himself up to his full height, "by the power vested in me, am the one entrusted by the laws of our realm to inquire into this, and I'll not cower, as too many of us did that day you scolded us for simply asking that the future of the throne be preserved through your marriage and the bearing of an heir or—or . . ."

"Or what?" she demanded. "Or there will be a treasonous uprising, led, of course, by my northern Popish subjects who are all cozy with my Scottish royal cousin? You are dismissed," she said, flinging out an arm and rising. "However, I vow to you I will see to these accusations you have made and give Meg Milligrew over to your questioning tomorrow, should I see a need. I am certain in your lofty position you have many more important things to see to now. Good day to you."

When the still-sputtering man left the chamber, Elizabeth reread the warrant, threw it to the floor, then collapsed in her chair with her head in her hands.

"Your Grace?" Cecil said, his voice so close he must be nearly leaning over her.

"I'll be all right in a moment. I'm thinking that I told Parliament that day that I will never be by violence constrained to do anything. Yet just now, I could have wrung that man's neck. Is that what could have happened to Hannah? That someone who is always in control lost his—or her—temper?"

"Over the years you have struggled to rein in that Tudor temper, and you will yet be victorious—in all things."

"I also told Parliament that fatal fashions are treasons, greed and lust, adultery and murder—and rebellions—in my kingdom. I told them that I do not fear death and that I have good courage, but this is wearing me down, Cecil. Yet, especially now, I cannot and will not turn this over to others to solve and punish."

"You also said to them that day, Your Grace, that England must take a stand for justice. You are doing that, always, even if it seems to some that you are obstructing that very justice. But you surely must hold to your pledge to let Whitcomb question Meg on the morrow."

She lifted her head from her hands and twisted around to look at him. "Hand Meg over to Whitcomb?"

"Not if we can clear her quickly and find who did put Hannah in that devil's liquor Hosea Cantwell's always pontificating about."

"Meg's gone to Gresham House with Ned, but I will see both of them, separately, the moment they return—Ned first. And, my friend," she said, rising to face him, "don't you dare add Meg's name to that diagram you have—not, at least, until I speak with her."

As she hurried down the corridor to meet with her council of advisors, Elizabeth prayed the day would not get even worse. The northern shires were yet Catholic and seethed with their desire to champion Queen Mary of Scots over their God-given queen.

Passing through her crowded presence chamber, she saw Hugh Dauntsey, whispering to Lord Paulet. She nodded to them and strode on until she heard Dauntsey call to her, "One thing I forgot, Your Most Gracious Majesty."

She halted so quickly that Lady Rosie nearly bumped into her. 'S blood, she didn't need Dauntsey calling out something private in this crowd. Though she gestured the man to her, she did not turn to him until she was in the corridor.

"The thing you forgot?" she asked, trying to keep her voice reined in. Meg and Ned weren't back from Gresham House yet. She felt twisted so tight about everything that she'd like to scream.

"Something I found in the bottom of the fatal starch bath when I drained it," he whispered to her. He held out a small black velvet pouch; she took it from his ink-stained fingers. "Not the pouch itself or it would be stiff as a board," he went on as if she were a dunderhead. "Within is something that must have slipped off in a struggle. Wet starch is quite slippery, they say."

"I will examine it and speak with you later."

She entered the council chamber, sat at the head of the long table, and nodded permission that others could be seated and business begun, but she kept fingering the pouch in her lap. Something small within, perhaps a thimble or an earbob. Unable to wait to see, even though Cecil began to speak, she opened the pouch and dropped the item in her lap.

She touched it, then turned it in her fingers. It was a ring, large, heavy, evidently a man's.

"Her Majesty has summoned us today," Cecil began, "to consider the northern shires and the dangers they could cause should the Catholic queen of Scotland become even more deceitful."

Definitely a signet ring, probably one used to imprint a coat of arms on wax seals.

"We are talking about a large number of rogues," Cecil said, "some nobles, some rabble, who may go to open rebellion, should Queen Mary give them either further covert or overt indications she would become the figurehead for such an uprising."

Elizabeth's stomach began to knot. Glancing down in the shadow of her lap, she wasn't certain what the figure on the raised part of the ring was at first, and she must not bow her head, or her men could think she was downhearted or fearful of her enemies. She looked straight ahead again at Cecil, who was still speaking.

"We must lay plans to keep our realm and our ruler safe, so the floor is open to reports and discussions."

Then she knew. She knew—and feared—the figure on the ring was a grasshopper.

"I swear to you, Your Grace, chief constable of London or not, the man is wrong!" Meg cried. She felt her skin flush hot; tears flooded her eyes, making two queens and two Cecils before she blinked. "Hannah was dead when I got there, and I didn't do it!"

"I believe you," the queen said as she rose from the table and walked around Cecil to come over to take her hand. Meg tried to keep some semblance of poise, but she clung to the queen's fingers. "Meg," Elizabeth went on, putting her other hand on her shoulder, "I'm just telling you what the constable has come up with. Since he's been looking in the wrong place, I fear he's jumped to the wrong conclusions."

"I treasure your support, Your Grace. I am so undone that—"

"Just listen now. Unfortunately, there is no denying the

two events witnessed by multiple persons that might be construed to mean you held a double grudge against Hannah. And that would make two powerful motives—disagreements with her over money and over a man."

"But I don't blame her for Ned's going back to see her—that's just him," Meg blurted as the queen stepped back. Meg wrapped both arms tightly around herself to shop shaking. "Though lately," she added, "Ned's vowed to change his ways."

"So he tells me. I spoke with him briefly just now. This formal accusation makes me even more desperate to solve this murder. You are not the only one at your wit's end."

"I don't mean to speak ill of the dead, Your Grace, but Hannah was a pinchpurse, and I'd tell the constable that if he asks. All that time it took Sally and me to gather those herbs—not that we didn't enjoy doing it—and she wanted my costs cut."

"Her stinginess would fit," the queen said, nodding and walking to the window where Meg had noted she often stood when she was deep in private thought. "Hannah seems not to be able to handle money well, though she must have made a pretty profit from her starch shop here. But now Hugh Dauntsey has a long list of those who had left ruffs to be stiffened, so her estate must return all those with the fees."

"Which means Dingen van der Passe will get even more business, with her competitor removed," Meg said. "But about my other supposed motive, Your Majesty. I was furious with Jenks at first for turning his devotion to me so swiftly to Ursala, but I certainly haven't murdered her, any more than I killed Hannah over Ned's attentions."

"Now that's roundabout logic, isn't it, Cecil?" Elizabeth asked. Then she added, turning back to Meg, "I know you were angry with poor Jenks at first, and even two days ago when you wouldn't let him carry you. You were sharp with him about carrying Ursala the night she was so distressed."

"Yes, Your Grace, but I've accepted that now—Jenks and Ursala. One more thing, though," she said, wanting badly to change the subject. Surely Her Majesty wasn't just stringing her along the way she had others she mistrusted like Hugh Dauntsey, Lord Paulet, or those northern lords who were still members of Parliament. Surely the queen really believed she was innocent.

"Yes?" Elizabeth asked when she hesitated.

"Did Ned tell you that Marie's having nightmares about meeting some woman in the gardens at Gresham House, Your Grace?"

Cecil looked up frowning as the queen nodded. "Marie must have seen Hannah there," Elizabeth explained to him, "when she came to Gresham House for money. Either while Hannah waited for the money from Sir Thomas or thereafter, perhaps Marie ran down to speak with her. Either the girl guessed who Hannah was or Hannah told her. If only, Cecil, we could see through the opaque swirl of starch water to the bottom of the barrel, eh?"

"We need to move even more quickly to keep the constable off our—and Meg's—backs," he advised.

Meg didn't like it when they discussed her as if she weren't here, as if huge decisions about her life could be made without her.

"You told Whitcomb we had other possible murderers in mind," Cecil went on, "so he'll be demanding to know who and how and why—and I can't see then how you'll protect the Greshams, at least until we discover who is guilty."

"If only," the queen said, hitting her fist on the window

ledge, "poor little Marie would have a nightmare that would jolt her back to reality."

"That's it!" Meg cried. She realized it might be a daft idea, but she was desperate now, and if it worked, she could continue to be important to this investigation without having it focus on her. "I know how to stage such a nightmare—with Ned's help. Hannah's not here to help us, but the cuckoo-pint is."

"What do you mean?" the queen asked, walking away from the window.

"Remember, Your Grace, how you staged a play at Nonsuch last year to get your painter Gil Sharpe to come clean on what had really happened to him when he was studying in Italy?"

"Of course."

"With Ned's help, we can use cuckoo-pint pollen to help Marie remember. She wants to badly—though there'd be hell to pay if her parents found out Sally sneaked us in at night."

"Not if I'm along," Elizabeth declared. "And they may thank us after, because there's going to be hell to pay for all of us if Marie doesn't quickly recall what she saw."

The last thing on earth the queen needed was an audience with the Marquess of Winchester, Lord Paulet, today, but she knew he hated Gresham, and since that could be one of the marks of Hannah's murderer, she agreed to see him briefly.

Despite his age, he nearly bounded into her conference chamber. Facing him alone but for her yeomen Clifford and Bates standing like silent sentinels inside the door, she was amazed to see the old man all smiles.

"Your Most Gracious Majesty, I knew you would heed my counsel!" he blurted after his bow.

She remained seated but remembered to raise her voice for his poor hearing. "In what respect, my lord?"

"I told you that you needed a larger staff, just the way things used to be when I was comptroller of the royal household and one of your father's chief financial advisors. I refer to your taking Dauntsey on and promising him if that goes well, there would be other assignments."

It was no news to her that Dauntsey would tat-tale to Paulet. She recalled seeing them together just before Dauntsey handed her the Gresham grasshopper ring. Of course, since she trusted both Dauntsey and Paulet as far as she could throw them, they could have planted the ring to incriminate her chief financial advisor they both hated. But however would they get a ring from Thomas?

Or did the ring in the starch indeed indicate that Thomas had lied to his queen about only seeing Hannah once and at his home? Men were capable of such lies to hide their lusts. Had he requested Hannah release her women, and had he lost his ring in their struggle for her life? It was just one more reason besides helping Marie to remember that she was risking so much this night to sneak her people into Gresham House after dark. Over Meg's protests, she was taking Ursala and her twin sister, Pamela, too, as key players. If this dark drama didn't work, perhaps nothing would.

"So," she said, refusing to go along with Paulet's hail-fellow-well-met demeanor, "thanking me for hiring your friend Hugh Dauntsey is the reason you have requested a private interview today? You are welcome, but I have many obligations, my lord."

"Destinations?" he said, cupping his ear with one hand. "Are you leaving the palace again, then?"

It amazed and annoyed her that he kept an eye on her. Did he have an informer telling him when she ventured out and who she visited?

"Tell me why you are really here, my lord," she said, raising her voice even more.

"As Hugh Dauntsey's mentor, I would offer Your Majesty the opportunity to make a great deal of money in the stock market," he said, speaking too loudly as usual. "He said you showed great interest. It is all quite high risk, but anything worth while having is high risk."

"An interesting philosophy. So, since you are no longer controlling my money, you yet propose to invest it for me?"

"It's quite obvious that you could benefit from someone with much experience to advise you in that and in other ways."

"Meaning you, sir?" she demanded, growing more angry by the moment.

"Dauntsey, as well. He's been making both of us a fortune speculating in stocks."

She was tempted to tell Paulet that Thomas Gresham had said Dauntsey was conducting his business illegally.

"Pray tell me," she said, nearly shouting back at Paulet, "what is the market practice called forestalling?"

He looked shocked. "Why—it's intercepting goods before they get to market, buying them direct from the herdsman for a cut price before anyone else can bid on them. But why—"

"And engrossing, my lord? What is that?"

Paulet's ruddy face blanched. "Ah—it's buying up the entire supply of something to resell at an inflated price, Your

Majesty. If you have interest in such practices, you can, no doubt, shave off more of what's called the overhead—"

"You, my lord, are in over your head with me and always have been," she cried, and threw her filigreed pomander at him. It bounced off his hip and rolled on the floor. She knew she should play along and try to give this man enough rope to hang both himself and Dauntsey with their double dealings, but she was at the end of that very rope.

"You've never trusted me, never favored me!" he pouted as if he were a spoiled child. Behind her, Clifford and Bates looked ready to lunge at the man if he made a move toward her, but it was she who rose and stalked him.

"Let me tell you why that is true!" she shouted at him. "Or perhaps if your long memory were not so very short, you could tell me. Who is it, my lord, what dyed-in-the-wool Catholic volunteered to escort the Princess Elizabeth to the Tower when her sister, Queen Mary, wanted her imprisoned there?"

"Why, she asked me, and I could not gainsay the queen."

"But you gainsay this queen, do you not, hanging about with the men who would force me to choose a husband, and with those northern lords who question my right to rule? Dare I ask in turn if you favor the Catholic Queen Mary of Scots over me, too?"

He looked as if he'd like to fall through the floor.

"I have it on the best authority," she went on, "that you volunteered to conduct me to the Tower when I was so afraid to go there—and enjoyed the task! No doubt, you might enjoy it again if another Queen Mary bid you do the very same."

"I—of course not. Never!" he cried, and nearly stumbled over his own feet backing away from her. "But then why do you abide me at all?" he choked out, then looked as if he'd like to eat those words.

"Because, man, I try to abide all my subjects! But let your memory take you even further back," she demanded, still advancing on him so that he backed into the door with a small thud.

"You mean—when your mother was accused of treason?"

"Treason, adultery, incest—anything that could be thrown at her, all false, all lies."

"I—I was just concerned with the king's finances, not with that," he gasped out.

"A dear friend of mine who is dead now told me that you were, in the words of Queen Anne Boleyn, 'a gentleman' through it all, unlike some of the other, newer breed."

"I was—yes, I was. I tried not to judge her."

"So in return, I do not judge you now—that is, on the issue of risky ventures in the stock market. But beware that you do not cross me, for you have quite used up your favors here, Lord Paulet."

Even as the man managed an escape, she felt torn about how she had handled him. On one hand, she had been wanting to tell him off for years. On the other, she'd alienated him now and, since she liked to keep her enemies close and unsuspecting, she might just have made her murder investigation ten times worse.

Chapter the Eleventh

MEG WAS SHOCKED TO SEE THAT THE QUEEN HAD evidently invited Ursala Hemmings not only to the palace but into her withdrawing room. Jenks brought her up the back staircase from the river, no less, a private way only the queen's most trusted servants knew about. And Jenks looked starry-eyed.

"Why is she here?" Meg whispered to Ned.

"Her Grace is going to use her in the little drama we're doing in the dark at Gresham House tonight," he whispered back. "Her twin sister Pamela, too."

"What? Don't tell me Ursala will also be sitting in a Privy Plot Council meeting!"

"This isn't a meeting, sweetheart. It's just rehearsal for tonight. Anyway, aren't you supposed to be off to see Sally?"

He darted away, showing Ursala where she would stand and how the miming would go so she could tell her sister later. One of the twins had to be at the laundry until dark to receive customers, so at least Pamela hadn't tagged along.

"Only the two of us will speak, and in whispers," Ned told the young woman, who, Meg had to admit, looked at least clean—actually, spotless—today, compared to the other time she'd seen her. "I've written a short script we must learn by heart," Ned added. Ursala nodded, eyes wide, while Meg just rolled hers.

The queen swept in with Lady Rosie close behind, as well as Clifford and Bates in her wake. "One of my yeomen will guard the gate," the queen told Ned, "and the other Marie's door to the main corridor. I don't put it past the ubiquitous Nash Badger to stay awake all night, and we don't want chaos. This all has to be beautifully organized.

"Oh, Meg," she said, noticing her at last, "you'd best set out for Gresham House to be certain Sally understands her part. She's to tiptoe down to the side courtyard door to let us in as soon as the moon rises, which, I am assured, will be eleven of the clock. And tell her not to be afraid, for if things go awry, it is the queen herself who will tell the Greshams why this needed to be done."

Meg dragged her feet to the door. She was loath to be sent away with Ursala taking such a large part, adored by Jenks, who never could hide his feelings. And fussed over by Ned. Worse, Meg felt she'd almost been replaced in the queen's trust and affections. Then, as she put her hand to the door latch, Her Majesty called, "Oh, Meg."

She turned quickly, hoping she'd be asked to stay at least a bit longer. Perhaps she would be included in Ned's playacting, too.

"You did leave some of the cuckoo-pint pollen we need to make Ursala and her sister glow, didn't you?" Her Majesty inquired.

"What's needed is with Ned, Your Grace. But I repeat that it's not to get in anyone's mouth. It will glow beautifully for your specters, but any bit of the herb could make one sick—or worse."

"Good," Elizabeth said, and turned away.

Hadn't she been listening? Meg's precious pollen was all she wanted when, after all, this entire dream drama had been Meg's idea. Now she was shuffled off to the side, even though it did give her a reason to see her Sally.

As she turned toward the door again, she heard Ursala speak. "Your Majesty, I been pondering something I'd best say. Jenks said I should."

Yet again Meg turned to watch the others. Ursala hung back from the queen a bit, half hidden by Jenks's big body, then went into a rocky curtsy. It reminded Meg how bad she herself had used to be at that.

"Yes, Ursala," the queen said, her voice calm and encouraging, even though Meg knew she'd been on pins and needles lately. "Speak up, for anything that can help us is greatly appreciated."

Meg pressed her lips together. Would the queen take this woman in if she kept clinging to Jenks? Would she even allow them to wed?

"I don't mean to speak poorly of anyone, Your Majesty," Ursala began as Jenks took her arm and moved her closer to the queen. " 'Specially not someone so grieved over her girl's condition."

Meg gasped. Was Ursala going to say something harmful about her? All she needed was this laundress chiming in on Chief Constable Whitcomb's dreadful accusations.

"Tell us what you recall," the queen urged Ursala, "no matter of whom you are speaking. We need to follow any and all clues."

"Well, I could swear I seen that Marie Gresham's mother afore—the lady standing by the child's bed that night I 'dentifed Marie. I seen her in Hannah's starch house, not near the day Hannah died or nothing, so I wouldn't want to get the lady in trouble."

Meg breathed a sigh of relief as Ursala seemed to speak faster and faster. Didn't she know not to rattle things off to Her Grace?

"Acourse," Ursala plunged on, "some ladies drop off their own ruffs, but I'm sure I passed her once on the stairs to Hannah's loft, I going up and her coming down. Told me to stand aside, she did, not dirty her gown, and me spending my whole life keeping gowns like hers clean, that's why I 'member her."

"Thank you, Ursala," the queen said—real sweetly, Meg thought. If *she'd* come up with that information in such a tardy fashion, Her Grace would probably have let loose a curse and thrown something. The last persons the queen wanted to see guilty—except for her, Meg hoped—were the Greshams.

"I can see you are going to be very helpful to all of us," Elizabeth told Ursala.

Meg snorted and lifted the door latch. Clifford usually did that for her, but he, too, was intent on the queen's exchange with Ursala. Tears in her eyes, for no one's plight but her own, Meg went out and closed the door.

Things went so smoothly that night that Elizabeth began to worry. Sally let them in promptly at the street door to the courtyard. No Gresham guards were there, where they left Bates behind, nor at the door to the great house itself. Sally, the queen, the twins, and Ned, with Clifford bringing up the rear, moved stealthily down a vast corridor and up the grand staircase, lit by only the fat candlestick Sally held and the full moon.

Since it was newly risen, it bloomed big as a ripe peach,

which appeared to teeter on the top of the roof across the courtyard. Its light washed into the windows of the grand house almost as if it were day.

In the dim second-story corridor, where moonlight did not reach, the queen half expected Nash Badger to leap from the shadows, but all seemed silent. No one spoke before they were in the antechamber to Marie's bedroom, when Sally turned to the queen to whisper something.

"What?" Elizabeth mouthed, bending to hear the girl's words.

"Sometimes Marie's mother peeks in on us. But usually not 'til later. Don't think she sleeps well, either. Marie's not had a bad dream tonight—not one where she woke or cried out, but she oft has one by midnight."

Elizabeth nodded, lifted her finger to her lips, and then turned away to whisper in Clifford's ear, "Man this outer door, and let us know immediately if anyone approaches. Just one knock on that far bedchamber door, and we will get under the girl's bed. With Sally's trundle out, we should have room. Then you hide behind drapery or furniture out here."

Clifford nodded as Sally slipped back into Marie's room, leaving the door ajar. Anxious, wishing Ned would hurry, the queen watched him dust Ursala's and Pamela's hair and shoulders with cuckoo-pint pollen. It did indeed glow in the dark, especially in the moonlight as its particles etched each of the women in shimmering silver.

How strange, Elizabeth marveled, that the Creator God had made such lovely, shiny dust a poison. It was like the fruit on the tree in the Garden of Eden, so alluring but strictly forbidden. It was also like the dual nature of people—the good and the bad all mingled.

And how much these twins resembled each other, another God-given miracle. Ned had arranged their hair the same and dressed them alike. In the darkness, would they remind Marie of the younger women in the portrait her father cherished? They were risking all on the hunch that Hannah had told Marie about her mother and that the child knew something of her aunt's murder.

They had told Sally she should slightly rouse Marie, and evidently she had. "Another dream?" they heard Sally's quavering voice within. "Here, sit up a moment, and let me get some water to wash your face."

That, too, was planned, since Sally had said Marie reacted so emotionally to having her face washed before. Besides, it gave Sally the excuse to step away from the bed, to clear Marie's line of vision.

The twins glided into the bedchamber, arm in arm, with Ned hunched down behind them so he could soon seem to rise from nothing. The queen crept in, too, hovering in the bedchamber's shadows. Goose bumps skimmed her skin, so she sensed how eerie this must seem to Marie.

The twins drifted closer to her bed, whispering nonsense words between themselves before one of them—she thought it was Pamela, but she'd lost track now—went from her sister's arms into Ned's as he seemed to appear from nowhere. They embraced each other, then she sank onto the floor with a breathy sigh.

"No," Marie whispered, then called out in a hiss of air that would have done a ghost proud, "S-S-Sally?"

As ordered, Sally stayed away from the bed. Ned was at his best, dark-cloaked with no dust on his person except what he had either apurpose or accidentally spilled on his hands, the only part of him that glowed. He now put those hands around the standing woman's throat, and when she went limp, he lifted her, then laid her on the ground.

The queen sensed Marie would scream before she even opened her mouth. Hell's gates, they'd gone too far. They would all be trapped here now.

Elizabeth lunged for Marie even as Sally did. Marie hit out, shoving the queen away, but threw her arms around her companion. Marie's mouth opened in a soundless scream.

"It's all right," Elizabeth whispered. "Sally's here, and you're all right, and you remember."

Looking dazed, Marie peered at her over Sally's shoulder.

"You do remember some things, don't you?" Elizabeth asked, perching on the edge of the bed.

Marie blinked, as if she still couldn't believe who it was she saw. Perhaps she thought she was still asleep, but at last she spoke.

"I—yes. I remember from a dream last night, not this one," the child choked out. "Some of it. I remember some of it. Are my parents here?"

"No," Elizabeth said, motioning the others away with her hand behind her back. "Just Sally and me, and we need to know everything you can recall."

Marie tried to peer around the queen as the players vacated the room, but Elizabeth shifted so she couldn't see. In reflected moonlight through the window, the queen saw tears track down the girl's face. Her heart went out to her for more reasons than she could say or share. Still, she must try. If she told her own dreadful truths, perhaps Marie would trust her.

"You lost your real mother so young you don't remember

her," Elizabeth whispered. "The same happened to me, so I understand your pain and longing. And years ago—the year I became queen—I heard from my aunt, too, my dead mother's sister, and risked everything to go to see her."

Wide-eyed, Marie nodded. She seemed instantly calmer. She set Sally a bit off to the side. "Was she a twin, too?" she asked, leaning closer.

"No, but I was desperate to see her. I lied to people, disguised myself, and went. And spent time with her—before she died."

"My Aunt Hannah looked just like my mother, Gretta," Marie said, her voice a monotone as if she were in a sleeper's trance. "Aunt Hannah told me so. My mother had a slightly rounder face, and their hair grew opposite ways from their parts, and Mother was left-handed and Hannah right, but they were so alike. My mother was an extension of herself, Hannah told me. They never lived apart until my mother fell in love with—with my father."

"You did know you were adopted, before Hannah told you?"

"Oh, they told me that, but I never asked about my mother—I just always knew not to."

Elizabeth nodded and blinked back tears herself. As a child, she'd been scolded more than once and even sent from court for asking her father or others about Anne Boleyn and her family.

"Did Hannah tell you those things when you first met her in the garden here or at her starch house? You did see her out your window and go out to see her, didn't you?"

Marie nodded, frowning. Elizabeth feared her memories might be slipping away again, but the girl went on. "I sent her gifts and epistles, but she didn't answer, so I had to go there. My last note told her when I was coming, so mayhap she let her workwomen go, because they weren't there."

"Did anyone else know you were going to see her? Could your parents have found out?"

"I don't think so."

"Could Nash Badger have known and told them? Or Celia, the glove perfumer?"

"She helped me, Celia, just for the purchase of the gloves, though I had to work through Badger after the first time Mother and I were in her shop. Then Celia sent word by Badger that he should bring no more notes, that she was afraid she was just too busy to deliver them."

Hadn't Badger said he never brought a message from Celia to Marie? the queen thought. No, in a way he had skirted that question, saying only that he'd never taken a letter back from whomever she was corresponding with.

"But Celia said she was *afraid* she was too busy?" Elizabeth repeated Marie's words.

"Yes."

"Why would she say it that way—afraid? Of what?"

"I don't know. She said Master Badger dare not come back again."

Badger had not told her that, Elizabeth thought, but perhaps that was because they were interrupted in the corridor when the Greshams returned. That reminded her that she must hurry now.

"Sally and I are here with you," Elizabeth assured her, "so you must not be afraid. Tell us, when you went to Hannah's starch house, what did you see?"

"I heard it first—someone with her upstairs."

"Voices?"

"No, a tussle—or maybe something else."

The queen clenched her fists so hard her fingernails bit into her palms. "Something else?" she prodded when Marie only frowned.

"I went into my parents' room one night when I was smaller. I saw what I shouldn't, with heavings and sighs and thrashing about."

"Oh. And Hannah's struggle—sounded like that?"

"I—I think so. When the sounds quieted, I waited, then crept the rest of the way up and peeked. But she was not there. No one came down the stairs, but no one was there, as if they'd flown away."

Marie's eyes were wide now. She didn't blink or cry as she had earlier but stared fixedly at a spot above the queen's head. For a moment, Elizabeth became aware of Sally again, silent, rapt.

"So what did you do?" Elizabeth asked.

"I went in, across the floor, trying not to slip on those brown flower bulbs—like Flanders flower bulbs, hyacinths and tulips."

The cuckoo-pint herbs that must have been spilled in the struggle, the queen surmised. She was about to ask another question when Marie went on in a clear voice, "Only she *was* there, in the starch bath with her mouth open in a scream and her eyes wide and staring up at me. Since no one was there, I was terrified I'd done it, but I couldn't have . . . or I'd remember that, wouldn't I?"

"Of course. No, you couldn't have done it."

"But I killed my mother when I was born!" she cried, reaching out to grip the queen's wrist so hard her hand tingled. "But I didn't murder her again then, did I, when I was floating in the white liquid of the birth? I saw puppies born once—in white stuff like that starch bath."

The girl sounded delirious, and yet the jumble of images—and fears—made dreadful sense.

"Marie, listen to me. No, your mother's death when you were born was not your fault. The childbed fever killed her, kills many, but it was not your fault. My brother's mother died like that, but it was not my brother's fault any more than it was yours. No one blamed him and no one blames y—"

"I do!"

These cries of anguish were the first time Marie had made much noise. What if her parents heard and came running? But she had to stay; there was more to know. The queen recalled that when she'd seen Hannah's body, the starcher's eyes and mouth had been closed, as if she'd died at rest. Had whoever plucked the corpse from the starch cared enough to arrange her features in repose before the stiffness of death set in? Who cared for Hannah that much and had the strength to lift her out? The same someone who might have had a tryst with her, one that went very bad?

Elizabeth's stomach began to cramp even more. Not Thomas! His signet ring had been in the starch bath. Or could Hannah herself have had it from him as some sort of pledge? Or had his lover Gretta had it, and Hannah inherited it? She must face him down on it tomorrow at dawn, as soon as she saw her Privy Plot Council again.

"Was the large window always open above the starch vat?" Elizabeth asked the now silently sobbing girl. Marie nodded, then just hugged Sally hard.

"Though my physician found no bump on your head, did you hit it somehow?" the queen asked, touching Marie's shoulder. She knew she should leave her alone now, but she felt so close to answers, to knowing.

"Ran," she choked out. "I ran and fell down the stairs, I

think, but I'm not sure. Maybe I hit my head—I don't know." She looked at Elizabeth again. "Did her killer go out the window? I ran outside and watched it, but—but . . . that's all I recall now."

Desperately Elizabeth hoped the murderer had gone out the window, because then it surely could not have been Thomas Gresham, not with that bad leg of his. She whispered to Sally, "Tend her close, and let us know how she is when Master Topside comes calling tomorrow. I pray she doesn't slip back, for she's made great strides. I must go now."

"If she don't recall," Sally said, "should I tell her you been here, e'en if her parents ne'er know?"

"If she believes that it was a dream, let it be," Elizabeth urged, scooting off the big bed. "If she recalls the truth, tell her the queen is on her side, no matter what befalls any of us, in mourning all those we've lost."

She squeezed Sally's shoulder and slipped out into the anteroom. Two ghostly women's forms were all she saw, until Ned and Clifford emerged from the dark.

"We must go now," she whispered, and indicated Clifford should ascertain the hall was clear. He looked out, then poked his head back in and nodded, so they all streamed out and hurried down the staircase to the door where Bates awaited.

As they emerged into the street near her coach, Elizabeth breathed a sigh of relief that tonight's plans had been both fruitful and smoothly accomplished. If what Marie had said was fact, though, a rough road lay yet ahead.

Elizabeth convened her Privy Plot Council before dawn the next day. Bleary-eyed, they stood around the long table, no one sitting since she remained standing. "We need to move quickly," she told them. "Marie Gresham has recalled enough of what occurred that, should the murderer learn how much she knows, her life could be in danger."

"Then Sally's, too!" Meg cried.

"I will find a way to protect them," Elizabeth promised. "I believe she is safe for now, because she evidently did not actually see the killer, so, I pray, the killer did not see her. But I have summoned you now because early this morning, these are the things that must be done. I am relying on each of you, for I have another meeting in this very room about the possible unrest in the northern shires."

Looking worried, everyone nodded. How much they meant to her, this stalwart mix of her servants of all kinds, her friends, indeed. "Jenks and Meg," she went on, "I want you to return to Hannah's loft and examine it both outside and in, specifically to discern whether her killer could have escaped out the window over the starch vat. Also observe carefully where someone could have hidden within the loft while Marie was in the room and thought no one was there."

"Maybe the same place he later hid the body," Ned said. "On the shelf behind those rolls of fabric."

"But those rolls would have been very difficult to place once one was already on the shelf. You two, should Hugh Dauntsey still be about the place doing his inventories, wait until he leaves so he doesn't see what you are doing. Also, I have a purse of coins for you to give to Ursala and Pamela for their help yesterday."

She looked at Jenks, who looked immensely pleased, then at Meg. If her herbalist thought her queen had not noticed how upset she was yesterday when Ursala was the center of attention, she didn't know her monarch after all these years.

"Ned," she said, turning to him, "I must ask you to try to trace this perfumer of gloves, Celia, though I doubt that she has returned to her place of employment after leading Meg such a merry chase."

"Yes, Your Grace, with pleasure. I'd like to give her a bloody nose for how she hit Meg."

"If you should find her, bring her here. I'll send Bates, too, so that the two of you can control her. If you cannot locate her, at least try to learn her full name, so you can find and visit her home. And if there is no trace of her from the original glover's at Eastcheap and Abchurch, using Meg's description of her, try other glovers in the area to see if she's been in for further employment. We must have it verified that Marie's notes went from her to Hannah—and learn why she refused to convey more.

"My lord Cecil, I would not have roused you so early on a day when we have national issues at stake, but I need you to do two things."

"Of course, Your Grace."

"First, send a message to Chief Constable Whitcomb saying that I have personally interrogated Meg Milligrew and believe she is innocent of all his suspicions."

"Oh, Your Grace," Meg blurted, "I thank y—"

Elizabeth held up her hand. "Second, my lord, everyone is to take a good look at the diagram of possible murderers you have been keeping—and then you are all to keep your mouths shut about the fact that the Greshams themselves could be guilty and must yet be watched. I've summoned Sir Thomas here forthwith for further questioning."

"But Sally's at their house!" Meg cried. "And what if their own daughter recalls that she saw or heard one of them?"

"We must move quickly, but both of them love their

adopted daughter desperately. And I tell everyone here, just as I would bet my life that Meg had naught to do with Hannah's death, surely neither did my honorable, rational Thomas Gresham."

"Where've you been?" Jenks demanded when Meg joined him at the back gate to Kings Street just at dawn. "You're late."

"I had to check the herbs in my drying shed," she told him, out of breath. "No telling how long we'll be out today."

They hurried to Hannah's loft but saw by the lights above—and by glimpsing him through the large window they were to examine—that Hugh Dauntsey was upstairs, even at this early hour, so they headed for the nearby laundry with the sack of coins for the twins. Jenks was so excited to be the bearer of such riches that Meg's heart went out to him. She knew what it was to be in love, though never with Jenks. And she had Ned where she wanted him now—didn't she?

Her heart overflowing with love for Ned, she could let Jenks go with her blessing. How protective Ned had been of her when he was assigned to find that glove perfumer. She couldn't hold out against him much longer, and, after all these years of fighting him, she didn't want to. She only prayed he felt the same—and that the queen would want a marriage between her two longtime servants.

"It's still so early," Jenks said. "Bet Ursala's women aren't even there yet. Ursala said she usually stays in the shop 'til they come. Meantime, Pamela stakes out bushes and grass in the field to dry the linens." He bounced the purse once in his big hands. "Ursala's the practical one. She'll divide these coins up proper."

"And maybe save some for a dowry?" Meg teased, and even laughed to see him blush as the first hint of sun slanted westward into their faces through the narrow street.

They knocked on the shop door and entered, blinking in the darkness until their eyes slowly adjusted. The shutters Ursala had opened the morning they were with her were still closed.

"Ursala?" Jenks called out.

"They're probably still all asleep out in back."

He shook his head. "Not with the street door unlatched—I told her to keep it secure. Besides, if they don't have their spots staked out by now in the field, she said, they'll have to dry things in here and it takes forever."

"So they've all gone there today, that's all. Oh, look. There's some laundry sticking out of that tub—" Meg got out before she realized what she was looking at. Not linens but a woman's body bent over with her head and shoulders in the tub. Jenks lunged across the room to lift the woman out.

Limp, heavy, sodden. Dead?

"No! Ursala! No, oh dear God, no!" Jenks cried.

The sack of coins spilled, sending shillings all over the floor as he cradled the sopping body in his arms.

Chapter the Twelfth

"IS THERE SOME CRISIS WITH INTERNATIONAL financial matters, Your Grace?" Thomas Gresham blurted the moment he straightened from his bow. Also standing, the queen and Cecil faced him across the width of the long table, Her Majesty directly before him with her secretary of state on her left. When they said nothing at first, he went on, "To be summoned so quickly, I just assumed—"

"Did you not think it might be something about finding Hannah's murderer?" she demanded, leveling a look at him that would have frozen the Thames solid.

It was obvious that Elizabeth was fighting to control her temper. He'd seen it unleashed before, but never, thank God, at him. Two days ago, when she'd confronted him, he'd escaped with a smack of her hand on the table, though he knew she was capable of so much more. She'd vowed then that they would work together to solve Hannah's murder, but he sensed she was against him now. He did not have the gall to simply stare back but had to say something. He felt as tautly strung as an archer's bow, ready to snap, but he must speak up for himself.

"I—having been your money man, as you have called me, for years, and having served you well—"

"I know you have served me well, and I need no reminder of your genius or loyalty to me. I have summoned you here to return to you some property you have lost and of which you cannot possibly deny ownership."

With that, she smacked not just her hand but a gold ring onto the table between them. His eyes widened as he leaned forward to look closely at it. He instantly knew—feared—what it was but took his time picking it up. It appeared to be coated with some sort of paste, which sat in the engraved lines and seemed to glue the grasshopper's wings together.

"Ah, my signet ring. I have several of them," he declared, his voice just a bit too defiant to sound natural. "Four, I think. Where was this found, if I may ask?"

"It must have slipped off your hand in the liquid," she said.

He frowned; his pulse began to pound. "When I washed my h-hands?" he stammered. "Did my wife or the girls find it and give it to you for some reason?" He got that much out before he realized that Anne indeed might have given it to the queen. He'd thrown such a ring at her in their bedroom.

"I am asking the questions here," she said.

He told himself to keep quiet, but he plunged on anyway. "Did Sally find it—or Nash Badger?" His mind raced. He'd dispatched Badger to inspect the progress of the exchange. "I think, Your Majesty, the ring was lost in my house, to tell the truth."

"To tell the truth," she echoed, her tone almost mocking. She gripped the back of one of the tall chairs as if to brace herself. "Thomas, the girls did not send it to me, nor did your wife or Badger. This was discovered at the bottom of the starch bath in which Hannah died, so I am assuming it will help me get to the bottom of the mystery of her cruel murder—with your explicit help."

His knees nearly buckled. He leaned so heavily on his walking stick that he swayed before he regained his balance.

"Well, my lord?" Cecil spoke at last. "How could it possibly have gotten there?"

"May I sit down, Your Grace?"

"I try not to parlay at my council table with those I cannot trust or those who mean to do me or my people harm," she countered. "Pray tell me that could not possibly be you."

"No, Your Majesty. That could not p-possibly be me."

But, he thought, could Anne intend to implicate him with the ring? Surely she was not still that jealous or hateful, but if he were executed for a murder, she would have the rest of his fortune and Marie all to herself. Yet when and how could she have put the ring in the liquid in which Hannah had drowned?

"Jenks," Meg cried as he continued to hold the drowned woman in his lap where he'd collapsed onto the floor. "Jenks! We have to go for the queen before word gets out. It's too much like Hannah's murder. We have to tell the queen!"

He only nodded, sucking in great breaths and sobbing. Jenks never cried, never collapsed under duress, never lost his mettle. How much and how quickly he must have loved this girl. Meg's heart truly ached for him.

Jenks was getting soaked now, too, as if he were drowning in his own tears. With Ursala's sopped hair flat to her head and her clothes clinging to her, she looked much smaller than Hannah had with her hair and garments stiffened by starch.

"You stay here with her, then, but lock this place up till I get back," she said, bending down to grip his shoulder. "Jenks, shouldn't we look in the back room to be sure we didn't corner the one who did this?"

Nodding, Jenks laid Ursala carefully on the floor. Not only had a lot of water sloshed out there and his coins spilled, but, Meg noted, several bulbous roots lay about. Her cuckoo-pint stolen from those sacks at Hannah's? That would mean the same murderer, indeed.

Swiping at his tears with his wet sleeve, Jenks drew both sword and knife and headed for the back rooms where the family lived. Meg prayed he wouldn't find other bodies there, but if the culprit were hidden within, she could tell from the set of Jenks's shoulders he was a dead man.

Crouching, weapons at the ready, Jenks banged the door open with his booted foot, then leaped inside. "Don't see anyone," he called to her. "Help me look around, under beds and the like."

"And on shelves," she muttered, starting to tremble. Every time she was sent to find someone, catastrophe struck: first Hannah; then that horrid glove perfumer, Celia; now this.

She helped Jenks search the three small rooms in which the family lived. Ursala had evidently inhabited the smallest chamber, one with no windows, while Pamela and her husband had the one on the other side with the common room between.

"Nothing," she said, straightening from peering under the last bed while he stood ready with his weapons.

"Nothing but my hopes dashed," he whispered. He seemed to wilt before her eyes as he resheathed the sword and knife. "Yes," he said, "hie yourself to the queen, before the constable is summoned."

Meg shook all the harder at the thought of having to face

any constable, the local one or the chief man, who seemed to dog her so. Everyone knew constables were laughingstocks, so maybe he was too inept to find Hannah's real killer. And he was part of the Parliament that wanted to give Her Majesty much grief until she agreed to wed. At least, Meg prayed, the queen would—she must—get to the bottom of all this.

"Jenks, I am truly, truly sorry," she said, turning back at the outside door only to see him lean against the wall, then sink to his knees beside the body again. Had he even heard her? "I'll find someone to fetch her family from the field, too," she added, and slowly opened the street door, peeking out to be certain no one suspicious was lurking. But when she stepped out, Pamela, rushing toward the door, bumped into her.

"Oh, Mistress Milligrew!" she cried. Meg seized her shoulders to halt her entry to the laundry, but she had no idea what to say to prepare her for what lay within.

"You been talking to Pamela?" the woman asked, confusing her even more. "No 'fense, but I been hoping Her Majesty would send Jenks. So's I told Melly—that's my name for her, and she calls me Lally—I'd stake out our ground this time. Peter's guarding it 'cause Pamela weren't feeling too good. Sour stomach, but we're hoping she might be with child and not really ailing."

Jenks came to the door, barring her way before she could see inside. "Pamela," he said, "I'm sorry, but . . ." His voice trailed off, and he gaped at her. "Ursala?"

All Meg got out was, "It's Pamela must have stayed here instead—"

"Ursala!" Jenks cried, and hugged the woman hard.

He might not have recognized Pamela drowned, Meg

thought, but he sure knew Ursala alive. The last thing Meg saw before she headed for the palace was the look of relief on his face, shining through the pain.

" 'S blood and bones!" Elizabeth shouted, losing her battle with her composure as she banged the chair into the table so hard it shuddered. "Thomas Gresham, I want you to tell me how your ring got in that starch bath in Hannah's loft! And just leave Anne, Marie, Badger, and even Sally out of this for now." She still felt a bit guilty for sneaking into his house last night, but she intended to ferret out his own guilt at any cost.

"The ring was probably Hannah's," he admitted. He cleared his throat. "That is, years ago I gave it to Gretta as a pledge of my love, and it provided a way she could buy things on credit if I was back here in London. Hannah took it from her the last time she visited her sister—when I was not there. I just thank God she did not also pilfer my and Gretta's infant daughter that day."

"Did she intend to pilfer Marie or her affections lately?" Elizabeth asked. She did not believe that of Hannah, since she had evidently not answered Marie's impassioned letters—unless she was just trying to get the girl to come to her or long for her more. Absence was indeed known to make the heart grow fonder.

"She dared not, Your Grace. Neither Anne nor I would have allowed it."

Which could have been a motive for murder, she thought, but she didn't say so. His countenance had gone from ruddy to ashen, and she didn't want him fainting at her feet. "Sit, Thomas," she said, and sat herself, though Cecil stayed standing. "Did Hannah use that ring that same way, to try to buy goods in Antwerp or here?" she pursued when he was settled. "It seems she was careless handling money."

"She threatened to use it to gain credit. I gave her money instead, and she promised to give the ring back."

"But, as far as you know, she kept it?"

He nodded.

"Ah, more truth slides out, as slippery as starch. Thomas, did you kill Hannah von Hoven to stop her from besmirching your good name financially or from blackmailing you or your family?"

"No, Your Grace! I swear it!" he cried, leaning forward over the table instead of sitting back as she would expect a guilty man to do. He looked so appalled that she wanted desperately to believe him, but she stiffened her backbone.

"Cecil, I heard the same song in this very chamber from Meg just yesterday," she said, without looking at him.

"What does Sally's mother have to do with this?" Thomas asked. "If I were you, I'd sooner question that friend of Hannah's who tried to make it sound as if my daughter were guilty, the one who said Marie kept staring up at the starch house window."

The queen almost revealed to him all Marie had told of her visit to the starch house, but she decided to keep her cards closer to her chest right now. "You see, it is possible that Hannah's killer climbed out that window and in again, perhaps in a fit of conscience to tenderly arrange her body," she told him. "I can envision you *wanting* to do that in honor of her ties and resemblance to her dead sister, your mistress, but I do not believe with that bad leg you *could* climb in or out a loft window."

He stared at her, gasping like a fish out of water.

"And that leg of yours is the only reason right now, Sir

Thomas Gresham," she plunged on, her voice becoming more strident as he tried to interrupt her, "that you are yet walking at liberty without having your movements and motives questioned by Chief Constable Nigel Whitcomb!"

"But I—you must know, Your Grace, that I would never—"

"I know you would never cheat me at finances, my lord, but am learning things about you day by day that I would never have believed a week ago. You may sit there and write out for me exactly where you were at what time the entire day that Hannah died—the day you were riding about the town to find Marie—and a complete reckoning of what words passed between the two of you the day she came asking for money at Gresham House."

With a quick knock, Clifford opened the door. She had told him they were not to be disturbed unless important news came from Jenks and Meg or Ned—or the northern shires were going up in flames.

"Some information has come, Your Majesty," Clifford intoned.

She rose and stepped out into the hallway; the big yeoman shut the door behind her. Meg stood there, disheveled and wringing her hands, looking as dreadful as the day she'd found Hannah's body.

"Well?" Elizabeth said.

"Because Hugh Dauntsey was still in Hannah's loft, Jenks and I went direct to the laundry. There we found one of the twins drowned in a vat. We thought it was Ursala, but it was Pamel—"

"Drowned, too? Dead?"

Meg nodded wildly.

"Is Jenks still there?"

"Yes, and there's water on the floor and some of my cuckoo-pint herbs, just like—"

"Write out directions for me to the laundry, then go find Ned, and both of you meet us at Ursala's as soon as possible," the queen interrupted. "You heard where to look for him, where he might be, and if you come across Celia without him, just avoid her. Meg, now!" she cried, and pushed her away.

"Clifford," she went on, "you will go with me to the laundry, while my lord Cecil stays here with Thomas Gresham. I must change my garments and summon Lady Radcliffe. I hardly want to draw attention to myself in these pearls and brocades."

"Thank God you're here!" Jenks blurted the moment Elizabeth and her two companions stepped through the door of the laundry. It was, the queen saw, too dark in here with the window shutters closed. The air was damp and heavy with death. They'd laid the body out on the worktable with a white cloth over the face. On a stool at Pamela's head sat an older man, evidently the dead woman's husband, with his hands gripped as if in prayer. Ursala was seated on another stool, with Jenks standing behind her, at Pamela's feet, one of which Ursala kept hold of as if she could comfort the corpse.

When the queen swept back the hood of her cloak, everyone rose, looking stunned and overwrought. "Stay where you are," she told them as she approached the body.

The tabletop was wet; how much this murder reminded her of Hannah's. She had no doubt it was the same killer, but felt furious she was no closer to knowing who that was.

"Ursala and . . ." the queen said with a nod at the man.

"Peter Browne," Jenks said, "Pamela's husband."

"Ursala and Peter, I greatly regret this dreadful turn of events. Both Ursala and Pamela have been of help to me, and I will see she is properly buried."

Ursala looked dazed, but Peter seemed to come to life as he squinted up at Clifford. Perhaps, the queen thought, he hadn't seen so large a man before. "Thankee, Yer Majesty," he said only.

"I didn't let anyone pick up the coins I dropped on the floor yet," Jenks put in. His eyes were bloodshot; he looked as if he'd been through a battle.

"All right," she said. "Now if Peter and Ursala would just leave me here for a few minutes to see to things . . . Jenks, perhaps you can continue to sit with them in their chambers."

"Yes, Your Majesty, right at the back of the building here. Peter?" he said, and helped the man up, then Ursala. "Oh, Melly, Melly, I'm so sorry," she sobbed into her hands as Jenks escorted them out and closed the door. Though their voices were muted, Elizabeth could hear Jenks talking quietly to them. Her brawny guard had come a long way from just serving her with shield and sword, she thought, then forced herself to concentrate, for she must not take long. She would send Clifford almost immediately for the constable, who, she had no doubt, would again send for Nigel Whitcomb.

"Clifford, open at least one of those pairs of shutters," she said, and gently lifted the cloth from the corpse's face. When more light shot into the room, Elizabeth gasped. The dead woman's lips were horribly red and chapped. Perhaps her mouth had been scraped against the wooden vat in which she had been thrust to die.

The queen examined the vat, then studied the wet floor

Meg had mentioned. Yes, scattered coins and several cuckoopint roots that had bounced into corners. "Rosie," she said, "scan the rest of the floor to see how many of those round bulbs you see."

"And pick them up?"

"No. They are a link to the other murder," she said, almost to herself. "Look," she said, pointing at the table next to the body. "Perhaps Pamela was setting the table for her breakfast, for there's a pewter plate, spoon, and cup. And what's this strange substance on the plate?" she asked, bending closer to study a small amount of dark, gritty powder with a consistency somewhere between soil and dust. "Rosie, ask Ursala to step back in here."

Elizabeth sniffed at it. Vaguely familiar. Then she recalled Anne Gresham's description of the imported *chocolata* cakes: little ones, round, brown, dry as dust and likely to break into dust, too, and bitter as can be without sugar.

"Ursala," the queen said, when Rosie brought her out, "is this dark dust something for breakfast or that you use to clean clothes here?"

The young woman peered closer. "Nothing dark cleans clothes. Never seen the likes. If it was here before, I didn't see it." She sounded as if she were in a barrel; her eyelids were swollen. To have lost her good friend Hannah and now her identical twin—which brought up other concerns the queen would have to consider. Had the murderer meant to kill Pamela or Ursala? Was he striking at female servants who worked for the queen? If so, was Dingen van der Passe in danger—or Meg?

"Here, I can taste it and probably tell what it is," Ursala said, and reached for the stuff.

"No!" Elizabeth cried, yanking her arm back. "It's best

left alone for now, that's all. And what might Pamela have drunk in the morning?" the queen inquired, picking up and looking closely into the empty pewter cup. Even in this dismal light, she could see the slightest trace of dark liquid rimming the inside bottom of it.

"Bread and curds and whey," Ursala said. "At least almost always."

Bread, curds, and whey were all light-hued, Elizabeth thought. The remnants of the drink and the spilled powder were dark—so dark.

She thanked the dazed woman and sent her back to Jenks. She'd like to know if it was *chocolata* powder or not, but she was taking no chances. It could be anything. Besides, there was cuckoo-pint on the floor, and Pamela's lips looked scraped raw. Meg had said even the pollen of the plant could be deadly.

If this was *chocolata*, who could have sent it here? It was ridiculous that laundresses could afford expensive stuff like that rare, secret Spanish import, let alone that they would know how to obtain some. Nor could households like this afford the sugar the bitter stuff needed. Her belly cramped again. The only people she knew who had access to the new Spanish fashion were, unfortunately, in the Gresham household, and if the drink was spiked with poison cuckoo-pint, several had access to that, including whoever killed Hannah.

"Clifford," she said, "open another pair of shutters. Rosie, come here and help me open her mouth with this spoon so we don't touch her sores. And, Clifford, bar the door to keep out any of her workers who arrive."

"Unless," Rosie put in under her breath, "like poor Hannah, she had agreed to keep them away to meet with the murderer."

"Not this time, I think, or Ursala would have known. No, the one who meant her harm just walked in through an unlocked door or managed to talk his way in for—or with—something."

Reminded of the dark dust again, not touching the powder, she brushed about half of it into her handkerchief and knotted it, then tied it to the cord of her pomander. Reluctantly she turned to her terrible task.

Shuddering, Rosie held the spoon, and with it they pried open the quickly stiffening jaw muscles to peer inside Pamela's mouth. "Could it be, Your Grace, that someone forced something hot into her mouth to punish her for telling on him or her?"

"Telling what?"

"Maybe, if the killer thought she was Ursala, for telling that she'd seen Marie Gresham or Anne Gresham near the site of the first murder. I don't know. I don't know about any of this. Ugh."

Everything seemed to circle back to the Greshams, Elizabeth thought. Though the light was still not good, she immediately noted two things about Pamela's death. One, like Hannah, she had swallowed or inhaled water, dark-looking water, too, maybe some of the *chocolata.* Two, though she was no doubt drowned, there had been an attempt to finish her off another way first. Not with strangulation this time, she would wager, but by poisoning, for the insides of Pamela's cheeks and tongue were as raw and red as a bloody, uncooked beefsteak.

Elizabeth rushed over to look again at the fatal vat of liquid. "Someone fetch a candle or two," she ordered as she stared into the darkish water where Pamela had been found. She didn't appear to be bleeding, so that wasn't blood in the water. Could it be *chocolata?* Cuckoo-pint herb didn't turn water dark like that but made it milky.

Rosie located a lantern, which Clifford lit with his flint. "Hold the light over the vat."

To Elizabeth's amazement, the water was not tinted at all. It had only appeared so in the wooden tub and dim room. How many times in this investigation had she found dead ends when she thought something might be a solid clue? At least, thank God, no gold signet ring glittered from the depths.

She told Clifford to fetch Jenks. "We must call in the constable," she told him. "You may stay to give Ursala support. If the authorities ask whether anyone else has been here, do not lie to them."

"Yes, Your Grace. I am grateful you're letting me stay with her—she's lost so much."

"At least, my man," she said, squeezing his rock-hard upper arm, "I believe she has found you."

"One more thing," Jenks said. "Peter tells me that a man as big as Clifford—first, he thought it was Clifford—used to be in this area a lot, loitering around the starch house. Wore black, he did, but for a red-and-blue-striped taffeta cap, and he had a Dutch accent."

"Dirck van der Passe," Elizabeth cried as both Rosie and Clifford nodded.

"Could be," Jenks said, " 'specially since I heard he admitted he was taking walks round here. But if the constable asks, should I say Meg found this body, too?" he asked, still whispering.

Elizabeth frowned down at the cuckoo-pint herb and recalled again Meg's warning about how poisonous it could be. "Don't be afraid for Meg," she told Jenks, "for I'm sure her time can be accounted for all morning—I'll vouch for that. What, man? Why are you looking at me like that?"

Her stalwart Jenks managed to appear even more shaken than he had when she first arrived. "She—Meg came running in late and out of breath to go with me this morning," he said, his voice a mere whisper. "Said she had to check her drying herbs first in the shed. Well, that could be, 'cause losing the profit from selling her starch herbs, she's got to make more money selling something."

"Ridiculous!" Elizabeth insisted aloud at the mere thought that Meg could be at all involved in murder, no matter what Constable Whitcomb had claimed. To cloak her thoughts, she added, "I can just pay her a bit more if she's fretting about supporting Sally, and the girl is making her own wages. Meg is happy for your new-fledged relationship with Ursala," she insisted as if they'd spoken of Meg's possible motive for a second murder. "I know she is, especially now that she and Ned are getting on."

"Oh, yes, Your Grace, that's sure," he said, but suddenly neither of them sounded like they meant it.

Chapter the Thirteenth

B THE QUEEN DID NOT RETURN IMMEDIATELY TO THE palace. Instead, after she sent Clifford to fetch the local constable, with Rosie in tow, she hurried to Hannah's nearby loft to see if Hugh Dauntsey was still there. The downstairs door was ajar, so she and Rosie tiptoed up the steps.

He wore forget-me-not blue with a matching cape as if he were at court instead of in this sad, haunted place. Rather than sitting at the table, he was perched on the single stool before the large window across the room. Head bent, he perused something on a long piece of parchment, perhaps his final reckoning of Hannah's earthly goods.

The queen's gaze skimmed the loft, which smelled of something fresh and looked well scrubbed. It had been stripped to the bare bones; the worktable, empty braziers, poking rods, wooden ruff forms, and the starch bath that had been Hannah's coffin were lined up tidily at the top of the stairs, ready to be hauled away.

Elizabeth held up her hand to Rosie for quiet and studied the big window from afar. She recalled how she had struggled to close it in her nightmare, but the breeze kept blowing into her face. Could that have been a sign she must open this investigation to consider those she did not want to blame, namely the Greshams?

Dauntsey had the window completely closed, and it didn't loom as large as it had when it was open. Yet the loft itself seemed to have grown in size and import since she'd seen it.

As Elizabeth climbed the last several stairs that brought her into view, Dauntsey looked over, started, and leaped off his stool.

"This place is not open for bus—Your Majesty? Here?" he cried and, rolling up his documents, strode quickly toward them.

"Do you think I need a coach or mounted entourage to go about my city?" she asked him as he bowed. "I was called to the scene of a tragedy near here, since," she said, watching him closely and drawing out her words, "a whitster was murdered this morn in somewhat the same way poor Hannah was dispatched in this very place—in this very tub." She walked over to knock her fist against the wood, glanced again into his concerned face, and went to look closer at the window.

"But—who died?" he asked, scurrying after her. "And by the same hand as Hannah?"

"I warrant so. I fear we've a filthy-hearted multiple murderer loose among those of my city who labor to keep all of us clean and fashionable."

She noted the window was nearly waist high off the floor. In that respect, unless one had a bad leg, it would be easy enough to climb in or out. It was nearly as wide as an oriel window or a big bay but hardly the height of one. Rather, it only came to the top of her head. She lifted the heavy metal latch and hefted the window as both Rosie and Dauntsey hurried to help.

"Stand clear," she said and raised it a few feet. Though made of leaded, mullioned sections, it was unique in that it lifted upward in one piece instead of swinging out in separate parts. "It's stuffy in here, Dauntsey. Did you see anything about the place to prop this open?"

"I—no, I have not. I used one of the poking sticks the other day—here . . ."

He fetched one quickly and brought it to her. It was a metal crimping iron to put S-curves in ruffs, but she'd seen similar ones for hair. It, too, was quite heavy. Too bad Hannah did not get to one of these for a weapon in time. Had she known her attacker, or had he—or she—simply taken her unawares by quietly coming up the stairs much as she herself had just done?

"Is there anything I can do to help with this latest tragedy, Your Majesty?" Dauntsey said, rubbing his ink-stained hands together. "I would be delighted to settle that estate, too. What is the name of the murdered whitster?" he repeated.

"There is no need, for this woman has heirs. She is—was—the sister of a woman you've met, Ursala Hemmings."

"Her sis— Not Ursala, then, but her sister?"

"She was an identical twin, you see, so it could be that the killer made a mistake. The victim this time was Pamela Browne."

He looked quite dismayed. "How dreadful for Ursala, first her friend here and then . . ." His voice trailed off. "Terrible. By the way, I have here for Ursala the pair of perfumed gloves you wanted me to save for her. I regret if I sound confused, but I've been so distressed by what Lord Paulet has suggested to me—that you have heard some dreadful rumor about my cheating at stocks. I assure you, I am no such charlatan."

No wonder, she thought, the man was so on edge with her. She'd known Paulet would tell his minion that she had hinted about illicit stock market dealings.

"It galls me greatly," Dauntsey said, clearing his throat, "that such a rumor might ruin my resurrected reputation with Your Gracious Majesty, for I am innocent of such murmurings. But what galls me more is that I can guess who is spreading such lies, and you always listen to him."

"You know a great deal," she countered, glancing out and down at the roof below the window. Though it did not appear so from the street, it was steeply slanted. A person would have to sprout wings to risk going out this heavy window, which could bang down if the prop holding it were disturbed. He or she would slide right off the shingle roof, not to mention being seen by a field full of whitsters.

"It was Thomas Gresham, was it not, Your Majesty?" Dauntsey went on. "I insist I must have an opportunity to answer such slanders. Why, if duels or jousts of honor were still fought at Smithfield, I would challenge him."

"Slap him across the face with the perfumed gloves?"

"I pray you are not mocking me, Your Majesty."

Thank God, she thought, the roof as well as the window could indeed help to clear Thomas Gresham, for with a bad leg and a cane, he'd never risk this. And a woman in skirts would have to be foolhardy and desperate to climb out, then back in.

On the other hand, whoever had killed Hannah could have heard a noise on the stairs and hidden in the room when Marie entered and saw Hannah, newly murdered. If not behind the rolls of fabric, then behind the big starch tub. It might be not only Marie's lack of memory protecting her but the fact that the killer knew the girl had not seen him or her.

"I am not mocking you, man, for I believe you have served me well with Hannah's goods so far. Besides, Sir Thomas's leg he shattered several years ago would keep him from accepting your duel, so I want to hear no more of such tripe. If you are both to serve me in the future, you must get on—with each other as well as with me." She finally stared full-faced into Dauntsey's strange eyes, something she tried to avoid. As if he did not want to face her, either, he quickly gazed out the window over her shoulder.

"You mentioned that the killer is targeting those who keep all of us clean and fashionable," he said. "Not only, Your Majesty, does that describe a particular person, but one who is ranting this very morning in the field out there. Did you note him well?"

She turned back toward the window, scolding herself for not looking out of it farther than the roof. Rosie came to stand beside her as Dauntsey peered out, too.

"The Reverend Hosea Cantwell," Elizabeth said. Occasionally, amidst the distant murmur of women working over their linens, she could hear his strident tones. She could see him, too, standing on a barrel in the midst of a field snowy with sheets.

"He may not pose the danger your rebellious northern lords do, Your Majesty," Dauntsey said, folding his arms over his chest, "but he's haranguing those of us who favor following your lead with courtly fashions, and on the very morning, evidently, that a whitster just happened to be murdered near where a starcher was killed last week. He's got quite a crowd, too, a captive audience, and when they hear one of their own has been punished by some invisible hand—"

"I do not need you to do my thinking for me," she clipped out, "but I'll see him arrested if he's preaching against me again. Let me have those gloves, if you please, man, and bring your papers to me soon."

He handed her the pair of gloves; they smelled of lavender and rich ambergris, the latter of which she'd seen on the perfumer Celia's worktable. "I yet need to sell these starching goods to the van der Passes," he called after her as she made her way around the items piled near the stairs. "Dirck is coming to look at these things and make a bid within the hour."

Perfect, she thought. The man had been seen in this area, and if he was culpable in or had information about these murders, this would be the perfect place for her to question him. Right now, she was going to see that Hosea Cantwell got down off his high horse.

"Whatever can we do, Your Grace?" Rosie asked, hurrying down the steps behind her. "We need Clifford or Jenks to cart Cantwell off, don't we?"

"We'll stop at the royal mews and see who's there. As my lord Cecil would say, it's time to stir the pot again. Then perhaps Hosea Cantwell or Dirck van der Passe will float right to the top."

Thomas Gresham could recall being in more pain only once before, when his leg shattered, and that had been physical instead of cerebral. This was turning into a dreadful nightmare.

"Here are detailed renditions of all the queen asked for, my lord Cecil," he said, and handed the sheaf of papers to the watchful man across the conference table. "May I go now?"

"I have no authority for that," Cecil said. "Stay while I glance through these."

"My building crews are expecting me on the site of the exchange today. The blocks of marble for the frieze above the front arches are being delivered."

"Then they will have to do without you."

"May I at least send my agent a note authorizing he sign for them?"

"And send him your signet ring to seal it with?" Cecil said.

Judas Priest. Gresham swore his father's old oath silently. This powerful man was hostile to him, too. He was lost indeed.

"Send the note, then," Cecil said almost begrudgingly, "but I must read it first."

"And my wife? May I not let her know at least that I am detained here for a while? That way, she won't worry something's amiss—even though it is."

"You may write your wife," Cecil said, still skimming the report he'd written, as if Gresham were some criminal.

Surely, Thomas thought, Elizabeth of England would not send him to the Tower to be questioned. He hated the place. In fact, he detested that entire end of town with the Thames rushing through the arches of London Bridge and all those small, crowded shops clinging to the very edges of it. It would be fine with him if the shops that would grace his exchange would sap the strength from that hodgepodge, where crowds of humanity shoved each other above the roaring torrent and criminals' heads were stuck on pikes.

He shuddered again. Surely, Her Grace did not believe he had murdered Hannah, even if the woman had been both a thorn in his side and a living reminder of his lost love. English law executed those adjudged a murderer in various ways, depending on their class, connections, and crime. Not being of the nobility, surely he would not be beheaded. The mere thought of his head displayed on the bridge for all to see horrified him. That shame would destroy the fame he had hoped to achieve through leaving London the grand edifice of his mercantile exchange.

He fought to collect his rampaging thoughts. "I will write my wife now, that she should not worry," he told Cecil.

"I'm afraid she will have to," Cecil said, turning to the next page of his report. "I want you to write her that you are here at Whitehall, and she's to come forthwith—without the children—to join you here."

"You don't suspect . . . don't think . . . that Anne aided or abetted . . ."

"I'll consult with the queen on that. Just write the note, Sir Thomas. Then I'll give you a comfortable room with a guard outside your door to rest up in until your wife arrives and Her Majesty returns."

Mounted on one of her favorite horses from the royal mews, a big bay, Elizabeth, with Rosie and four grooms also mounted, headed a block away to see if Cantwell was still raving. Indeed, he was. They heard him before they saw him as they stopped at the fringe of the field behind four oaks, which were rattling their brown leaves in the rising wind.

"You women of England must take a stand for decency!" Cantwell was shouting. His clarion voice carried well on the breeze. The queen had always wondered how he would sound when he preached, and now she knew.

"If there are starchers among you, renounce your tasks of

stiffening neck ruffs for stiff necks, ruffs as large as cart-wheels for the queen, her nobles, and even the upstart gentry who would ape their betters. But are those who are slaves to style really their betters?"

"The rogue is as good as urging them to sedition," she told Rosie. "Remind me not to exile him to the northern shires so he can preach more rebellion there."

"Remember," Cantwell shouted, punctuating his words with grand gestures, "it is far better to have a millstone tied about your neck and be cast into the sea than to mislead someone to sin. And you laundresses and whitsters who labor to wash the fine and fancy linens of others, their ruffs or the tablecloths whereon they feast daily at bacchanals—"

"I doubt," the queen muttered, "that these women have a clue what that means. And it's a lie from the pit of hell, which this man evidently thinks he has the keys to."

"—or the bedsheets of sin in which they cavort" he railed on. "You will answer for it, all of you, in one way or the other. Do you not think the hand of God passed judgment on the poor starcher who was murdered recently? And only today another of your ilk was so judged, when a laundress was drowned in her own laundry tub."

"I'm not even sure that is common news yet. I want that man brought to me," Elizabeth ordered her men, "but dismount to take him. I do not want horses' hoofs sullying the work of these hardworking, good Englishwomen."

Three of the four grooms dismounted and were about to wade into the crowd when the queen commanded, "Hold a moment!" To her amazement and amusement, despite what the rogue had been saying, she saw what was going to happen before he did.

Some of the women behind Cantwell had lifted a so-called

sheet of sin between them and were creeping toward him. Before he knew it, as the laundresses made a circular move that reminded Elizabeth of a Maypole dance, they had wrapped the man in linen and pulled him from his perch. She could hear him shouting, muffled now, and, if she stood in her stirrup with a hand on her sidesaddle, she could see him writhing on the ground as they rolled him like a great, growing snowball.

"Let him be for a while, men, then bring him to the palace," Elizabeth ordered. "And if you haul him to me in a linen net, be certain to pay the woman whose sheet or tablecloth you take."

Despite her predicament with the murders, the queen shouted a laugh as she dismounted and handed her horse's reins to the still-mounted groom. She shot a swift glance up at the window of Hannah's loft and saw that Dauntsey had been watching, though he quickly turned away. Could this be where Marie had stood to stare at the window? And had she seen someone there she could now not recall?

"With me, Rosie," she said. "Perhaps we shall yet snag another suspicious man. I intend to question Dirck van der Passe on the very site of Hannah's murder."

Despite Hugh Dauntsey's vehement protests, Elizabeth sent him away. Rosie didn't like it much better when the queen had her lie down in the now empty starch tub in which Hannah had been drowned. "And do not show yourself until I say, 'I can picture poor Hannah there even now,'" Elizabeth instructed.

Then, hoping Dauntsey would not dare to warn her prey that she was lying in wait for him like a spider, she sat down on the single stool by the window to face the door. Outside in St. Martin's fields, her grooms had rescued the disheveled, furious Puritan cleric, only to cart him off toward the palace. Though the women had bested Cantwell, they did not celebrate but whispered in clumps, probably about the dreadful demise of one of their own.

She heard footsteps on the stairs, and her heart began to pound. Who had Hannah been waiting for, perhaps in this very place, someone she'd let her women go home for, so she could face him or her alone? Thomas with that haunting adoration for his lost Gretta, which still shone in his eyes? He might not make it in or out the window, but he could hide within. Marie had said she'd heard what must have been a liaison gone wrong or an attempted rape—if Marie had not already hit her head and been hallucinating.

Dirck van der Passe appeared up the steps, all six feet plus of him. Suddenly she didn't feel so brave, but she would face him down at any cost.

"Your Majesty?" Dirck said, squinting into the daylight streaming in behind her. "I—Hugh Dauntsey said meet him here to buy some starching goods, *ja,* he did."

She walked closer so that he wouldn't see Rosie in the tub. "You knew where to find the place, I warrant," Elizabeth said.

"I been by before. Ve settled that. I vas just walking."

"This is where poor Hannah died, you know. She fought for her life here, choked half to death before she was drowned in her own starch tub. The murderer hid at first, then crept out from where he'd secreted himself. He took poor Hannah out of her starch bath and put her on the shelf. Did you know all that, Dirck?"

"No, but you know all that?" he whispered, his eyes darting around the room.

"I know all that because there was an eyewitness."

"Ja?" he said as his jaw dropped.

"An unseen one, one we've kept hidden but who will now testify so we can arrest the killer. It would be better for him if he came forward to confess, for he'll not escape now."

She hadn't meant to say all that, especially about a witness, but she would have Marie and Sally well protected. She probably should have bluffed everyone she suspected days ago—told them they had been accused by a hidden eyewitness—but she hadn't been sure about Marie for a while.

"Drowned there?" he asked, pointing at the tub, which was behind her and the other stacked starching goods.

"It was under the window then, but yes," Elizabeth said. "I can picture poor Hannah there even now. Can you?"

At her cue, Rosie sat straight up as if the dead had been called to rise on Judgment Day. Dirck jumped back and stumbled over a brazier. Two poking sticks went rolling under his big feet to send him to his knees, but he was gibbering all the while, "I swear I know nothing, nothing of it. I'm an honorable Flemish knight," he cried, his eyes still wide on Rosie.

"I'm telling you, you were seen," the queen accused.

"Ja, 'tis true I knew vere her shop vas, even stopped some of her customers from going in—gave them promises of better prices at our place, took some of the ruffs there myself before they went up her stairs. That's all I did, I swear by all that's holy!" he cried, still on his knees, gripping his hands together as if begging for absolution.

" 'S blood," she muttered. That confession wasn't the one she wanted, but it was one she believed. He looked distressed enough that he would have blurted out a murder, too, wouldn't he? She herself had let slip about an eyewitness, so she had to send for Sally and Marie to be brought to the palace.

It took Meg nearly three hours to get to Eastcheap and locate Ned. He said he'd sent Bates back to Whitehall to report their lack of a prisoner. He had, at least, discovered that Celia no longer worked for the same glover and had not returned home—if he could believe the two women she'd been living with.

"But I tell you," he said to Meg as they hurried westward toward the palace, "if I couldn't get them to talk, no one could."

"Turned on the charm with the ladies again?" she managed to get out between gasps. She had a stitch in her side from running.

"Meg, my Meg," he said, swinging her around to face him. "My stock-in-trade is to convince people to like me and to believe in me."

"You're a great success at both, especially with the ladies who flock to—"

He gave her a little shake as others bustled past where Kings Street met the Strand. "If we are going not only to get on but to get together, Meg Milligrew, you must accept that and trust me, trust that my career depends on, as I said, being liked and believed. I'm vowing here and now, though, that it is only you I care for deeply, only you I—love."

He'd said that as if he had a bitter taste—pure poison—in his mouth, but she nearly melted to a warm puddle on the cold cobbles anyway. She'd be willing to give him all the years of her life to prove that and to learn to say it better. She believed it already, though, because he'd never said the like before, not to her or anyone else all the times he'd had his trysts and tumbles, not that she'd heard of, anyway. And she'd been watching Ned real close for years.

"It's not just, just," she said, fighting for words herself, "that I look like and can sometimes sound like the woman you adore and can never have—Her Grace?"

"I do adore Her Grace, so I shall amend my vow. I shall still keep her on a pedestal but keep you in my life and in my bed, if you will allow it."

"A marital bed, Ned Topside."

"Of course. Didn't I say that? I do want much more of you than your fair brow and those seashell ears you've let me fondle and kiss before. I'll ask you again later, when death is not our business but life—together."

"Now that was the prettiest speech you ever gave in any play, my love, and I'll hold you to it," she said as they set off again.

Holding hands, even in the thickening crowd, they rushed toward the vast grounds of Whitehall. Just as they broached the Kings street entry, Meg heard a cry. "That's her. There! Seize her!"

She wondered if a female cutpurse was loose in the crowd. Or had one of the queen's own guards spotted someone suspicious trying to get into the palace?

A burly man stepped between her and Ned and chopped his arm down to break their grips. From behind her, two other men took her arms and turned her away from Ned, who was shouting her name.

Everything blurred. Sounds, sights, smells. The world began to spin out of control.

"Margaret, alias Meg, Milligrew," an agitated voice intoned, "you are under the aegis of the chief constable of the

City of London for questioning under duress for the murder of one Hannah von Hoven."

"Ned!" she screamed as the crowd, the accusations, the entire scene seemed to suffocate her. "I demand to see the queen!" she shrieked. "I am a servant of the queen. I demand to see the queen!"

But she was hustled off so quickly in the opposite direction, she knew that no one who could help could hear her.

Chapter the Fourteenth

AS SOON AS THE QUEEN RETURNED TO HER ROOMS in the palace, she summoned Cecil. "My lord, we must send some guards to watch Marie, and Sally, of course, for safety's sake. I have let out to Dirck van der Passe that there was an eyewitness to Hannah's murder. I doubt he is the murderer, but word could spread. If Anne Gresham protests her daughter being closely guarded, that is just too bad, for someone could creep into Gresham House to get to Marie. 'S blood, I've proved that."

"Perhaps Lady Gresham won't be there when the guards arrive, as I sent for her nearly an hour ago."

"Good. But not Marie and Sally?"

"I had no idea—"

"Sometimes it seems that everything conspires against us," she cried, smacking her hands into her skirts. "Are Ned and Bates back yet with word of the glove perfumer?"

"Ned sent Bates back to say they'd had no luck, but Ned was going to pass himself off as Celia's friend at her old residence."

Elizabeth heaved a huge sigh. "Which means Meg might miss them both. My lord, send Bates at once to Gresham

House at the head of a mounted and armed entourage. He was there with us that night, so he knows the way. Charge him to protect the girls until I arrive to fetch them in my coach, for on second thought, they would be even safer here."

Cecil rushed from the room before she realized she'd forgotten to ask where he'd put Thomas and to tell him that Hosea Cantwell was being held here. At least, the Gresham family would soon again be under the royal roof, where she could keep an eye on them and interrogate them further.

She untied the handkerchief that held the dark powder. Was it her imagination that the substance seemed to glow in the shadows? She carried it into the early afternoon sunlight pouring through her window. Now she could see that the grit was composed of three distinct substances: white specks, perhaps sugar, as well as a dark brown—the *chocolata?*—and a coarser tan grain, the latter, no doubt, the ground poison herb.

If only Meg were here to identify it. Who had so carefully prepared this mixture, then given it to poor Pamela and convinced her to try it? Or had a drink made with it been forced down her throat before she was drowned? Strangest yet, surely not many knew cuckoo-pint herbs were poison. That made her fear the van der Passes might yet be involved, though Dirck had merely confessed to drawing away Hannah's customers. Was he guilty of eliminating her and then dispatching someone he feared was an eyewitness?

Cecil hurried back in with Ned. "Did Meg find you?" she began, then saw that Ned was not only disheveled but bloodied.

"Hell's gates, man, what happened?" she cried, rushing to him. It must have been something extreme. Ned was always protective of his appearance, and now his eye was nearly swollen shut and his nose had been smashed crooked.

"The chief constable's men—took Meg." He was gasping and breathing through his mouth. He had a split lip, too.

"*Took* her?"

"Accused her—of Hannah's murder, arrested her. I tried to stop them—big louts—all of them."

"Perhaps," Cecil said, "after the two days he was promised, Whitcomb felt he had a right to question Meg."

"He had no such right! Ned, where did they take her?"

"I know not. I tried to follow them, but they hit me. I fell and— Doesn't Whitcomb have a jail or interrogation rooms somewhere?"

Elizabeth summoned more guards and commanded them to inquire in the city guildhall where to find the chief constable, then to demand in the name of the queen that Meg Milligrew be released.

"Whitcomb's trying to spite me, just the way Cantwell did," she told Cecil, and began to pace as Ned went out to tend his bruises. "I defied the Parliament, so they are trying to vex and challenge me in any way they can. I have Cantwell being held here, so I will have you interrogate him."

Elizabeth put both hands to her head, pressing hard as if to keep her thoughts steady. "I fear Whitcomb will try to accuse Meg of Pamela's death, too, for I believe the residue I found there was a deadly concoction made from sugar, *chocolata* powder, and Meg's poison cuckoo-pint. He might know naught of that, but he'll see the roots on the floor at the second murder scene, just like at the first."

"But you said you had the *chocolata* drink at Gresham House, so that leads back to them, too."

"If Meg or Anne Gresham—or the van der Passes, for that matter—is proven guilty, I face great loss. If it's Thomas, the entire kingdom will suffer. I must move now, but I'm not sure in which direction. As soon as we discover where Meg's being held, I've a good mind—"

The knock on the door startled them both. Clifford opened it.

"You're back!" the queen cried. "Did you fetch the local constable to the murder site?"

"Yes, and he sent information forthwith for the chief constable, as you had thought he would."

"Send someone back to the local man and ask him where the chief constable is now. Hurry!"

"Also, Lady Anne Gresham is here, Your Grace, demanding to see her husband," Clifford said, as he turned toward the door.

"She can't have arrived already from my summons," Cecil said, frowning. "Not enough time has elapsed, so she must have come on her own."

"I pray the girls are safe."

"Shall I show her in here or take her to her lord?" Clifford asked. "I heard he's already here under watch."

"We shall do both," Elizabeth declared. "Have her held in the hall for a moment, and bring Thomas in the back way to await her here—but send that man to the local constable first," she insisted. Clifford nodded and rushed out.

"We need to know what passes between the Greshams," Cecil said.

"Exactly. Though I regret it has come to this, you and I will eavesdrop on their reunion behind the door to my withdrawing room. My lord, I am getting desperate, and we must not only stir the starch pot again but slosh it all out on the floor."

"I had naught to do with Hannah von Hoven's death," Meg insisted, the moment the two big guards half-escorted, half-shoved her into the small, dim room where Chief Constable Nigel Whitcomb sat in a large chair behind a small table.

"I must admit those charges were not correct, mistress," he said, with a thin smile twisting his lips.

Thank God, Meg thought. He must have realized his great error. Her biggest worry then was that she'd seen two of his big oafs turn on Ned and beat him in the face with their fists just before they blindfolded her.

"Well?" Whitcomb said, his tone still goading. "Not going to ask the chief constable what he means by incorrect charges? My, but you're clever with the queen's herbs, eh, even ones that can be used to dispatch your rivals in romance?"

"What? I demand, if the charges were wrong, that I be released forthwith, so that I—"

"You'll demand nothing!" he shouted and banged his fist on the table. His beard quivered when he spoke. "The charges were wrong because now I have a second murder of another rival I vow I shall link you to. Cuckoo-pint on the floor of both your deeds—did you not think I would know or could not discover what it was and that it could be deadly? Her Majesty believes she can gainsay and buck me—all of Parliament—but she cannot protect you now, mistress."

Meg's insides cartwheeled. "A second murder—you mean Pamela Browne's?"

"I mean you accidentally dispatched Pamela Browne, I judge, instead of her twin sister, whom your former betrothed, Stephen Jenks, has deserted you for and—"

"No! That's a lie from the pit of hell!"

"Best watch your tongue about the pit of hell," he threatened, pointing a stiff arm straight at her. "Those judged guilty of murder are executed in this land, young woman, and I shall have great bearing on your conviction. Speaking of warrants," he went on, looking suddenly more amused than angry, as if he were toying with her, "the additional one against you will be drawn up as soon as I can visit the second murder site myself, for I've had to rely so far on the local constable's description of things and his questioning of those there."

"I didn't kill Pamela Browne. Stephen Jenks, the man you mentioned, the queen's own man, will testify to that—that I was happy for him and Pamela's twin sister, Ursala. Just as Ned Topside, the queen's chief player, will tell you that—"

"I understand at your arrest you were holding hands with the aforementioned Topside, so I've no doubt you've also cozened him to support your false claims. I expect all Her Majesty's servants would stand behind your story, as the queen herself tried to do.

"I once meant to work with Her Majesty," he went on, "even tried to placate her with an offering of a portion of the first dead woman's estate. But she is stubborn to the core, much too willful for a woman, who should listen to the men of her Parliament, however high she thinks to sit in this land."

Meg gaped at the man. His words could be construed as treasonous. If he detested Her Grace so, she had no doubt he'd like to make a scapegoat—or sacrificial lamb—of someone who loved her dearly.

"Anne!" Thomas Gresham cried as Elizabeth heard the door to the corridor open, then close. The queen had ordered that Anne be brought in, then left alone with her husband.

"Why are you here?" Thomas demanded. "Is Marie here, too?"

Their voices carried easily through the door set slightly ajar, the queen thought with approval, and Cecil nodded from the shadows as if to second that. Good, he could hear, too.

"I wasn't sent for but came of my own accord," Anne said. "And I didn't want Marie out in the streets, even with me, so of course I didn't bring her. I have something to tell you, and since you are lingering here, I had no choice but to—"

"I am not lingering but have been detained. The queen has questioned me further about Hannah's death," Thomas admitted. "But, for the good of our daughter, I am asking you to stand with me in this, not against—"

"For the good of our daughter?" she said, her voice bitter. "I'll tell you about the good of our daughter. If you'd just listen for once, I need to inform you that this morning I dismissed that horrid watchdog of yours, Nash Badger, at least exiled him from our house. If you want him at the site of the exchange, that's your business, but Marie just told me about the letters he carried for her. The man's betrayed us. If he had come to us at once, her running away and getting in this plight could have been avoided."

"He was no doubt only trying to please Marie—as we both do. Have you forgotten not only how beguiling but woebegone she can be?" His voice grew tender when he spoke of the girl, though Anne seemed to have enough venom for both of them.

"Beguiling? Then, I fear, she must have inherited that trait from her other mother—the one you wish lived instead of me!"

"Let's not start all that ag—"

"You're always on Badger's side—on your own side! I

never could abide him, with his tobacco-drinking breath and stinking hands. I finally got out of Marie that he's secretly been carrying her letters. Did you know about those? Well, did you?"

"Marie gave the queen a draft of such a letter, and Her Majesty read it to me."

"Oh, fine, you never tell me anything, either. You and the queen are closer than you and I! Have you been trying to protect Marie or Badger?" she raved. "Or, more to the point, yourself in all this?"

"Never mind shifting the subject. I'll tell Badger to keep clear of you, but I need him at the house as a jack-of-all-trades and even a bodyguard when I go out. Look, Anne, I know that tobacco smell is—"

"He's taken to trying to cover it up—and those smelly hands—with perfumed gloves, at least when he goes out. Perfumed gloves! I'm sure he'll be laughed to scorn if he wears those at the construction site."

They went on arguing, Thomas telling her she had to put the past aside and stand by him now. He warned that she herself might be considered a person of suspicion in Hannah's death if she continued to be so vitriolic. Anne exploded at that, but the queen was beyond heeding her ravings.

For, several moments ago, more jagged-edged pieces of the puzzle had begun to fit horribly into place. Badger's incongruous gloves could link him to Celia for more than just serving Marie. Badger had access to the *chocolata* as surely as Anne and Thomas had, for he had found the imported cakes for Thomas and had even carried the brew made from them in for the queen to taste. Thank God, that was not poisoned, as poor Pamela's quaff must have been.

Besides all that, Badger had always seemed to hover close, from that day Elizabeth had first visited Thomas at the construction site of the exchange. Did Badger intend to protect his master at any price, and so had secretly decided to silence Hannah before she caused him harm? Or had Thomas hired him to do so?

Even though Cantwell was waiting to be interrogated, the queen knew she had to find and question Badger. But first, she had to get to Marie and Sally to be certain they were safe from him. He must know that Marie was regaining her memory. She had already caused him to be questioned by the queen about the letters and dismissed by Anne, partly at least, for secretly carrying them. He might fear the girl could identify him or would tell others more—the very reasons Ursala might have been targeted for death.

Elizabeth drew Cecil away from the door before she whispered, "Badger may be the link not only to Celia but to the killer."

"At the least, it's dangerous to have him at large, especially since the Greshams are both here."

"I'm going to Gresham House now, and not in my coach. One of my barges, a working one without all the royal trappings, will be faster. Anne may have thrown Badger out of the house, but the girls are there alone until Bates and my guards arrive. You stay here, question Hosea Cantwell, and try to deal with the Greshams."

"Your Grace," he said as she started away, "remember badgers bite."

"I appreciate your coming down to see me—both of you," Nash Badger told Marie and Sally the moment they joined him in the Gresham gardens. "I know it's a bit brisk today, but I see you two clever girls are well protected from the wind by your cloaks and hoods."

Despite the biting smell that always came from Badger, Marie was glad he was still around. The housemaid had told her and Sally that her mother had scolded the poor man terribly and had ordered him to leave, but that must have blown over now. She was puzzled, though, that he wasn't with her father. Both her parents had left the house separately, so why was Badger still here?

"We saw you gesturing to us when we looked out the window," Marie explained. "We're not to venture out, but the courtyard doesn't count."

"Precisely, Mistress Gresham. You always were a sharp one, and Sally also, eh, girl?" he said with a nod and a smile.

Marie knew that Sally liked Badger, too, not because he'd done errands for her but because he treated her as if she didn't have a mark or scar on her face. Some of the other household servants had been shocked by her appearance and had whispered behind her back.

"You do know, do you not," Badger said with a glance up at the second-story windows, "why they don't want you to go out, especially today?"

"No. They don't really tell me much about—important things."

"Ah," he said with a sigh. "Well, I warrant it's because your poor departed Aunt Hannah's body is being laid to rest today in Southwark at the parish church of St. Saviour, just across London Bridge. They no doubt wanted to be certain you didn't go there to pay your final respects to the twin sister of your dead mother—your real mother."

"But she died a whole week ago," Sally put in.

"Yes, but with the inquest, they held her body for a while. Besides, the coroner and constable had to be called in . . . So sad," he added, and shook his head, looking mournful.

"Is that where my parents went?" Marie asked, gripping her hands together. "I know they argue about her—my real mother—sometimes."

"Oh, no, they had separate errands, I believe. They wouldn't go there. I doubt if anyone will, so it will be a sorrowful and lonely burial. Frankly, before your mother left, she warned me most sternly not to tell you about the graveside service, but I thought you would want to know anyway. I believe you spoke privily to your aunt when she was here in this very courtyard, pleading for money . . ."

Again his voice trailed off, and he shook his head. So that was why her mother had scolded Badger this morning. He had always been so kind to her, and her mother had resented his familiarity. Worse, just this morning, she had pried out of Marie the truth about sending letters to Hannah through Badger and Celia and no doubt blamed Badger for that favor. Oh, dear, she had probably partly caused the tongue-lashing Badger received, though he didn't look the worse for wear over it—much better than she herself took her mother's lectures.

"I would love to attend the service in my aunt's honor," Marie admitted, "but after all the trouble I caused last time I ventured out, I just don't know."

"Oh, I understand you wouldn't risk a scolding just to honor your dead mother, as well as her sister. Celia, who was willing to help you before, and I will go in your place," he said, indicating the side gate to the street. "She awaits me there. We'll be back soon, before your parents return, so that we don't get in trouble. It's not far, as we'll go over the bridge, right past the shops with all the pretty goods for sale."

"But surely St. Saviour way across the river was not Hannah von Hoven's parish church," Sally said.

"Ah, no—I believe the queen has paid for things, arranged them there, though she'll be too busy to go, of course. At least the two of us, myself and Celia, though not related to poor Hannah, will be there, and we'll tell you all about it, secretly, of course, when we return."

"You're sure you won't be gone long?" Marie asked, pulling her cloak tighter around her as a chill swept her, along with a wild idea.

"Not over an hour. Out that door and back in it soon."

"Sally, will you go with me?" Marie pleaded, turning to her frowning friend. "I so long to go. I will never be able to visit my mother's grave—too far, and they wouldn't let me. It would mean so much to me to go to my aunt's resting place!"

"Do you dare disobey them again?" Sally asked. "I, too, promised the queen that—"

"You vowed you'd stay with me and watch over me," Marie argued, "and that's exactly what you would be doing. Master Badger, will you take the two of us?"

"Only if you're ready to go right now. As I said, Celia awaits, and time is fleeting for us to get there on time."

"We're dressed warmly enough, but we don't have our purses."

"Do not fret for that, for Celia and I will pay for any need and you can reimburse us later."

Badger edged away, toward the side gate. Marie made to follow, but Sally tugged her back. "You know," Marie said to him, "I longed to go with you to Celia's shop and with her to my aunt's starch house. I—I think that's why I must have gone there alone the day she was killed."

"I sensed that," Badger said. "I always knew how much you cared not only for your aunt but for your real mother."

Marie now pulled Sally along. "If you're certain we'll get back quickly. No time to shop on the bridge," Marie said, "though I've thought about that, too, when I was cooped up—so dearly protected here, that is."

"Don't give any of that a thought now," Badger comforted as he swept open the gate for them. Celia was standing right outside as he had said. She looked happy to see them. Marie had never had a chance to thank her for passing on the letters, but she'd tell her now.

Suddenly, down the length of the outer walls of the large house, Marie saw a group of horsemen pulling up in the front street with a great clatter, at least six men.

"Who could that be?" Sally asked. "They're all dressed alike."

"Some foreign visitor's entourage. A diplomat to see the exchange today," Badger said as he motioned them on to where they could cut down an alley. "They're evidently confused about meeting your father here instead of there. Let's move sprightly now, if we intend to be on time. Come on now, stick close to Celia and me."

Elizabeth took Clifford and Rosie, in simple garb like herself, along with their horses and commanded that the working barge be put in as close to Gresham House as possible. If she'd taken the one with her coat of arms, cloth of gold, and crimson velvet seats, she would have drawn a huge crowd when swiftness and secrecy were what she needed now.

"The landing 'neath London Bridge be closest, but too dang'rous with this high tide right now," the head oarsman told her.

Elizabeth gazed ahead at London's only bridge as it spanned the broad Thames. The twenty arches made a cauldron of the current, which only trained boatmen called bridge-shooters dared to challenge. Unfortunately, it was a place of suicides, demented souls who leaped into the foam and whose battered and bloated bodies were found miles upriver where the tidal surge spent itself, or, if it was going back out to sea, were lost forever in the Channel. Worse, she'd heard terrible tales of untended children dropping from the back windows of the houses above the shops. They were sucked down, battered, and drowned against the wooden platforms called starlings that protected the piers and arches.

"All right, then," she called to him over the roar of the river and the noise from the busy shops and houses on the bridge itself. "Put in at Old Swan Stairs near the bridge, and we'll ride straight up Fish Street to Gresham House."

After disembarking, Elizabeth, Rosie, and Clifford went on horseback from the river landing. When she was half a block from Gresham House, she saw her yeoman Bates riding toward them, waving.

"I am surprised you spotted me!" she told him.

"I was in that side street. No other woman sits a horse like you, Your Majesty."

"Have you put a cordon of safety around the house?"

"Best brace yourself. When we arrived at Gresham House, it was too late."

"For what? What has happened?"

"The two girls are missing, or at least the household staff has not turned them up yet. I was just starting to search the area."

" 'S blood! Do you know aught of Nash Badger?"

"The maid who cleans Marie's chambers says he was ordered to leave the house today—that she saw him leave."

"He left alone, I pray."

"Yes, but he must have returned shortly, for she saw him in the gardens, speaking with Marie and Sally but moments ago. I'm sure that's who she said, the one who took a terrible scolding from Lady Gresham today."

"You are certain they are not in the gardens now? It's a large area with much autumn overgrowth."

"We looked, but the girls went out with him, the maid says, evidently that same gate we used at night, the one I guarded for you. The maid rushed downstairs to tell the man who oversees the household staff to stop them, but by then they'd vanished into thin air."

"He's taken them somewhere, and I fear for their lives. Let the household staff continue to search in the house, but order the guards to send out a hue and cry for them in this immediate vicinity. Someone must have seen two girls with a man in broad daylight!"

"You don't think he'd take them to the van der Passes?" Clifford put in. "That Dirck van der Passe could be involved."

"We'll send someone there in case that's true. I don't know where else—unless Badger discovered Meg's jailed and talked the girls into a visit to her or some such, but I still don't know where that could be. Wait—Cecil said Nigel Whitcomb used to be head of the Skinners' Guild. Send someone to inspect their guildhall. It's not far from here on Dowgate."

Bates clattered on ahead as the queen, Rosie, and Clifford followed. They rode around the vast walls of Gresham House and dismounted at the side gate where the girls and Badger were last seen. It was locked.

"Shall I pound on it until they let us in, Your Majesty?" Clifford asked.

"No. Just let me think a moment."

Elizabeth stepped back into the arched shelter of the doorway and looked up and down the side street and then into the alley that cut off almost directly across from the gate. Would they have gone into that, to disappear quickly from possibly being spotted from the upper floors of Gresham House? Unlike when Meg had chased Celia down an alley, there were no coins or drops of blood to follow.

Chapter the Fifteenth

MEG LOST THE LAST REMNANTS OF HER PLUCK when Constable Whitcomb's big guards forced her neck and wrists into the stocks. It was not a public pillory but one set in a large stone cellar beneath the chamber where she had been questioned before.

She wasn't even certain where in town she was, since she had been blindfolded shortly after they dragged her away from Ned near the palace. At first, she'd feared they would put her in one of the city prisons. But, she'd reasoned, Bridewell was for political prisoners, and Newgate held felons, while the Fleet, Marshalsea, and the Tower were under the ultimate control of the queen.

No, Constable Whitcomb didn't have her in a regular city or state prison. That was news as bad as it was good, because it would make her much harder for the queen to find, if—in all the chaos of the murders—she was even looking for her. But Ned would try to find her, wouldn't he?

The building in which she was being held looked more like someone's place of business, the kind that had the living quarters overhead. Surely she wasn't being kept in the constable's house. And nothing was stored in this spacious cellar, so it probably wasn't a shop above. A meeting place, perhaps?

All she did know was that the wooden *O* of the stocks hurt her neck and the smaller holes pinched her wrists as, bent over, she was forced to face the chief constable again. One of his louts pulled up a chair for him and he plopped himself in it.

"Perhaps I have your attention now, mistress," he said.

It hurt Meg to look up, so she stared down. The two support posts of these stocks were stuck in holes in the stone floor. She could see Whitcomb's shoes and the white ceremonial cane of his office resting across his knees. Why, he even wore his red cloak in this cellar. Surely he didn't mean to beat her while she was trapped and bent over in a private place like this, and him in all his fancy garb—or judge her, either.

"Any more of your failure to address or answer me courteously," he went on, "any further back talk, and I will have your pretty little ears nailed to the stocks. Do you hear and heed me, Mistress Milligrew?"

"Yes."

"Yes, what?"

"Yes, Constable."

"Yes, Chief Constable," he corrected. "Then listen carefully, because after having one's ears nailed, the next step is their being cut off. Why, I had a servant girl here, oh, about a fortnight ago, it was," he went on, stretching out and crossing his legs, "who got off quite lightly for giving her masters and her household poison. Both her ears were cut off, and she was branded on the forehead with a *P* for 'poisoner.' But you see, she cooperated fully, and her victims did not die. Now here, Mistress Milligrew, I find a more dire tragedy, one in which, under my aegis, the full penalty for poisoning must be brought to bear. Do you know what that penalty is?"

"No, Chief Constable."

"My, but you are ill informed. It's burning at the stake, to be precise—especially, no doubt, for a double murder. Now, to business," he went on when she gasped. Her throat went dry, and she began to sweat in this chill place. She had to force herself to listen as this vile man droned on.

"I've had a bit more time now to examine the circumstances under which the second victim of the same murderer—or shall we say, murderess—died. Are you quite ready to answer my questions, then?"

"Y-yes, Chief Constable."

"How pleasant to find you so helpful, so obedient. Would that your royal mistress were so. Do you know you greatly resemble her? Do you?"

"I would not p-presume to say so, but, yes, Chief Constable."

"So perhaps I shall imagine I have her here instead of you, doing precisely what I bid, all meek and mild."

This man, Meg thought, was mad. Her knees began to shake so hard she could barely stand. She feared for her very life—but not that she would burn. Whitcomb could never afford to let her get that far, carted through the streets to a place of public execution. He could hardly let her escape to tell the queen the things he had just said, though, she supposed, he could deny it. However bad this got, she'd just concentrate on her beloved Sally, cared for and safe at Gresham House.

Marie saw Sally's eyes were as big as plates, though she kept her hood pulled close about her face. Cutting through back alleys that Celia seemed to know well—Badger had said this was her part of town—they soon went back onto Fish Street with the grand London Bridge in sight directly before them.

This time of day, shoppers crowded its two-cart width, and drovers with their flocks and herds streamed toward them into town. As they neared the bridge, Marie thought it looked as if it writhed with people. Beyond its other end, across the river, rose the large Gothic church where her Aunt Hannah would be buried. Marie's eyes misted at the mere thought of honoring her mother's sister as she was laid to eternal, silent rest.

Meanwhile, life here was suddenly so exciting! Her gaze darted from face to face as people hurried past. Even the sound and scent of the captive sheep coming at them, baaing and bumping their way toward Smithfield and slaughter, was astonishing.

"Oh," Sally cried, tugging at her cloak and pointing, "why does the water foam up by the bridge?"

"It's the tidal river rushing through the arches," Marie told her, proud she knew all about it though she'd seldom seen it.

"Are these shops or houses, hanging out over the edge?" Sally asked as they made their way along the bridge itself.

"Both," Celia cut in before Marie could answer. "Some of the best haberdashers in town, and the place where I work now, too, a real nice glover's."

"Oh, you're not at the old place?" Marie asked, but Celia

must not have heard her in the noise. She saw Badger shoot Celia a frown, though.

From time to time people came to a complete stop, packed like salted fish in a barrel, but Badger soon shoved folks aside. Marie and Sally followed him farther out over the water, with Celia pushing from behind.

"Will we make it in time in this crowd?" Marie shouted to Badger. "You said we'd only be gone one hour."

"No worry!" Badger yelled as they neared the center of the bridge. "Now don't look up, you two."

Of course, they both did. There above them, stuck on pikes, glowered the rotting heads of criminals. Marie felt sick to her stomach. She remembered overhearing the housemaids tell how Sir Thomas More's daughter had paid someone to drop her beheaded father's skull into her apron, so it could be buried with his body. Yes, Marie was risking getting caught, too, honoring her mother's memory at Aunt Hannah's burial today.

Instead of staring at the heads like Sally, Marie looked out through one of the breaks in the buildings. She felt less shaky if she just stared at the fine view of the river and the town.

"In here," Badger said suddenly, and produced a key to unlock a door. Above it, in the biting breeze, swung a sign shaped like a yellow glove. When the girls hesitated to enter, Celia pushed them in from behind and shut the door. That muted the bridge noise, though Marie could still hear the roar of the water through the back windows of the shop.

"Why are we stopping?" Marie demanded. "We'll be late. Is this Celia's new shop?"

"It is," the woman said, securing the latch and banging closed the shutters to the street. "The master goes home for two hours in late afternoon each day, and I watch things. Now don't you fret we'll be late, Mistress Marie, as there's a cut-corner way out the back to where you're going."

At last the search paid off, for one of the queen's guards had reported to Bates that a woman had seen two girls with a man—but with a large woman, too.

"Then perhaps it wasn't Marie and Sally," Elizabeth said, her hopes dashed.

"It sounds like them, Your Majesty," Bates insisted. "They were cloaked and hooded, but the size of the children was a match."

"The one girl in a blue cloak and the other—the smaller one—in a brown one?"

"So the woman said. Saw them cutting from an alley off Fenchurch but then heading down Fish Street toward the bridge."

"The bridge? Perhaps they are being taken out of town, but why would they go willingly?" she asked, thinking aloud. "Badger could be going to hold them for ransom, but if he is the one who already drowned two women and is now heading for the river . . . Remount! We're riding for the bridge!"

Rosie, Bates, and Clifford went with her, and the other guards clattered behind. The bridge was packed at this hour as everyone rushed to do late-day shopping and the last herds of beasts were brought in for the big Wednesday sale of meat on the hoof at Smithfield tomorrow. She'd been learning much more about that place and the dubious legality of its sellers and traders, for it might be one way to imprison Dauntsey.

"Halt!" Elizabeth cried as they neared the north gate to the bridge. She raised herself in her saddle to scan the shifting swells of people and animals. "We'll make no headway en masse without harming someone," she called to her party. "Bates, take two guards and ride the bridge, looking for the four of them—or two hooded girls. Call out to those in the shops lest this is quite harmless and they've simply sneaked out to go shopping, but Sally should never have allowed that."

As soon as the three riders were gone, she turned to Clifford and Rosie. "You two, come with me. We will take the barge to the other side of the bridge and look for them to exit there. The rest of the men are to stay here to watch for two girls who might emerge from this end. If we do not find them that way, before the drawbridges are closed for the night, we will do a shop-to-shop and house-to-house search of the entire span."

The three of them rode along the riverbank to the Old Swan Stairs where the barge awaited; they stared at the nearby bridge while the crew loaded their horses. The queen shaded her eyes into the sinking sun. Things had been going so poorly of late in this quest for the killer, she could only pray this would not be some dreadful dead end.

Badger and Celia shoved the girls out of the shop, into its small back room. A single window, set ajar, overlooked the river. Gloves, uncut leather, and fur pieces were stacked on shelves and thrown on a small worktable with cutting tools, maybe Celia's. With the roar of the water under the arches, they had to shout to be heard.

"Badger, I demand you take us to the church forthwith!" Marie insisted, trying to sound as commanding as her mother always did. She cursed the tears stinging her eyes. "I don't want to be late for my aunt's burial."

It was when Celia hooted a laugh right in her face that Marie knew she'd made a terrible mistake trusting these people. She had actually thought there might be a back walkway the shop owners used to avoid the bridge traffic, but that was a lie. Was everything else Badger had said untrue? Maybe he was so angry at her mother that he intended to hold her for ransom. Everyone knew her father was as rich as King Midas. Perhaps the queen would pay a pretty penny for Sally, too.

"You must let us go at once or I shall tell the queen herself," Sally put in, stepping closer so their shoulders bumped. It touched Marie that the younger, smaller girl was yet trying to protect her, when this was all her fault.

"That poxed face of yours may scare some," Celia said, yanking Sally's hood back, then pulling her hair, "but not us. You don't want to be pitched in the water, girl, you just leave off, 'cause our bus'ness is with Mistress Marie here."

Panicked, Marie darted for the door. Everything happened so fast. Celia seized the struggling, shrieking Sally and stuffed a glove in her mouth. Badger grabbed Marie with hard hands and dragged her into a corner of the small room. All she saw there was a wooden closestool. He shoved it aside with his foot, revealing a square drop hole in the wooden floor, which looked straight down to the river, raging through the bridge arches below.

To her horror, Badger pulled her hands behind her back, threw her to her knees, and thrust her head and shoulders down through the horrid hole, then drew her back up a bit so he could shout in her ear.

"You'll tell me what you know now, what else you've blabbed to your mother and the queen about the day the starcher was killed! I want to know now or you just might slip through this hole, and that'll be the end of you."

"We'll just say she fell right through," Celia yelled on her other side. "Poor girl, slipped, just trying to use the jakes."

Marie gaped at the white foam below. It seemed to reach for her, fill her open eyes and mouth as she drifted in it, sinking, screaming silently. Aunt Hannah's face in death . . . She imagined her mother's face dead from childbed fever . . . No. No, the queen had said that was not her fault.

"What if she don't talk?" Celia asked. "The stocking man will have our heads like those out there on pikes."

"Shut your trap! She's going to talk, right, Marie? Who did you see at your Aunt Hannah's that day she drowned?"

"No one—I heard them, struggling," she cried.

"Louder!" he demanded. "Heard who struggling?"

"I was on the stairs. I started up to see her, but heard it—a man with her. Then when it . . . was quiet . . . I came up to see if she was all right."

"And saw what? Saw who?"

"No—no one was there. She was floating . . . dead."

Marie felt she was floating, pulled under as the thick, sticky memories roared forth to drown her. Trying to swim upward, through the starch, she remembered now: She hurried back downstairs after she saw Hannah floating. On the stairs, she fell and rolled, hitting her head, but she got up and rushed into the field to stare up at the window. Through it, she saw someone lift her aunt Hannah's body from the starch tub. She should have tried to pull her out, but she'd been a coward and fled. Through the window, she saw someone dressed like Badger, short like Badger—but if she said that, he would drop her through this hole. Maybe he meant to do it no matter what.

"What else did you see?" he shouted, shaking her like a cloth doll.

"N-n-nothing. The sun shone off the windows in my eyes. Everything was gone then, from my head, after I fell. That's all I recall, I swear it!"

"We've got to hurry with the rest of this," Celia said. "The glove maker will be back soon. That's enough to tell the stocking market man."

"Just the stocking man, remember?" Badger hissed at her.

"What's the difference? These two won't be round to tell!"

Who are they talking about? Marie wondered, panicked as she stared down at the white chaos pounding against the pillars. The glover sold stockings, too?

"I still say she's worth a fortune alive, no matter what he said about final revenge," Badger argued. He eased up slightly on her neck. She turned to see that Celia had bound Sally with a roll of ribbon—and that her friend had managed to cut nearly through her bonds with a pair of scissors she had somehow got a hand on.

"I remember something else," Marie added, hoping Badger and Celia didn't look Sally's way. "Let me sit up. I can't breathe."

Badger loosed her slightly, though he didn't let go of her. She knew she would only have one chance to pull off this trick, and if she failed, she and Sally were gone for good.

Marie shrieked in Badger's ear. Sally, free now, gave a shout and rushed Celia, knocking her sprawling facedown on the floor, swinging the big scissors at her like a knife. As Badger startled, then tried to get up, he loosed Marie. Instead of fleeing, she yanked him back and shoved. He ended up with his posterior from shoulder blades to the backs of his knees stuck in the drop hole, struggling not to fall through all the way.

Marie tried to help Sally, but the girl seemed a much better brawler. Celia's wrist was bleeding, but she grabbed Sally. The scissors went flying. The woman backhanded Sally, slamming her into the wall. Furious, Marie pounded Celia's back, but she knew it would do no good to scream for help unless the glover returned. The outside noise was still deafening.

Somehow Sally righted herself and scrambled for the scissors on the floor just as Badger got himself out of the drop hole.

"There's a big club out in the shop," Celia screamed at him, holding her bleeding wrist. "Fetch it to use on them. We have to hurry—"

The moment Badger ran out to get the club, Marie slammed the door behind him and shot the bolt. At least it would take him a moment to break the door down, if he dared, since Celia had said the glover would be back soon. Now, at least, it was two against one.

Sally had the scissors again, and Marie grabbed another glove-cutting tool. They swung them in large arcs to back Celia toward the open hole in the floor, but she cleverly skirted it. Still, she tripped over the closestool that Badger had shoved aside and crashed backwards into the wall, then sat hard on the floor.

"Grab her!" Sally shrieked as they heard the first bang on the door. "Push her halfway down and let her hang there. He's going to get back in, and then we're cooked."

Together, as Badger battered at the door, the two girls grabbed handfuls of Celia's hair, then shoved and pushed her head down into the hole to her waist, though her hips and wide skirts stopped her fall. Her arms had also gone through, but she spread her legs in the riot of skirts and petticoats to try to hold herself there.

"These tools won't be enough against him," Sally cried as

she stood with Marie, staring at the splintering door. "Not with that big club. He must have drowned your aunt and now wants to drown us." She ran to the single window overlooking the river. "There are boats out on the water, and there's a ledge outside. Someone will see us out there and help."

"Over that water—I can't," Marie said as Badger cracked the wood of the door, then bashed at it again with his club.

"We have to. Now! Come on!"

After a grueling interrogation, Meg was left, bound to a chair, in the upper room where she'd first been questioned. If she hadn't known she was innocent of the murders of Hannah von Hoven and Pamela Browne, she would think by now that she was indeed guilty.

The chief constable was a haranguer and a tormentor, skilled at instilling terror. Yet she had no doubt he'd carry out his threats. Ears nailed to the stocks next time, he said, if she didn't admit her crimes. Then the third time he questioned her, if she didn't confess, ears cut off and forehead branded. He'd had his man show her the hot branding iron and singe her hair with it. Then, he vowed, when it was too late for the queen to gainsay or disprove all she'd confessed, he'd see she had a public execution by burning at the stake.

Despite her horror, exhausted, Meg floated into a half-sleep. She recalled that Ned had fondled and kissed her ears and called them seashells. He'd brushed his lips so tenderly against her "fair brow." Ned had loved her complexion. And he'd said that he had burned to lie with her abed and love her forever.

She heard his luring voice even now. "I'll ask you to

wed again later, when death is not our business but life—together." But now, still, death was her business, and the death just might be her own. Yet how close she had been to being Ned's, in body as well as in heart, after longing for him all these years. How close but now so far . . .

She dozed but was wakened by voices—distant, stern, especially one man's. Was she still dreaming? Those were not Ned's cultured, ringing tones but a rougher voice, though one of authority and purpose.

Her hopes soared until one of Whitcomb's louts rushed in and stuffed a rag in her mouth that made her gag so violently she almost couldn't hear that new voice. But yes, she could catch words if she held her breath and concentrated hard on not choking.

"Queen's demands . . . where . . . Milligrew . . ."

Yes! Yes, the queen had sent someone to rescue her from this place, wherever it was. After gasping for air and nearly dry-heaving, she held her breath again. Whitcomb's voice, strident, strong.

". . . for questioning . . . mountain of evidence . . . until someone else confesses . . . bound over soon enough . . . my sworn duty . . ."

Meg prayed the queen's man would not leave her here. Had he come alone? Hadn't guards been sent, too?

It seemed so silent now. A door closed distantly, thudding an echo in this room, in her heart. She strained to hear more voices, even horses. But nothing now. Nothing.

The oarsmen had to row hard to fight the current as the queen's barge headed across the river to the Southwark side. This close to the bridge, a gap-toothed maw sucking in the river, it wouldn't take much to be swept closer and battered against the wooden starlings that protected the pillars. Elizabeth shuddered as she recalled nearly being capsized here when she tried to solve a woman's murder seven years ago. Meg had rescued her in a rowboat; now Meg's daughter's life might be at stake. How things seemed to come full circle, she thought, as she prayed that both Meg and Sally might be safe.

"Your Grace, look!" Lady Rosie cried, pointing just past the center of the bridge. "Outside that window on a ledge. Two women are outside that window over the rapids!"

Elizabeth squinted into the sinking sun, then shaded her eyes with both raised hands. Prayer so quickly answered? Goose bumps gilded her skin.

"I think it's them!" the queen cried, first to herself and then to her chief oarsman. The two were either small women or children, though neither had a cape or hood—no, the smaller girl was waving her brown one like a banner.

The queen pointed and screamed louder, "It's them, the girls! Row the barge closer in case they fall! Row for that arch just beyond the center!"

Her men didn't have to tell her it was dangerous, but they bent to their oars. The royal barge was too big to shoot through the arches, but it would take a bashing if they went sideways to block the rush of river. The queen saw that other river craft had spotted the girls, too, but dared not sail or row close.

She stood, bracing herself against a post that held up the plain awning, as the flow and tilt of water rocked the barge. Hoping the girls would see her, the queen waved broadly. They had gone out on either side of a window onto a narrow wooden ledge; each was clinging to a faded blue shutter.

Yes, she was certain they saw the barge, saw her. Thank God!

In waving her cloak, Sally nearly toppled and had to let it go. Like a brown autumn leaf, it sailed to the foaming water and was instantly sucked down. The shutter she clung to swung away from the outer wall, with her hanging on, feet flailing while the roar of the rapids drowned her screams.

Chapter the Sixteenth

HORRIFIED, ELIZABETH WATCHED SALLY HANG ON for her life.

"Closer!" she urged her oarsmen on the barge. "Put us under her."

At least the girls were on the lower level of the bridge's buildings, for some rose to three stories—but, even if Sally hit the awning, the fall was too far, and if she missed and went into the river... She prayed the shutter would hold Sally's weight, that she could get her feet back on the ledge.

"Marie, don't reach for her!" Elizabeth shouted up as the Gresham girl tried to lean over to help. But she was certain they could not hear her.

Clifford and Rosie ran to the queen when they saw they would hit the bridge. With a huge bump and crash, the barge banged once, then again, into the wooden starlings. The impact of the water pinned them, shoving them sideways, sweeping over the bow, soaking them with spray and waves while the oarsmen fought to control the craft. Rocked as if they rode a leaping, bucking horse, Elizabeth tried to steady herself by linking arms with them.

"Shout to them not to jump!" Elizabeth ordered Clifford. "Someone will come, and if Sally slips we are under her."

"Don't jump!" he bellowed, leaning back to face upward and cupping his free hand around his mouth. "Someone will come! Sally, we are here if you fall!"

We are here if you fall. Elizabeth's thought echoed his frenzied words. Hannah had been killed in water; Pamela, too. Now Sally and Marie might drown, the fault of England's reputedly wise queen, who had not protected them soon enough or well enough.

Fury and anger stoked her strength. At any cost, she had to save them.

The room was growing dim as daylight ebbed outside. Still gagged, the rag now soaked with saliva and tears, Meg heard another new voice in the room next to hers. Her spirits fell: This was not Ned, either. It was probably a man delivering something to Whitcomb. Despite the harsh tone and unlearned speech, though, the new voice reminded her of Ned's. Straining to hear, she sat up instead of slumping against her bonds.

"Eh, then, we be sent by the local constable from St. Martin's fields, one Gideon Banks," the new voice said. "Got more news of the murder of the second woman for you."

They must be in the room just outside this chamber. *Was* it Ned? She'd often enough heard him adopt different voices in his acting, but he usually took the lofty roles of kings or generals, not some rough commoner.

"Say on," Whitcomb ordered. "I've got the culprit here but can use more evidence to break her."

"Oh, break her, eh? I always 'mired—Geoff here done,

too—how a bold fellow like yourself can keep the peace through power."

"You got her 'prisoned here," another new voice put in, " 'spite o' her workin' for the queen?"

Holy heaven, Meg thought. Geoff sounded like Jenks. Ned had brought Jenks! If only she could cry out to them.

"How in hell," Whitcomb said, "did you get so beat up, man?"

"The queen's men," Ned said. "They came to the local constable, looking for her herb'list. We wouldn't say where she was being held—didn't rightly know then."

Meg's heart went out to him, for Whitcomb's bullies had hit that handsome face hard. At least the chief constable had not been there when his men dragged Ned off, so he didn't know what he looked like one way or the other.

"Speaking of hell," Ned went on, "there's gonna be that to pay if 'n you don't hand that herb'list back, 'cause the queen depends on her mightily."

"That so? Mightily? Good!"

Meg could picture Whitcomb gloating. Ned was taking the wrong tack here, because the chief constable loved to be reminded he was hurting the queen by hurting Meg.

"This be a real fancy place, this Skinners' Guildhall," Ned said, blessedly changing the subject.

So that's where she was! Nigel Whitcomb used to be head of the guild of skinners; he evidently still had access to it.

"Good place to skin a guilty cat, I'd say," Whitcomb said, and guffawed. Ned and Jenks laughed right along with him, but then Meg heard a door open and a fourth man's voice.

"Chief Constable, we brought the things you needed for—hey, then. You there. You're the man was with the murderess we brought in from St. Mar—"

The rest was drowned in a chaos of shouts, overturned furniture, and the slamming of bodies into walls and doors. Meg imagined she could hear fists striking flesh and bone. As far as she could tell, it was Ned and Jenks against Whitcomb and one of his men—maybe more. She had never prayed so hard in her life.

"Look," the queen cried to Clifford, pointing. "Near the far side of the arch across the starling. A wooden ladder affixed to the stone!"

"Hard to reach," he shouted back, "but I'll try for it. I'll take a couple of the oarsmen to make a human chain, in case I fall climbing over the starlings."

Above them, Sally had managed to swing the shutter back toward the wall, but she hung between the wooden slats and the building. Marie looked frozen in place like a statue, wide-eyed, looking not at Sally nor the barge but just beyond at the seething waters. She edged farther out as if she meant to jump. What was so dreadful inside the open window that she did not try to go back to safety?

Suddenly the queen's head cleared. She beat down her own fears.

"No," she told Clifford, "the oarsmen need to stay with the barge. You and I can make it to that ladder and up to the bridge."

"But, Your Grace," both he and Rosie chorused.

"You can go first," she told him, taking off her cloak and handing it to Rosie. "If the ladder holds someone as big as you, it will hold me. I'm in my riding skirts. I can do it."

The bargemen held the craft somewhat steady as Clifford climbed onto the starlings and helped the queen out. It actually felt better here at first, off the pitching deck, but she saw new dangers. Waves lashed the soaked planks, and stray debris, including tree limbs and boards, had jammed here.

The spray reminded her of a great rainstorm. Standing under the vaulted arch, she recalled that day her royal sister had sent her to the nearby Tower through the river entrance called Traitor's Gate. There, in driving rain, the young Princess Elizabeth had sat down and refused to go in that way—with Lord Paulet insisting she must obey the queen. Now she was queen, and yet she was not free, not safe.

Once the two of them had stumbled and crawled their way to the ladder, sometimes holding to each other, sometimes bending over and scuttling sideways like crabs, they saw that the bottom three rungs were not only waterlogged but crumbling.

"They won't take your weight!" she shouted at him. "Boost me above them."

"Your Majesty, I cannot—"

"You can and will, man! You'll be here to break my fall. Now!"

He hoisted her up to grab the fourth rung, then higher, so she could get a foothold. It felt so strange to have a man's hard hands on her person, her back, waist, and hips.

She looked up as she climbed. What if she got to the top and this went nowhere, or she could not get over the edge of the bridge?

For the first time, she saw people gazing over at her from above. Someone threw a rope down; she wrapped it around her left wrist in case she fell, but she was hardly going to let them haul her up on it. At least this side of the bridge was sheltered from the flying spray of the other side.

Riding skirts or no, they were still a problem—heavy, a burden each time she went up another rung. A problem to be a woman and rule, she told herself, but she could do it. No matter how demanding the men of her Parliament became with carpers like Cantwell or renegades like Whitcomb, she would survive and thrive. Even if the northern shires exploded in rebellion, she would put it down. Her life would be spent helping all who were loyal in her kingdom, men and boys, but women and girls, too.

Many hands pulled her up over the wooden rail in an open spot between shops and buildings. People gaped at her, but at least they didn't recognize their queen, looking like a drowned rat.

"Did you fall from a boat? What . . . How?" the growing crowd peppered her with questions.

Exhausted, she righted herself, pushed away, and shoved through the crowd, running toward the other side of the bridge. But exactly what building to enter to find the girls?

Then she saw a yellow glover's sign and ran for that door.

Meg feared the worst when the sounds of the fight halted in the other room. She wished she could scream for Ned through her gag. What if he had been bested and Whitcomb or his man came in? But no, Jenks was with him, and she'd never known him to lose a fight.

Tears of gratitude blinded her when she heard both familiar voices shouting, "Meg? Meg Milligrew, you here?"

She tried to answer them but began to choke again. The door to the room banged open against the wall. Ned stood there, his once handsome countenance bruised and bloodied anew. Jenks towered behind him, not looking so good, either.

They rushed to her and had the rag out of her mouth in a trice, but she was so dry she still couldn't talk and only coughed and gasped. Jenks sliced her bonds with his knife, but it was Ned who lifted her in his arms.

She held hard to him, pressing her cheek to his, even though her arms were numb and his face swollen, black and blue and slick with blood.

"He . . . going to torture and maim me," she tried to say. "Hates . . . the queen."

They took her out into the large front room but headed toward the back of the guildhall and out a rear door. Bless them, they must have sent that earlier fellow to look around the area, but how did they know she was here?

No matter now. She had never felt safer. The queen and Sally would sure be shocked when they heard what she'd been through.

The door to the shop was closed but not locked. The queen burst in. The other glover's shop came to mind, where Celia struck Meg, then led her a merry chase out the back door. But the back door here was splintered and led to a small room in chaos and a window overlooking a steep fall to fast-flowing water.

She heard several others behind her, but once she saw that the shop was empty, she didn't look back. Hands on the ledge, she thrust her head out the window.

Like part of the carved stone of the bridge beneath, Marie stared fixedly into the roiling waters and Sally yet held to the shutter. Who to save first?

"Marie, I'm here. Just stand still. Sally, I'm going to swing the shutter out, then into the window and help you inside.

Don't be afraid, now," she said as she glanced down at the barge, still held under the window by raging waters and her valiant men. "If you fall, they will catch you below."

Holding her breath, Elizabeth slowly, steadily pulled the shutter toward her and grabbed Sally's shoulders, then pulled her through the window, head first. Others pressed into the room, taking Sally from her as she turned back to Marie, still unmoving, pressed against the stone wall, staring down.

"Get back," the queen told the people in the room, and motioned them away with one arm.

Though no one knew who she was, they obeyed, but for one tall, thin man who demanded, "What's going on here? This is my shop. Just what is going on?"

One of her guards she'd sent to ride the bridge appeared, too. "Clear this room, but for this girl," she said, pointing at Sally, collapsed and panting on the floor. Again, she leaned out the window and turned toward Marie.

"Marie," she said, when there was only the sound of rushing river again, "give me your hand. Slowly, just give me your left hand."

"I heard her struggling, then drowning, and didn't try to save her," she said, still not turning or moving. "Are Badger and Celia gone?"

"Yes, they're gone." Celia, the queen thought. She should have known the woman with Badger was Celia. "It's just Sally and me. Give me your hand now, and I'll take you to your parents."

"They didn't kill her, you know, kill my Aunt Hannah. I was afraid they did, but they didn't."

"I was afraid they did, too." She was still terrified of the connection between Thomas and Badger—afraid that her financial genius might have hired Badger to rid him of a problem—but she said only, "Give me your hand, Marie. Your queen is commanding you take my hand."

"But through the window—of the starch house—I saw who killed her."

Elizabeth jerked so hard she grabbed the ledge and held on tight. "Who, then?"

"Someone dressed like Badger," she said. "Badger's height."

"Are you sure it was not him?" The queen leaned way out and over. She had Marie's hand now, but she was afraid to tug at her. The girl went even more rigid. *Dear God,* Elizabeth prayed, *don't let her throw herself off, for I could never hold her.*

"Yes," Marie mouthed so quietly that the noise drowned her words. "I remember now that I could see through the window he wasn't Badger, even when he picked her out of the starch and carried her away."

"You remember that now?" she said, trying to sound soothing when her heart was about to beat out of her breast. She tried to move Marie closer, but the girl didn't budge beyond letting the queen lift her left hand.

"Yes, and his voice wasn't Badger's when he struggled with her—when I heard them and should have helped her."

"If his voice wasn't Badger's, whose was it? Come here and tell me, Marie. It's cold out here, so come in with Sally and me through this window and get warm."

"I looked through the window of the starch shop," she repeated. "I wanted to fly, to climb through the window, but I was frozen—afraid."

"Everything's all right now. This isn't the same window. You don't have to be afraid of what you find in here."

"I didn't cause my mother's death. You said I didn't," she insisted, turning to look at Elizabeth at last.

"No, you did not. Nor did you cause your aunt's in any way. Sally needs you, Marie. Come in here with Sally."

The girl moved at last, shuffling sideways closer, though the queen feared she still might fall or jump. Then she wrapped the girl in her arms and pulled her inside, collapsing to the floor beside Sally with Marie sprawled across her lap.

The three of them huddled there, the two girls sobbing and Elizabeth weak with relief. Finally, sniffling, Sally said, "Even if Badger didn't kill anyone, he's still really mean. He's a killer, too, 'cause he was going to kill us, going to drop us down a hole under that closestool to the river."

Elizabeth glanced at the crude wooden jakes. The wooden closestool itself had been shoved back over the hole hastily but not positioned properly.

"We cut both him and Celia, Your Grace," Marie put in. "With scissors and some other glove-cutting tool."

"Maybe if they're bleeding bad," Sally said, "you can follow their path, but I guess it's getting dark outside."

Elizabeth glanced around the dimming room. She had not noted it before, but perhaps that wasn't just the water she had dripped on the floor. It could be smeared blood. At least, if she found Badger and Celia, which she doubted after they'd done all this, their wounds would prove the girls' story.

"I wager one thing," Marie said, seeming fully alert at last. "Their cuts might slow them down if you mean to chase them, Your Grace."

"'Cause," Sally added, "bet we know now who hurt Marie's aunt."

From the mouths of babes, the queen thought, sitting up straighter, then scrambling to her knees. "Tell me," she said. "Marie said it wasn't Badger she saw in the upstairs starch house window, lifting Hannah—that it was a man in Badger's clothes. Who, then?"

"He's called the stocking man," Sally said, and Marie nodded.

"But who's that?" the queen countered.

"One time, Sally, don't you remember that Celia said the stocking *market* man?" Marie said. "And Badger got angry at her for that, like she gave too much away?"

"The stocking market man," Elizabeth echoed, still sitting on her haunches. "Did they say aught else about him?"

"Two things," Sally said. "One, that the stocking man would have their heads if they didn't get things out of us. Two, that Marie was worth a fortune no matter what the stocking man said 'bout final revenge meaning more."

"Final revenge . . . the stocking man . . . the stocking market man," Elizabeth repeated in a monotone while her mind raced. She felt fury flood her again. Why hadn't she reasoned that out before? But she had needed the motive to put all the pieces together.

She stood in her sodden skirts and shoved her wild hair back from her face. "Guard!" she called. The splintered door, which no doubt told another tale of horror, opened immediately to reveal not one but three of her yeomen guards, including Bates.

"One of you stay here to be certain these girls are taken by my barge to Whitehall to be reunited with Marie's parents," Elizabeth ordered. "Bates and Stiller will go with me on horseback." She would have to ride astride, but, truth be told, she preferred that.

She walked to the still-open window. The royal oarsmen had managed to pole or row the barge away from the bridge.

She pointed back toward the Old Swan Stairs, where they had put in earlier today. Though dusk was falling, they saw her, waved, and bent their backs to row.

"Where are we going, Your Majesty?" Bates asked as she accepted the man's cape he offered her and wrapped it around her shoulders. It came only to her knees.

"To see the stocking man," she told him, striding for the street as he and her other yeoman, Stiller, hurried along behind her. "And the first place we're looking is Smithfield Market. Nothing quite so fatal a fashion as final revenge, but I shall turn it to queen's justice."

Chapter the Seventeenth

DESPITE DEEPENING DUSK, THE QUEEN AND HER two yeomen started for Smithfield. At least the bridge was not so crowded now. They must ride nearly the width of the City, and she hoped the gates would not be closed before they went through.

Approaching night had greatly cleared the streets. Despite the fact she had only two guards, she was relying on surprise to take Dauntsey, if Badger and Celia had not managed to get to him first. If she could trust what Marie had finally recalled she'd seen through the starch house window, Hannah's murderer had not been Badger himself but someone wearing his clothes. How clever of the popinjay Dauntsey to exchange his usual flamboyant fashion for Badger's plain garb. No wonder eyewitnesses noticed no one unusual.

Besides, both Dauntsey and Badger were short, nearly the same height. Another thing had finally hit her, too. Those dark smudges on the linen rolls of fabric that had been placed to hide Hannah's body and perhaps the killer, too. The rolls had bluish blurs on them, which she'd attributed to smears from the dye in Hannah's gown. But could they have been ink stains from Dauntsey's fingers?

Elizabeth had no way of knowing how much of a head start Badger and Celia had or even if they were heading for "the stocking market man's" place at Smithfield. If not, she might have to drag the wretch out of Paulet's house. Worse, if Paulet were also involved, she'd have to bring him down, and that would cause more upheaval in Parliament.

"Where at Smithfield is Dauntsey's establishment?" Bates asked as they turned onto Thames Street to follow the river westward.

"I don't know," she admitted. Giving up on keeping the man's cape she wore pulled over her head like a hood, she let it flap behind her. Should anyone recognize their queen in hot pursuit, she would be gone before they could blink. "I just know he needs to be arrested and questioned," she told her men. "If we snare Badger and Celia, that will be a bonus, but I'll have a hue and cry out for all of them by dawn."

As they rode past the corner of Dowgate Street, on which sat the Skinners' Guildhall, Elizabeth hoped her men had found Meg. She wondered if Nigel Whitcomb would back down when she insisted his prisoner be freed. She'd like to toss him in prison, and drum him out of Parliament, too, but perhaps she was going to have to handle the Lords and Commons as she did potential suitors—coddle rather than confront them. She might be her father's daughter, but these were not her father's times.

"Will we go to the palace for more men?" Bates asked over the clatter of their horses' hooves on cobbles.

"I'm trying to decide whether to send Stiller for help or keep him with us."

"You don't intend to ride into Smithfield this time of day—night? We should go for help, and you can remain at the palace while guards go out to find—"

"Bates, I favor and trust you to help me keep order, not give me orders."

"Yes, Your Majesty."

Her horse was in a lather, and so was she as they rode through Newgate and plunged outside the city walls. It was even darker out here, for lanterns or torches were fewer and farther apart.

With their horses wheezing from the pace she'd set, they cut up St. Sepulchre's Alley. Smithfield lay beyond, a large, dark pentagon under the slope of night sky.

When the breeze shifted, the sudden assault of the stench almost staggered them, but Elizabeth discovered that if she took several deep, dusty breaths, the potency lessened. She remembered Meg saying she sometimes, her nose being overfull of them, couldn't smell the sweet herbs she handled; it must hold true for reeking aromas, too. The sounds of vast herds kept here until the big Wednesday market tomorrow blew at them with the smell.

Their mounts tried to pull back, even as the three of them reined in. Torches at sporadic distances framed the field; their lights flared doubly, reflected in the wooden water troughs at which the animals drank. Now and then, the sharp silhouettes of watchful herdsmen cut through the lights.

"Bates, walk up and ask one of those fellows if he knows the location of the stock market office of Hugh Dauntsey. If the man doesn't know who Dauntsey is, describe him—peacock-hued clothes and strange, pale eyes."

He dismounted and walked away but was back in a trice. "The clothes were the key," he called to them, sounding almost jaunty as he remounted. "Hugh Dauntsey lets a two-story building at the corner of Long Lane, across the field."

"Let's go, then," Elizabeth insisted, and turned her horse the way he indicated.

They picked their way along between water troughs, which helped to pen in the herds, and the encircling buildings. Despite how her stomach knotted and her pulse pounded, the queen fought to stay calm. No more jousting knights in mock battle here, but at least no martyrs' screams as they were burned to death—murdered—either. It was, she hoped, the perfect place to catch a killer.

"Must be that building there," Stiller said, pointing. "Look, lights upstairs and down."

"A bull's-eye," she said, noting that one of the shutters stood ajar. "Stiller, I will ask you to take these skittish horses around to the back door of the place and block any rear exits with them. Bates will go with me, but we will try peeking in that front window first to see who is within."

Stiller yet hovered while Bates looked as if he'd like to argue again, but he dismounted and helped her down. "Draw swords, both of you," she ordered, "and one of you give me a dagger." She held up her hand to Stiller, and he handed his to her, hilt first. He dismounted and led the three nervous horses away while Elizabeth and Bates peeked in the dusty window.

She gasped. Indeed her bad fortune had turned, for, in the light of a single lantern, Niles Badger slumped at a table, looking exhausted, filthy, and bloody. She could not see Celia or anyone else. She wondered at first if he was unconscious, but he lifted his head and one arm, then put to his mouth a small carved wooden object with a bowl and a stem from which he seemed to be sucking smoke.

"Even if Dauntsey's in a back room or upstairs, I want to take that man now," she said in a normal voice, to be heard over the noise of the animals. "He looks too beaten to fight back, or else I'd send for more men. Let's try the door, but if it's locked, you kick it in. I don't think the herders will hear with all this noise. If Dauntsey or Celia should be here and dart out the back, Stiller will stop them."

Among the lowing, snorting cattle, someone was singing "Bonny Barbara Allen" in a fine tenor voice. A dog barked. In that instant, sounds and scents seemed to assault the queen more clearly. She thought she even smelled the smoke Badger was drinking.

Her efforts to slowly lift the latch failed. It stopped partway up.

"Let me try a trick with the sword before we startle him," Bates said.

Elizabeth nodded and went back to peer in the window. Wreathed in smoke, Badger looked as if he'd topple over in a stupor. This might be easier than she'd feared, but she deserved a boon in all this.

She watched Bates jiggle his sword tip in the crack between the door and the frame. "Now!" he cried, startling even her as he slammed the door open and, sword raised, vaulted in.

Elizabeth rushed behind him, closing and relatching the door. Badger leaped straight up, then seemed to droop back over the table. Though the queen was wearing a man's cape, he evidently knew her instantly.

"You—here!" he cried, and started coughing so hard his shoulders shook.

"Is Dauntsey here, too? And Celia?" she demanded.

He shook his head. "Fled. I was too weak with blood loss from those two little bitches."

She almost slapped him, but she needed him to talk, and

he already looked ashen. Still holding the dagger in one hand, suddenly exhausted herself, she sat on the other bench across the table from him. Between them lay wet, bloody cloths he'd evidently tried to use for bandages. The smell of his tobacco was strong, but she preferred it to the stench of the animals.

"Tie this man, then watch the staircase, Bates," she said. "He looks done in, but he's not to be trusted. We don't need him trying to dive out a back window the way he forced the girls to."

Badger looked surprised at that. The yeoman took his smoking piece away and put it on the table, then tied him with torn cloths to the room's only chair, which he shoved to the end of the table, close to the queen. Quickly she glanced about at stacks of parchment neatly aligned on the shelves. Several big leather-bound boxes sat on the floor; those should be searched, too. Yes, this looked like a place of business and not some sham. She wondered, if she'd come in pursuit of a stock market criminal instead of a murderer, was enough evidence here to have Dauntsey arrested and convicted?

"Unless you want to be charged with double murder," Elizabeth told Badger, rapping her knuckles on the table, "you'd best tell me all about your relationship with Hugh Dauntsey. I take it you're working for him as well as for Gresham, but Dauntsey has your true loyalty."

"Paid better," he said with a snort. "Gresham' s filthy rich, but Dauntsey paid better. Can I make a bargain with you, then?" His voice was slow and barely audible. "I explain things, and you let me walk out of here—if I can."

"No bargains. By noon tomorrow, I'll have him as well as you in prison being examined by much more skilled interrogators than I. How long have you worked for Dauntsey?"

"Let me put it this way, Your Majesty," he said, strangely rolling his eyes upward before he looked at her again. Was he going to faint? "My first big task for Dauntsey was shooting a firearm at Gresham in Flanders the day his horse crushed his leg. I was to kill him and missed."

A hint of a rueful grin crimped his mouth. "Dauntsey was furious at first," he went on, " 'til he realized how much pain the man was in, even after his leg supposedly healed. He relished that, making him a cripple. Decided to take his reputation, too, ruin his family 'fore killing him . . . so my missing him that day worked out for the best."

His words slowed even more; he seemed to drawl them. Again his eyes rolled upward before he squinted across the table at her.

"You need medical help, Badger, so answer my questions quickly, and we shall get some for you."

"I just need a puff on that pipe—if I'm to go on."

Elizabeth nodded, and Bates came over to put it to his lips. The man drew on it greedily before Bates put it down again. The big guard peeked out through the front shutters and rechecked the latch on the door. He went to peer out the single back window. "Can't see Stiller since there are shutters closed from the outside," he reported, then returned to his post at the bottom of the stairs.

"I assume," Elizabeth questioned Badger, "you took Sir Thomas's signet ring and made certain it appeared in the starch bath in which Hannah von Hoven drowned?"

He nodded almost imperceptibly; his head lowered, and his eyes closed. She must know so much more and couldn't let him slip away before she learned the truth—if he was telling the truth.

"Did you harm and drown those two women or did Dauntsey?"

"They were just pawns to him . . . it's Gresham he's hated for years. Dauntsey killed the starcher to set him up, the whitster to shut her up. Rich bastard Gresham got Dauntsey's position, ruined his dreams, kept close to you. I just did what Dauntsey said, set things up, got the ring, the *chocolata* drink he took to the laundress—told her it was sent from you."

His shoulders heaved; he coughed again. Over the muted noise from outside, Elizabeth strained to hear him.

"Dauntsey found out," Badger went on, "about the poison roots from the other starchers he did the books for. But he did the drownings," he said, lifting his head and turning to give Bates a long look.

"Say on," she prompted, when he seemed to forget her.

"I can't—can't."

"Then I'm going to have to throw you over the rump of a horse and have you taken to the palace, where—"

"One more pull on the pipe, that's all."

She leaned toward his chair to put it to his mouth herself, then took it back and set it down on her side of the table.

"He loved to do the drownings, craved it—like I do that pipe," Badger whispered, as if to himself. "Said so, more'n once. Boasted he drowned a playfellow, a pretty little girl, years ago in a fishpond and . . . the passion of it was like nothing else . . ."

Elizabeth's lower jaw dropped. That last about the passion of murder by drowning—Badger could not have made that up. She couldn't let this man die, because she'd need him to testify against Dauntsey when they found him.

As Badger slumped forward in his bonds, she told Bates,

"We must look swiftly for more evidence, then get this man to my physician at Whitehall."

"I'll glance upstairs and try to call out a window there to Stiller."

"All right. I'll stand at the bottom of the stairs to keep an eye on this one, and you can shout down to me what you find."

Bates went quietly, quickly, up the narrow stairs, which were lit from above. Their prisoner had sat up again but kept shaking his head and rolling his eyes upward, as if he could see through the ceiling and floor over their heads.

"Be careful up there!" she called to Bates. She gripped her dagger so hard her fingers cramped. She couldn't stand this place any longer. The sounds of the penned beasts awaiting their fates outside, the smell, dust, and tobacco smoke seemed to suffocate her. Striding to the stairs, she shouted up them, "Bates? Did you call out to Stiller?"

"Come up here!" he cried at last, when she was getting so panicked she was about to leave Badger and shout for Stiller herself. Bates sounded nervous; he, too, was hard to hear over the outside sounds.

She glanced at Badger. He looked unconscious, his head lolling forward. His eyes were closed, and he drooled. Grasping her dagger and holding her skirts close, she went up the narrow, dim stairs to the small landing. There she tried to look out the back window. Her dark reflection as well as more closed shutters on the outside of the glass kept her from seeing Stiller or the horses.

She would quickly see what Bates had discovered, then send him outside to fetch the other guard. She went up a few more steps until her head was even with the floor upstairs. A single lantern hung from a wall peg in the short hall. Why hadn't Bates taken the light with him into the two small, darker rooms, which both had their doors open?

"Bates? Where are you? What is it?"

"Here!" he called gruffly over the continual hum of noise from outside.

She went up the rest of the stairs and looked left, into the room from which Bates had called. She expected to find Dauntsey's illicit gold heaped in a trunk, or even the murderer himself, hanging from his own noose, trapped . . . a suicide.

It all happened fast. On the floor of the room at her left, she saw Bates's legs stretched out in spilled water—or blood. And next to him, with her back to the door, sat a headless woman!

Elizabeth screamed. Beheaded? In horror, the queen bucked back into the wall.

No, no, it was a woman on her knees with her head thrust in a bucket.

Dauntsey leaped to the doorway at which she stared.

She screamed again and lifted her dagger, but he heaved a bucket of water and lunged at her. Wooden . . . hit her face . . . water exploded over her. Before she could see, he wrenched her weapon from her hand and seized a fistful of her hair, which tumbled loose from its pins and snood.

She thought he might shove her down the stairs, but he yanked her head back, forcing her to stare into those rimless, invisible eyes. She read hatred there, teetering on madness.

"This will top them all," he said through gritted teeth. His voice—he'd spoken for Bates and sounded like him. "My most thrilling drowning. How much do you think the northern lords will pay me for a dead Tudor queen?"

"You and Paulet—"

"That bumbling fool knows nothing of all this," he hissed.

All this . . . Buckets—he had six or seven big buckets in the room he dragged her into, and the woman who must be Celia was drowned in one.

Elizabeth fought hard as he tripped her and threw her to her knees—thrust her face into a big bucket. Cold water. His strength surprised her. Hannah . . . Pamela. Had it been like this, wanting to breathe but knowing that meant death?

She held her breath until she thought her lungs would explode. Pain in her scalp. Clawed and kicked. Grabbed some air before he shoved her down again. She reached blindly for a nearby bucket. Tipped it empty, smashed it backward at him.

He went off balance. She hit him again with it, shoved him, rolled away into Bates. He was bleeding from his head. She scrambled to her feet, bounced off one wall. Lifting her sopped skirts, she tore down the stairs, one flight. Turn corner, down the rest.

Outside. Get outside. Find Stiller. Scream for people—her subjects outside to help. Get help . . . help . . .

She heard Dauntsey pounding downstairs after her. Badger still slumped in his chair. The door. She'd latched it herself. If he caught her here . . .

But as she jerked at the latch, she heard him stop across the room at the bottom of the stairs. She glanced back; he opened a big box. "All right, then," he called to her, strangely calm, as she lifted the latch, "I'll just provide a little distraction, like poor Badger did that day he shot at your damned lackey, *Sir* Thomas Gresham. I thought you'd rather be drowned in private, but if you, oh great and glorious queen, always need an audience, so be it."

A firearm. He had a matchlock!

She tore outside, screaming for help. Stiller came barreling around the corner of the building, but a herd of baaing sheep blocked him from reaching her and blocked her escape toward him. Cattle had shifted closer; she had only one direction to flee.

At first no one heard her cries. Then a few herdsmen looked her way. She must look wild, demented, pointing back toward Dauntsey, forced to run forward into the field.

Darting behind the first water trough she came to, she bent down and peered over it as light in the open door silhouetted Dauntsey and the firearm. Marie had stared at Hannah's lighted window. She'd seen Dauntsey, but in Badger's clothes, lifting Hannah from the tub. He'd drowned her, hoping to blame Gresham. After Marie came inside, he'd lifted Hannah out and onto the shelf, because that was something Thomas would have done. Perhaps he'd hidden himself on that shelf while Marie was in the room.

Elizabeth saw that Dauntsey had lit the wick that would ignite the gunpowder in the pan. Could Dauntsey aim and hit her from this distance and through the wooden trough?

She heard Stiller's shouts. Her yeoman was wading thigh-high through sheep toward Dauntsey as if through deep water, but, unfortunately, the path between her and that madman was now clear.

Just as she opened her mouth to scream for help again, the matchlock belched a flash of light and noise. He'd fired not at her but into the air.

At first the cattle seemed to go still as stone. Several shifted, snorted; some began to bump into others in a growing panic. She heard the warning shouts of several herdsmen and Stiller's voice again, ordering Dauntsey to put the firearm down.

In that short time, he must have reprimed and loaded again, for one more blast followed. As one great beast, the animals bolted in a churning mass as all hell broke loose in a wild rampage of horns and hoofs around her.

Pressing herself between two drinking troughs, Elizabeth was forced to stand; that made her a better target, should Dauntsey shoot a third time. Instead, swinging at the beasts with the butt of the matchlock, he fought toward her, into the edges of the writhing herd, which now forced Stiller even farther away. On the side of the troughs temporarily holding back the onslaught, though that put her closer to Dauntsey, she edged along while the water in them rocked like waves.

Then she realized what the human beast intended. Amidst the chaos of the crashing cattle and sheep, the water trough reminded her of Hannah's starch-tub coffin—of Ursala and Pamela's washtub.

Dauntsey reached the troughs and pursued her down the line of them. In the deafening noise and rising dust, she saw she must face him alone. If she could only fight her way to the sturdy tree trunk that was the memorial to martyrs here, she could climb it and be safe, but it was too far away.

The animals slammed into the barrier of the troughs, overturning some toward her. The two closest still stood, but soon she would lose her last bulwark of protection. Water slopped over the edges in swift surges as some beasts slammed into them before they swerved away.

Trapped by the circle of surrounding buildings with only narrow escape routes, the mingled herds seemed to be circling, swinging toward the center of the field where they had been penned in. Dauntsey was almost to her. Only two troughs yet stood against the rush, and Elizabeth had to either stand and face him or be trampled. Her hand on a quaking tub, she turned and pointed directly into his frenzied face.

"Stand back from me, Hugh Dauntsey! You are finished here!"

He seized her wrist and shouted so close in her face that his saliva speckled her. "For years, I wanted to torment and kill Gresham, but you'll do! You've ruined everything, but losing you will ruin him, too!"

Holding to the trough, she wrenched away, kicking out at him. He went down. She did, too, hitting hard on her elbows and knees—but found herself sheltered by a tipped trough even as its water slammed into and over her. She saw Dauntsey battered down and trampled, a shocked look on his face before his entire body disappeared in the mad rampage of beasts.

She threw herself backward into the tipped trough. Knees curled up, arms tucked against her chest, Elizabeth huddled, tears streaming down her face, praying this would not be her coffin. The animals rushed past or vaulted it in churning dust, trying to rend her apart, like her enemies trying to crush her under the weight of her duties, her fears . . .

But then, when the herdsmen had rushed past, attempting to retrieve and pen in their stock, Stiller found her, shaken and stunned. He fell to his knees, leaning close to peer into the darkness of her shelter.

At first, she blinked back tears and simply stared at him. Yes, this was how poor Marie must have felt when she hid within herself, stunned, haunted by the evil deeds of others. But queens could not hide or waver.

"Your Majesty," Stiller whispered, horrified, still hacking in the dust, "are . . . are you . . . all right?"

"Of course I am," she insisted, though her voice shook.

"Just soaked so thoroughly by this tipped water my face is all wet. Stop staring, man, and get into that house to help Bates. Quickly now, for I saw that he's been hurt."

He gaped at her but obeyed. With a silent prayer of thanks for her deliverance, Elizabeth Tudor rolled to her knees and stood, trembling yet triumphant.

Epilogue

JANUARY 23, 1571

SIR THOMAS GRESHAM'S MERCANTILE EXCHANGE WAS completed at last. After a sumptuous banquet at Gresham House, the queen with her nobles made an official visit for its opening.

"I recall the first day I saw this grand edifice, Thomas," she told him as he helped her down from her coach amidst cheers from the crowd in the street.

"I do, too, Your Grace," he said, nodding. "It was barely a foundation then, and that traitor Badger, long imprisoned now, hovered close."

The entire city seemed to hover close along her journey here today on freshly graveled streets. Church bells clanged, houses were decked with carpets and bunting, and people ran along behind the queen's coach and entourage. How she loved her people, even the rowdy, blue-gowned apprentices and the pompous lines of guild members, bowing and doff-ing their caps. If only she had gotten her hands on the former chief constable from the Skinners' Guild before he'd fled north, some said to Scotland. She'd have skinned him for what he had done to Meg and for his mockery of justice in her realm.

From the balconies above, lutes and guitterns began to play but were drowned out by the royal trumpeters here for the occasion. She could barely hear Thomas when he spoke. "But I hope you do not harbor thoughts of those difficult times that shortly followed that first visit here, Your Grace."

"How I wish I had Marie's faulty memory for those days, but all is well that ends well." They waited for her ladies to arrange her cloak before they entered the building. She was as gorgeously decked out as the exchange was today, in her new fashion of white satin with cloth-of-gold accents and white ermine on her black silk cape. She still favored huge ruffs, now not cartwheels but standing ones, with dangling jewels and pearls, though she wore black pearls today—and knew that, too, would begin a new trend.

"I am pleased that you and Anne seem to get on well, Thomas. She is proud of you, I warrant," she added, patting his arm. Slowly, with him limping and leaning on his walking stick, they entered the inner courtyard through the arches, under the proud Gresham grasshopper emblem.

"Somehow Hannah's death gradually helped to heal our marriage," he admitted, raising his voice above the noise. "And, of course, our united joy for Marie-Anne's happiness in her betrothal."

"Sally is thrilled about the coming wedding. She will make Marie a fine, loyal maid over the years—much as her mother has served me."

To be certain her servants were here, too, Elizabeth glanced back, past her retinue of nobles. With the lords and ladies came her dear Cecil and his wife, Mildred. She intended to bestow a great honor on her friend next month, for she planned to ennoble him as Baron Burghley. Behind the Cecils, over to the side, stood Jenks and his wife, Ursala, pregnant with their third child. Beside them, she glimpsed Meg and Ned, whispering together. Ned's nose had never recovered from the fisticuffs he'd engaged in to help save Meg from Whitcomb, but he was all to the good for it—not so vain, and he played the villains even better in court dramas.

After a tour of the courtyard where England's financiers would bargain and trade for goods, Thomas led the queen and her company up the stairs to the second floor with three sides of shops. Though it was not yet dusk this chill day, the entire area glowed with the wax lights she had heard Thomas had ordered to be displayed. In turn, he'd given the lucky shopkeepers a year's free rent.

"Look at the bounty!" the queen called to the press of people coming up behind her. "Let us support Sir Thomas's grand endeavor with our choices and our coins!"

Everyone, especially the women, mobbed the pretty shops. It was worse, Elizabeth thought, than that wild melee of animals she'd lived through at Smithfield the night that murderer Dauntsey was trampled to death and her big yeoman Bates was knocked over the head so hard it took him days to recall who he was. Ah, but Elizabeth of England always knew who she was, and since that horrible night when she fully came to grasp the power of revenge, she had used her might more judiciously, even when Parliament was driving her to distraction.

God knows, she'd lived through terrible trials since her Privy Plot Council had solved those drownings five years ago. Plague, plots, rebellion, even excommunication by the pope, which she, like her father before her, considered a badge of honor. She intended to live through much more to rule and reign.

She, too, strolled the booths, admiring their delights.

Rolls of thick-piled velvet and shimmering silks in the newest shades of dead Spaniard, popinjay blue, lady's blush, and lusty gallant. She made a special stop at the van der Passes' new shop to admire their array of goods.

When she caught Dirck's eye, she told him, "I hope that no one hangs about your shop to lure your buyers away."

"Vould serve me right, Your Majesty, but I learned my lesson."

"So have we all," she said to herself as she turned away. Though she was but thirty-seven, she felt she had come far, not only to mount the throne but to keep and tend it. And she would face whatever was yet to come.

She nodded to Cecil, who sent a runner to the trumpeters. When their fanfare began, everyone turned to see what was happening. With one hand raised, Elizabeth called out in her clarion voice, "On this special day for London and our realm, I wish to bestow two favors. To my beloved people, I declare that each Sunday on these grounds in good weather shall be presented a concert by the queen's musicians at no fee to which all are invited. And to my loyal servant and founder of this mercantile exchange, Sir Thomas Gresham, I give a special honor. I do proclaim this is henceforth the Royal Exchange of England, to be designated and so called!"

Cheers went up as word spread through the crowd. The queen, with Thomas, walked to the balcony and waved to the press of people in the courtyard below. Again she smiled at those closest to her, couples all: the Cecils; the Greshams; Marie and her betrothed; Meg and Ned; Jenks and his Ursala, her hand tenderly placed on her breeding belly. Why, even the Queen of Scots had a son, but none of them had, nor ever would have, Elizabeth's dear lover England.

The cheers and the music swelled again as several stepped

forward to present her with keepsakes from the shops. "I wish I could give you all gifts so you could begin a thousand new rages of fashion," Thomas said to Elizabeth as he put his arm around his wife's waist.

"Even a queen can't have everything," she told him, and blinked back tears to force a smile. But, she thought, turning away to wave again to those below, her best royal fashion would ever be to rule alone with charm and might.

AUTHOR'S NOTE

ALTHOUGH WILLIAM SHAKESPEARE WAS ONLY EIGHT YEARS OLD at the time this story ends, and this series may not stretch far enough to encompass his heyday in London, I am honoring his works in this book by including more than one set of twins, something he had great fun with in his plays. He also portrayed constables as bumblers and fools. I have studied Shakespeare for years and did my master's thesis on his *All's Well That Ends Well*, so he provides rich research for this mystery series even without appearing in it.

As for the concept of twins in my story, besides the von Hoven and the Hemmings sisters, Clifford and Dirck greatly resemble each other. Meg has for years (and in other books in the series) served as a double for the queen, and on it goes. But the real twinship in the story is the light and dark sides of everyone, the good and evil, like the pretty, glowing pollen that is also poison. That is the fatal fashion of mankind.

Among the things Thomas Gresham left behind at his death is a portrait of twin girls by a Flemish painter. This hangs at Titsey Place Manor House in Surrey, once the country home of Gresham's uncle John. The two girls in the painting are not identified, so, taking into consideration that his mistress bore him a child, I have imagined who the twins might be.

The Royal Exchange that stands in London today is the third building with that name on that site. The Gresham building burned in 1666 during the Great Fire of London; its replacement went up in flames in 1838. It was rebuilt in 1844, during the reign of Queen Victoria. The Royal Exchange is still one of the traditional sites from which new kings and queens are announced and sits today in the heart of London's commercial district.

Britain's first public lavatories were built in the forecourt of the new Victorian Exchange in 1855. These were, no doubt, water closets that were a far cry from the jakes used on London Bridge or in tall castles over rivers in Tudor times. However, Queen Elizabeth would not have approved of the early Exchange privies, as they were exclusively for male use.

Like William Cecil, Sir Thomas Gresham was one of the men on whom Elizabeth relied heavily for good advice. She cried openly when she heard Gresham had died at age sixty in 1579.

His widow, Anne, twice tried to overturn his will to get more money. She also failed to make repairs on the Exchange until Elizabeth issued an order saying that "the queen will take great offense if so beautiful a monument is suffered to decay."

Yet Anne Gresham remained a problem, petitioning Parliament to grant her more money from her husband's will, which provided her with the generous annual income of £2388 and £751 from the Exchange itself, a goodly fortune in that day. Parliament rejected her demands, but she did manage to have a more expensive funeral than her husband had seventeen years before.

HERE IS AN EXCERPT FROM *The Hooded Hawke*—

KAREN HARPER'S NEW ELIZABETH I MYSTERY

Now available in hardcover from St. Martin's Minotaur

ST. JAMES'S PARK, LONDON
MONDAY, AUGUST 1, 1569

ALTHOUGH SHE WAS RIDING SIDESADDLE WITH BUT one hand holding the reins, Elizabeth Tudor spurred her horse to a faster gait, forcing the others to keep up with her. Her crimson hair spilled loose from her snood, her skirt flapped, and the hooded hawk perched on her leather-gauntleted hand spread her great gray wings as if to fly.

The queen was desperate to escape the palace, where problems proliferated like rabbits, or rather, she thought, like rats—perhaps even the sort that leave a leaking ship. She heaved a huge sigh.

"Your Grace, what's amiss?" her dear friend Robert Dudley, Earl of Leicester, who alone kept pace beside her, asked. "Do you feel well enough to test the new hawk?"

"Of course I do! I've led you a merry chase this far today."

Even her longtime court favorite's fervid attentions hardly helped her disposition, however dashing he looked ahorse. He was attired much too grandly for riding and flying her new gerfalcon, the breed fit for a king. Robert, whom she had called Robin all the years they had known each other, had given her the hawk as an early birthday gift. 'S blood, she was nearly thirty-six, she realized, and shook her head, which tumbled more tresses free.

With the excuse of testing the prowess of the bird, the queen had brought a small entourage on a morning's robust ride. She could not wait for her summer progress through Surrey and Hampshire that she had just decided on last night. Though she'd chosen hosts for the journey who needed testing themselves, it always heartened her to be out among the common folk of England.

"This looks to be a good spot with a bit of open ground," she announced as she reined in. "We shall fly Swift here."

Being watchful to keep the bird facing the wind so she wouldn't beat the air with her huge wings, the queen dismounted with Robin's steady hand on her free arm and her loyal guard Jenks holding her horse. The queen's handsome, young falconer, Fenton Layne, four other guards, and two of her ladies-in-waiting hastened to follow their sovereign's lead.

St. James's Park had most often been used by the Tudors to hunt deer; by ordering the surrounding marshes drained, her father, King Henry VIII, had created access to it near his country retreat of St. James's Palace. Elizabeth seldom used the old redbrick edifice, but she loved the crooked, wooded lanes and ragged bits of open meadow. It was but a half hour's ride from her main London palace of Whitehall, though she seldom managed a visit.

For each time she snagged a few hours for herself, more couriers came with news of Mary, Queen of Scots's plotting, though Mary was now England's "guarded guest" in the north of England. Or messengers rode in with word of Spanish hostilities on the seas. Worse, couriers conveyed rumors of possible rebellion in England, a future uprising led by her own northern lords, men who were entirely too close to Elizabeth's Catholic cousin Mary in more ways than one. And almost every time William Cecil, her trusted chief secretary of state, called on her, it boded only bad news and dire dangers.

"The sun and wind feel good," she told Robin. "I pray this mild weather continues as the court moves south next week. We'll go first to Oatlands, then to Guildford and Farnham, even to the River Meon and clear to the south Channel. I seldom see the sea with its vast waters, fresh and free."

"You've made a little sonnet upon it. Our queen is a poet and doesn't know it," he teased, obviously trying to lighten her mood, though, since she'd declared she would not wed him, Robin had moped about a great deal himself.

"I need diversion, it's true," she admitted quietly, so the others would not hear. "With all this wretched talk of attacks on our meager navy by those Spanish bullies who think they own the seas, I look forward to hearing from Captain Francis Drake. I shall send word he is to meet us at one of our destinations on the progress."

"Rough, untutored sea dogs, all those captains from the west country," Robin muttered, his tone taut. "Drake and his cousin John Hawkins—they're all pirates at heart, so beware you do not trust or heed Drake overmuch."

"Robin," she said, as she stroked the gerfalcon's gray back to calm her, "I swear, but you sound jealous—or envious." She sighed again. "But I am envious, too. To be land-bound, England-bound, as I shall ever be, is right for a queen, but I would like not only to see the sea but go to sea."

He hooted a laugh but stopped in midyelp when she glared at him. He quickly sobered. "It's a hard life, Elizabeth," he whispered, using her first name as he did only in their moments of privacy.

" 'S blood and bones, everyone thinks I am coddled and spoiled, but I know much of a hard life, and you'll not tease or gainsay me on that."

She turned away from the others pressing close and put her hand to the feathered and tufted green felt hood that covered the hawk's head. Instantly, her falconer, Fenton, broad-shouldered, blond, and blue-eyed, stepped forward to be ready to take it from her when she freed the bird to fly.

But before she snatched off the hood, she heard something that made her pause. Thunder on this clear day? No, hoofbeats, distant ones but coming closer. Swift sidestepped on her hand, still blinded by the hood and snared by the leather jesses that tethered the bird's ankles to her fist. The small bells on the jesses jingled as the foot-and-a-half-tall bird of prey tensed in anticipation.

The queen frowned into the sun to see who approached. When she was young and exiled from her father's court for being Anne Boleyn's daughter, she had learned to fear a quick, unheralded approach by anyone, for it usually boded ill. Queen she might be, but some things still haunted her heart.

Robin, too, turned in the direction of the hoofbeats and covered his eyes to squint across the little meadow. Four riders burst from the line of trees. Behind her, Elizabeth heard Jenks and several others scrape their swords from their scabbards.

"It's Cecil and his men," she called to them, but her pulse did not stop pounding. "He must have news that could not wait."

Still holding the hawk, Elizabeth strode to meet her chief

advisor as he reined in several yards away. She recognized those with him, all Cecil's underlings, a scrivener, two guards, and his favorite courier, Justin Keenan, a handsome man, who often rode back and forth with important documents between Cecil and the court when he was elsewhere on queen's business.

"Bad news, my lord?" she called to him.

Though only forty-eight years of age, the man was out of breath, but then Cecil's strength was in his intellect and loyalty, not his body. He was thin with a shovel-shaped brown beard, which was turning as silvery as frost.

"Only the news that you yourself created, Your Grace, in your suddenly ordering the court to prepare for a progress," he got out in one ragged burst, bowing briefly before rising to face her eye to eye. "Before word reaches those I hear will be your hosts, I need to speak to you about the wisdom of it all."

"Cecil, I am indeed going on my annual progress. I refuse to let either Englishman or foreigner think that threats to my kingdom rile me in the slightest, nor will my concerns about Queen Mary of Scots stop me. She is under my control, although I warrant she hardly realizes that yet, even if her dangerous allies mayhap do."

"But to be out of the capital with the threat of the northern rebellion possibly exploding in support of a Catholic queen to replace you on the throne—"

"I am heading south, not north, dear Cecil. Granted, you must needs stay behind in London at least for some of the time, to keep an eye on that serpent of a new Spanish ambassador de Spes. And I am taking along my second-least favorite cousin, Thomas Howard—the great and grand and glorious Duke of Norfolk, at least in his own eyes. That way he can't get into mischief with Mary or the fomenting rebellion, for I'll have him tied to me like this," she added, and lifted her wrist with the bird to show it was firmly tethered by the straps she held.

"But your plans to stay at both Loseley and Titchfield, hosted by Catholic hosts of highly questionable loyalty..." He cleared his throat, then lowered his voice even more. "I realize you have ever had a policy of keeping your friends close and your enemies closer, but with the Spanish so on edge far too near our borders here or even in the New World—"

"I planned to explain it all to you when I returned after flying my new falcon. Look you, Cecil," she said as she whipped the hood from the bird and, loosing the jesses, cast her skyward. Swift's great wings spread as she leaped free, beating the air, circling to climb to a great, soaring height from which she would see and strike her prey.

The queen could tell Cecil still felt thwarted and overthrown. "Yes, Your Majesty," he said, his voice hardly audible over the cheers of the others. "Not only do all your enemies make a fatal error if they believe you are off on a mere jaunt of summer diversions, but—" He stopped and hacked into his fist.

"But what?" she asked, as she watched the gerfalcon swoop like a shot toward some feckless prey they could not yet see.

"I was just thinking that, though that gauntlet is still on your hand, this supposedly carefree royal progress you propose is indeed throwing a gauntlet down in the face of all your enemies, be they English, Scottish, or Spanish."

"And so, as ever, we understand, trust, and support each other perfectly, my Cecil."

Pointing up at the diving hawk, she turned and shouted to everyone, "Look, Swift has already flushed something!" Lifting her skirts, with the others in pursuit, she set off at a run toward where the bird had plunged to earth for its kill.

ALSO BY KAREN HARPER...

The First Princess of Wales

A NOVEL

Joan of Kent, daughter of a disgraced earl, is sent into the court of King Edward III in the hopes of redeeming her family's disgraced name. Naïve and high-spirited, Joan is unprepared for the devious maneuverings of her fellow courtiers. She learns that it was the royal family who betrayed her father. Joan targets Edward, Prince of Wales, for her revenge. But what begins as strategy soon grows into love. Will Joan allow her real feelings for Edward to take precedence over vengeance? And, if so, what will be the price?

ISBN: 978-0-307-23791-0 / $14.95